GHOST SEASON

GHOST SEASON

A NOVEL

Fatin Abbas

W. W. NORTON & COMPANY
Celebrating a Century of Independent Publishing

Copyright © 2023 by Fatin Abbas

All rights reserved
Printed in the United States
First Edition

For information about permission to reproduce selections from this book, write to Permissions, W. W. Norton & Company, Inc., 500 Fifth Avenue, New York, NY 10110

For information about special discounts for bulk purchases, please contact W. W. Norton Special Sales at specialsales@wwnorton.com or 800-233-4830

Manufacturing by Lake Book Manufacturing
Book design by Beth Steidle
Production manager: Julia Druskin

ISBN: 978-1-324-00174-4

W. W. Norton & Company, Inc.
500 Fifth Avenue, New York, N.Y. 10110
www.wwnorton.com

W. W. Norton & Company Ltd.
15 Carlisle Street, London W1D 3BS

1 2 3 4 5 6 7 8 9 0

To my mother, Afaf, and my father, Ali—
with all my love and gratitude.

GHOST SEASON

DENA PICKED UP THE CAMERA BAG, LIFTED THE TRIPOD under her arm, and, in the courtyard, stopped to look up. The light was mellow, caressing surfaces: the thatched roof of the gazebo that stood at the back of the compound, the clay walls of the storage room, the pale canvas of the tent set up by the office. Light like this was rare—it was only because of a haze of morning clouds, which might melt away at any moment—and so she hurried across the yard to the kitchen, where she found the boy Mustafa sweeping.

He glanced at her and smiled and then his eyes returned to the work. There were few formalities between them now. She didn't have to ask, as she used to, whether she could switch on the camera. He knew why she was there, that her work was watching him, and he'd accepted it, though not without some lingering bewilderment.

She unpacked her things—headphones, a piece of paper to check for white balance, batteries—then turned on the camera and framed the boy sweeping dirt. Sweat trickled into the crease of her one shut eye, and through the other she watched his arms move, the cloudy sunlight hitting them just-so, reflecting the smooth skin just-so against the brown mud of the kitchen wall behind. At his feet the dust swirled up luminous from the uneven ground, rising, then unfurling out in a shadowy motion, the cloud thinning then dissipating in the morning air.

"Look," he said, shading his eyes. Dena watched him through

the lens. "There'll be rain later." His hand remained above his brow for an instant, and then he reached for the broom again.

In the background, echoing through her headphones as though from a faraway place, she could hear a tune pulsating on the radio, and behind that the sound of water splashing in the street. The scent of baking bricks and dung came and went, carried by the river breeze, and still she looked, drifting between the face, the hands, the dust, the moving broom, so lost in looking that the pulse in her aching arm no longer felt like pain but only rhythm.

∫

IN THE OFFICE Alex sat on a stool too low for the makeshift desk, a map spread out in front of him. The room was the only one built out of concrete in the compound. It was cramped, barely big enough for the table, chair, and a metal filing unit set against the left-hand wall. A poster was pinned above it, showing the logo of the organization: a white globe floating above two green palms raised upward as though in prayer.

He'd spent the morning reading an agricultural report, but, bored, had pulled open one of the maps lying on the desk. He never got tired of looking at maps. He leaned forward on his elbows, eyes tracing the northern border, a line bolting straight across the Sahara. His gaze drifted down, following the river to its source as it meandered through the thick yellow belt of desert to the capital, where it split in two, a branch curving up toward the Ethiopian highlands in one direction and the other continuing south toward Lake Victoria. He stopped at a dot marking the town he was in now—Saraaya, at the boundary between North and South. Here the desert merged into grasslands, swaths of pale green that became darker and denser toward the tropical south of the country.

He'd come to this town to make a map, sent by his organization to chart farmlands, villages, grazing pastures, water wells, district lines as part of an information-gathering mission. The maps that existed were outdated, drawn up by the British more than fifty years ago and still used by the local authorities; a good map was needed to give direction to the organization's aid efforts in the area.

It was late November. He wanted to begin, but two weeks into his stay he was still waiting for official permission from the authorities. And his surveying equipment, which should have arrived a week ago from Khartoum, had been shipped to the wrong town, two hundred kilometers away, and was only now on its way over.

A shadow blocked the light coming from the yard, and when he looked up he saw William, the translator, looming in the doorframe.

Teeth flashed in a smile beneath glinting eyes. "Good morning," said William.

A fresh, zesty fragrance wafted into the office. William had been drenching himself in cologne lately, and Alex thought it had something to do with the pretty new cook who had started working in the compound.

Alex raised his nose in the air and sniffed. "Has my translator turned into a lemon tree or what?"

William grinned, his long, handsome face bashful. "It's a new cologne," he said in a lilting accent, drawing out the vowels. "Maybe you could do with some yourself."

It occurred to Alex that he didn't make a very pretty picture. He sat shirtless, his chin overgrown with stubble, his light hair dangling in wet tendrils around his ears. Sunburnt skin was peeling off his nose. In contrast, William was a picture of elegance: His shirt glowed crisply white against the dull clay walls of the compound. His hair was buzz-cut close to his scalp so that the line between it and the broad, dark forehead was almost impossible to discern.

"Any news?" asked Alex. "About the authorization?"

"Not yet," said William. "But soon. Any day now."

It was the same answer that William always gave him.

"It's been two weeks. How much longer am I supposed to wait?"

He was suddenly irritated by the neatness of William's white shirt.

"I'll talk to them again tomorrow," said William. "But I can't rush the authorities. They will slow things down even more if I push them." He stepped out into the yard. "I'll be in the kitchen. Call me if you need me."

He closed the door before Alex had a chance to say more.

⟋

WILLIAM WALKED PAST the plants and the old tires and the sacks of sand piled by the gate. He saw Dena and Mustafa by the storage room, heard the rhythmic swoosh of Mustafa's broom like an accompaniment to the tempo of the music coming from the radio.

His heart clattered in his rib cage. He had tossed and turned all night in bed thinking of Layla—there, now, in the cool darkness of the kitchen. He had plotted and considered what he was about to do: walk into the kitchen and, under the pretense of seeking a glass of water, linger to make conversation about the weather, the crops, the seasonal arrival of the nomads. Then he might venture into more intimate questions: ask her where she lived, about her family.

He stopped by the office wall, smoothed his white shirt, ran his tongue over his teeth. Since meeting Layla his body was not his own, existing only as she perceived it in his imagination. Now, in anticipation of her presence, he was suddenly aware of his long legs, thin and gangly as a camel's. His too-big teeth. His clammy hands, which were as broad as bird traps. His dark skin, black as water on a moonless night.

He took a deep breath and turned right along the office wall, glanced through the doorway at Alex's back, passed more plants potted in rusty oil drums. He waved to Dena and Mustafa across the yard, but the turmoil in his chest was growing. By the time he reached the kitchen door his gait was stiff and his eyes were wide. His jaw was clenched in a manic smile. He walked in blindly and stepped to the orange water cooler, poured himself water and drank. His throat gurgled and the glass wobbled and his Adam's apple bobbed. Only when he dropped the empty cup on the counter with a clatter and looked around did he realize that Layla wasn't there.

∫

"HOW'S THE FILMING?" The question came abrupt and electric through the headphones, startling her.

She didn't answer but felt his shadow lingering. Finally she pressed the Stop button and pulled the headphones from her ears. She'd been following Mustafa around the compound all morning, and now they'd ended up near the two beds in the courtyard, him sitting on a stool with wet knees above a large metal basin full of bedsheets in bubbling water, her crouching opposite him.

"It's fine," she said, looking up at Alex. There was an eagerness, an intrusive familiarity in the bold gray eyes.

Mustafa stopped washing for a moment and flicked his hands into the dirt, drying them. Drops of water flew everywhere and Dena shielded the camera with her arm.

"What's it about, your documentary?" Alex asked.

He was shirtless in the heat and she glanced at the few scattered hairs on his chest, noticed a dark mole beneath a pale nipple. She looked away, more embarrassed by this physical intimacy than he seemed to be.

"I've just started filming," she said.

"What's it for?"

"It's not for anything. It's for me."

He paused, bewildered. "But what are you going to do with it when it's finished?"

Again her eyes wandered down to his torso, to its easy nakedness.

"I don't know yet. Maybe nothing."

He watched her fingers on the camera's dials.

"What's the point of making a film if it will just sit there?"

The question vexed her. In this poor, troubled corner of the country there was room only for victims and saviors.

"And your map? What's the point?"

He seemed to register the challenge in her question, but his tone was casual when he answered. "It's simple. Information. The more information we have the better, right?"

She smiled, not a friendly smile.

There was a sudden brightening, a glinting of the rim of the metal basin, and she realized that the clouds were thinning and the sunlight was getting stronger and she would have only a few more minutes of good morning light left to film.

"Do you mind?" She gestured toward Mustafa, who had been following the tense inflections of the conversation, though not the words, which he only half understood.

"Of course," said Alex, spreading his hands. "I'll let you get on with it." He turned away and she watched as he ambled back to the office, his tanned arms and neck seeming to belong to a different body from the ghostly torso that connected them.

MUSTAFA CLIMBED UP on one of the beds and unhooked the mosquito net from the bamboo frame, then dumped the material on the mattress. He went over to the other bed and did the same. It was almost noon. Dena had put away her camera and gone to the kitchen to prepare lunch for everyone. Layla had not shown up today, and no one had eaten anything all morning.

He heard the pop and fizz of hot oil, and the smell of falafel drifted out of the kitchen doorway. The radio was still playing under the gazebo, though Dena had tuned in to the BBC station, and now the presenter's English speech drifted over the courtyard, staticky, sonorous, the words rippling over Mustafa mysteriously.

It was Thursday and the football championship final was tonight. There was only one place in all of Saraaya that was showing it: Omar's juice stall in the market, and it would cost him three hundred pounds to watch the game. But he had no money. Just last week he had spent all of his measly savings on buying merchandise for his underwear venture in the market. He had given his mother the rest of the fifteen thousand pounds a month he received for performing daily chores at the compound—cleaning and taking out rubbish and washing. His mother was widowed with two children much younger than him, and so most of his wages went to help her.

His friends wouldn't have any to spare. His mother would think it a waste. And she had given him a thousand pounds last month as a present for his twelfth birthday, which he had spent already. He listed in his mind the things he remembered buying: three bottles of Coca-Cola, two sweet pastries at the market, a pair of battered sunglasses from his friend Ibrahim—eight hundred pounds in total. But he couldn't remember what he had spent the remainder on.

He picked up the nets in his arms and crossed over to the mudroom used for storage. The air was stuffy in there, dusty. Cartons were stacked against a wall all the way up to the wood-beamed ceiling. Piles of blue tarpaulin sat in one corner, on top of an old, damaged generator with rusty gears. Cracked earthen pots were lined up underneath a wooden table by the door. Alex's belongings—a blue backpack and a small suitcase—were wedged in between them. On top of the table sat a rolled-up mattress and plastic bags full of bedclothes, pillows, and old newspapers. Mustafa stuffed the mosquito nets into one of the bags and went outside again, heading toward the beds.

On the way William hurried out of the office and caught up with him. "Where's Layla today?" he asked in Arabic.

"I don't know," said Mustafa. "She didn't come in this morning."

"Did she say anything yesterday?"

Mustafa shook his head. He had seen the way William's eyes followed her around the compound. How he tripped over his long legs when he noticed her watching him.

William drew closer. "Can you find out where she lives?"

Mustafa considered, sensing an opportunity. "Maybe. But."

"But?"

"It's another chore."

William stared at him. Then he understood. He pulled notes from his back pocket, counted them out.

"Here's two hundred pounds."

"Four," said Mustafa.

"Four? You're a thief."

"It'll take up half my day finding out where she lives. I have to ask around, go looking, find the house . . ." He tried to think of other ways to convey the magnitude of the errand.

"Fine, fine. Here's four," said William, adding to the notes. "Do it today. Tell me if she's coming tomorrow."

Mustafa took the notes and folded them in half. The game. A bottle of Coca-Cola. He smiled. He stuffed the money carefully into his pocket.

"I'll go after I finish here," he said. William patted him on the head and returned to the office.

He was dragging one of the beds toward the gazebo when there was a loud thumping at the gate. He continued pulling the bed until it was under the shade of the thatched roof, parallel to a hammock strung up between two poles made of tree trunks. When he walked back into the light he saw William standing by the gate. There was the sound of voices, but he couldn't see who was outside the door. William opened the gate farther and three men walked in, struggling to carry a heavy bundle wrapped in sackcloth. Nilot men, tall and dark like William, wearing faded, dusty vests, T-shirts, and cutoff trousers.

William spoke to them in Nilotic and directed them to the middle of the courtyard, by the bed. They laid the bundle down on the ground. Crouched over it. As one of them spoke he pointed to a location beyond the wall, his words visible in the excitement of his hands, fluttering up constantly, drawing a scene. The other two men sat quietly, listening and nodding occasionally.

When Alex stepped into the yard William called him over. One of the men drew open the top of the sackcloth. Mustafa couldn't see what was inside. Alex's eyes went wide and his face became suddenly paler. William covered his mouth and nose and drew his head back. Mustafa crossed over to the group. Something sweet and rotten in the air. Dena stepped out of the kitchen, drying her hands on a dishcloth.

"What is it?" she called, coming over. Mustafa wedged himself in between Alex and William.

One of the Nilot men was removing the sackcloth now, gingerly lifting the corners. The two men who stood on the other side of the bundle moved back as he threw the cloth open.

The stench rose, rancid and sweet and sulfurous, more a taste than a smell, filming their tongues. The skin—or what remained of it—was black and rutted in parts. It had melted onto the rib cage and flakes of it hung dryly on the bone; below it the scorched piping of the intestines spilled out. The arms stretched upward above the head, charred fingers coiling. Legs dry as wood were bent with the feet floating stiffly in the air. The lips had been burnt off, leaving the teeth protruding in a silent screech below the blackened stump of a nose and closed eyes.

The heat and stink concentrated around the grisly flesh were stifling. Dena stepped outside the circle. Alex covered his nose with his arm. William pulled his shirt over his face. Mustafa stood up and stepped back, breathing through his teeth. The three strangers were covering their noses now, too, swatting away the fat, buzzing flies that spun above the corpse. The even drone of the BBC presenter's voice washed over them. In the brightening sunlight the rough outlines of the body were stark against the brown dust of the courtyard floor.

Alex spoke over Mustafa's head to William, his voice muffled by his arm. "Where did they find it?"

William translated to the men, two of whom sat squatting along one side of the body. They were strong-muscled, their arms and faces splotched with dung ash. The same man who had spoken to William earlier—with high cheekbones and small, deep-set eyes—answered, the pitched syllables of the language moving fluidly back and forth between him and William.

"They were out grazing cattle upriver," said William, turning to Alex. "They found it in the grass, along the left bank."

"Do they know who it is?" asked Alex.

"They say word's been put out that a body has been found, but no one's claimed it yet."

The space of the courtyard contracted into the tight circle of people around the corpse. There was a movement and when Mustafa looked up he saw Dena, at the foot of the body, uncapping the lens of her camera and lifting it. The looming glass eye caressed the dead flesh, moving slowly, up and down, along the stiff curves of the legs and arms and torso. For a moment everyone's attention shifted to the thin woman with the camera. One of the two strangers sitting along the left side of the body whispered something to his companion. They stared up at Dena. Then their eyes returned to the corpse.

William spoke again. "They came to ask if we can drive them to the cemetery in the pickup truck. It's too far to walk, and they want to bury it."

"Did they go to the police?" asked Alex.

"They went there this morning. The police said the body's unidentifiable and there's nothing they can do about it unless someone comes forward. They will investigate, but they told them to bury it."

They all looked on in silence. A donkey cart rattled by in the street. A burst of music came from the radio, marking the end of the news program.

"I'll get the keys," said Alex, and stood up and went into the office.

One of the men leaned across the body and pulled the sackcloth over it. Everyone rose. The sun suddenly disappeared behind a tufted cloud, and the stark shadows of the walls, the gazebo, the colorful flags strung up along the periphery of the yard grew hazy as a dimness fell over the compound. A breeze drifted through the courtyard and the gate creaked languidly but insistently. The sackcloth covering the body quivered, wafting up, and William stretched forward and pulled it down again. Dena switched off her camera and held it dangling by the handgrip. Two of the herdsmen knelt and pulled the cloth taut around the corpse, then gripped the outstretched arms and feet. They lifted the body, and when Alex came out of the office, now in a blue T-shirt, he and William followed the men out through the gate.

Outside, the street was quiet in the midday heat. A stray dog trotting by slowed, then paused at a wary distance and tilted its head, scenting the flesh. Three women walked past on the opposite side of the road balancing plastic tubs of water on top of small padded cushions on their heads. They turned carefully, keeping their long necks steady, to watch the group of men maneuvering the brown bundle into the bed of the battered truck parked outside the compound. Standing just inside the gate, Dena and Mustafa suddenly felt a cold, wet pattering against their skin. They looked up at the sky, which was low and heavy with rain, the sun that was glaring only minutes ago nowhere to be seen.

∫

WILLIAM, OUTWARDLY CALM, kept telling himself that he was imagining things. He stood—Alex fidgeting nervously to one side with a shovel, the three herdsmen opposite him leaning on theirs—in a cemetery on the outskirts of town. It wasn't clearly demarcated so much as a patch of brown land that blended into a broader patch of brown land, the only indication that bodies were buried here the slight mounds of dirt rising from the earth, here and there the occasional misshapen headstone.

The shrouded corpse lay a few feet away, to the left of one of the herdsmen. It had been found kilometers out of town, surely far from where Layla lived. Things were flaring up again with the rebels, who were somewhere in the area, and probably the corpse had some connection to those troubles. There would have been news from her family if she'd disappeared.

Still, from the corner of his eye William was aware of the corpse's fingers straining against the fabric, as if wanting to tear through the shroud. He looked away, past the herdsmen and the corpse, to the tracks of dirt road near where the truck was parked, and farther along to the line of homesteads hugging the earth in the far distance, marking the southern periphery of the town. The drizzle had stopped, but the sun was still hidden behind a layer of clouds.

"Should we bury it here?" asked one of the herdsmen, the same one who had done most of the speaking at the compound. The other two looked at William—the question was addressed to him. This was one of those times when he wished he could escape the burden of his own authority. He was from here, but his work, its educated nature in a place where most people were farmers and cattle herders, separated him from the locals. He was just a translator, but in Saraaya that meant being a big man.

He lived in a town whose strategic importance in the war was in inverse proportion to its provinciality, its cut-offness, located, as it was, in the middle of nowhere—desert to the north and endless swamp and grasslands to the south—but here, at least, he'd been able to make a decent living for himself. Anyway, that's what he told himself. He'd been lucky, getting this job. He had a way with people, a talent for making himself likable (only with Layla did his powers seem to fail him), and because of it he knew how to get on with the police, the security men, the nomads, the Nilotes, the NGO staff, and expats like Alex whom he had to look after during their stays here.

Besides, at thirty-three, his desires were simple: He wanted a wife, children, his own home. He'd wanted more once, back when he was still a young man in Khartoum, where he'd turned up at the age of twenty, accounting diploma in hand, determined to make something of himself. He'd ended up in manual labor, working on construction sites in the city, on the extravagant, garish edifices that were rising up with the oil money spurting from wells all over the South.

In his first weeks in Khartoum—shaved, shoes polished, fake gold watch glinting on his wrist, accounting diploma carefully secreted in a plastic folder—he'd assaulted the offices in the central districts.

"We don't need an errand boy" was the bewildered response of the secretary in the first office he stepped into. He still remembered her: eyes winged with eye liner, round face wrapped tightly in a purple headscarf that cascaded elegantly on one side onto her shoulder. She was confused by his nice clothes. They didn't fit the pitch-black skin and the gangly frame that broadcast him as a Southerner.

The plastic folder crinkled as he reached into it. "I have a diploma." He handed it to her. She skimmed it. "I see . . ." She glanced left and right as if looking for a rubbish bin to throw it in. She leaned forward. "I'm sorry. No one will hire you for office work. I'm telling you this to save you the trouble. If you're looking for errand work, you might find something."

William stared. He replaced the diploma.

"Thank you," he said, and walked out.

In the next office, and the next, it was the same. Wide-eyed secretaries confused by his perfumed, elegant presence. His polished shoes. His spotless white shirt. The confident air with which he strode forward for a handshake. "Hello, my name is William Luol." Like an executive. Not a Southerner. Everywhere the same answer. No. We don't have anything. Nothing. Each defeat emboldened him rather than set him back. He swaggered more. Flourished his diploma. Boldly stared down the secretaries. Demanded to speak to their bosses. The more desperate he grew, savings quickly dwindling in his pocket, the more persistent he became.

Until one day he had no money left to pay rent for the house that he shared with his cousin and three other men from their hometown. So he joined his cousin on the construction sites. Every day from six a.m. to six p.m., then back to the two-room shanty. Fava beans for breakfast, lunch, and dinner. Washing out back with a hose attached to a tap that supplied them, in the summer, with water heated almost to the boiling point by the sun in the large metal tank that sat atop the neighbor's house.

The cinema had been his only escape in those days. He went there once a week, to watch Bollywood films with the little money he managed to spare. Doe-eyed heroines with bare midriffs and pierced nostrils. Handsome heroes garlanded with necklaces of flowers. Green pastures and palaces and ornamented doorways, far removed from that ugly brown city with its brown roads and its brown telephone poles. In the darkness of the cinema, discarded plastic bottles and bags snapping and crinkling beneath his feet, clusters of young men holding their breath when a bare arm, a throat, flashed on the screen, the exhaustion of the week would drain out of his body, out into the open space of the valleys in front of him, the hills and mountains, wash away with the waterfalls gushing their torrents.

Those films had, more than he realized, shaped his idea of love. He'd been back in Saraaya for three years. There was no shortage of eligible women and he could have easily been married by now, as his mother wanted him to be, but there was something about the way marriage was done here that put him off. Cattle exchanged for wife. That was it. It was a transaction, an exchange of goods, not love. And he wanted love. He'd given up on wealth, on success, and was disillusioned enough to understand that not everything was within his grasp. That life treated you differently based on where you were born and who you were born to, and there was nothing you could do about it. And so with age (he felt not exactly old, but too old and too young all at once), he had readjusted his expectations. He was intelligent, educated, likable, handsome, even, but a Southerner nonetheless. All he wanted, all he hoped for now, was a wife, children, a home.

For the first time since his return he had felt that he was really, truly in love. Why Layla? Perhaps because she was, on some level, inaccessible: After all, he was a Nilot and she was a nomad. Perhaps unconsciously he sought to reenact a complicated plot line from one of his Bollywood films, star-crossed love triumphing against the odds.

The appearance of the body that morning, and the coincidence of her absence, had left him stunned. Up to that point the worst that he had been preparing himself for was disappointment—it was possible that she would reject him. But was it possible that she was no more? It was a terrible thought, especially with the corpse's fingers straining there, still, against the fabric. So he kept telling himself that it wasn't her. It couldn't be.

He nodded at the ground, to the place the herdsman had indicated.

"Here's fine," he said. He lifted his shovel, ready to dig.

"But what if it belongs to the nomads?" asked the second herdsman, a long piece of grass waving from his mouth. He was older than the others, quieter.

William lowered the shovel. He hadn't even thought about which cemetery, actually, they were standing in.

"If no one's claimed the body, it's better to bury it. Doesn't matter where. Anyway, the nomads bury their dead quickly, within twenty-four hours."

The herdsman reached up and took the grass out of his mouth. "But if it's in the wrong cemetery—"

The other one, hands dangling over the handle of the shovel planted in front of him, interrupted him.

"It's all burnt up. You saw it. We can't know which cemetery to bury it in if we don't know who it is," he said.

"What are they saying?"

William turned to Alex, suddenly aware of being crowded, pressed upon; there was nothing but empty space around them, and yet Alex had somehow ended up only a few inches away from him, so that William had to step aside. He looked down now at the stubbled face, the raw lips, the gray, anxious eyes. The over-sized T-shirt made him look thinner, even, than he was.

He wished now that he had left him back at the compound. For the past two weeks Alex had been pushing William to speed things up with the authorities so that he could start on the map. William had resisted, not out of negligence but because he had no control over how long it would take for the paperwork to be processed; the authorities took their time, and more than that, because they were the authorities. His job was to help Alex, serve him even, but there was something about Alex's persistence, the way he followed him around, head craning, eyes squinting against the light, asking, "Why's it taking so long?" and "Can't you talk to them again?" and "What am I supposed to do in the mean-time?," question after question, without pause, and William try-ing hard to be polite but firm, not wanting to antagonize Alex but also itching to put him in his place, to make it clear that Alex just didn't understand how things worked here and it would be best for both of them if he left things up to William.

Now Alex's fear—he kept fussing with the shovel in his hands and glancing over his shoulder at the wide-open land behind them, as if they might be ambushed out of thin air—didn't move William; it irritated him. He explained that they didn't know who the body belonged to, the Nilotes or the nomads, and so they were debating which cemetery to bury it in.

Alex looked left and right—at the shallow mounds of graves on one side and then the other.

"It all looks the same," he said. "How do you know which cemetery's which?"

William pointed to five large stones, each about two feet wide, set in a row, separating the Nilot cemetery from the nomad burial grounds. They were easy to miss. The burial grounds were littered with stones of all sizes, some used as headstones, but everyone knew the configuration of these.

"Does it really matter where it's buried?" asked Alex.

William gestured to the herdsmen, who, though they couldn't understand a word, were engrossed in the exchange.

"They think it does," he said. "If it turns out the body belongs to the nomads, and it's buried in the Nilot cemetery, maybe it's a problem. And vice versa."

Alex's lips came together.

"Can't we just bury it in between?" he said.

"In between?" asked William.

"Yes. In between the two cemeteries. Like, in the middle."

William translated to the herdsmen.

Two of them spoke at once.

"In the middle? Not possible."

"It's one thing or the other."

"But if we don't know . . ." It was the elder herdsman.

William looked at the corpse, then up at the surrounding flat land, sparse tufts of grass receding with the end of the rainy season, earth and sky two pale slates reflecting one another. Where was she, where could she be? He looked at the corpse again. It wasn't her; it couldn't be.

"Let's just bury it here." He wanted to be done. He stepped forward, his shoes sinking into the soft earth, and thrust the shovel into the dirt.

"Here?" asked Alex, dragging his shovel behind him. "Are you sure?"

"Yes," said William. "Come on."

Two of the herders began digging, and Alex joined them.

The handle of the shovel was hot in William's hands. He dug without pausing for breath, dirt plashing against dirt, dust rising and coating his white shirt, stinging his eyes, aches running up and down his muscles, but he didn't stop—the pain in his arms focused his attention, concentrated him so that for moments at a time he forgot about Layla.

ſ

THROUGH THE AMBER TINT of his sunglasses Mustafa saw Jane sitting on a low stool in a bright-orange dress with a kettle in her hand, at her usual spot by the butcher's. A plastic rose bloomed from a braid in her hair. Her bottom spilled over the edges of her tiny seat as she sprinkled pinches of cinnamon into boiling water. A handful of men were gathered around her, sipping tea from small glass cups.

Jane pointed at his sunglasses. "What are you, a fruit fly?"

"They're new," said Mustafa, smiling. He fingered the sleek frame of the sunglasses, nudging them up the bridge of his nose. They slid back down. Jane laughed, her cheeks dimpling, tiny squares of teeth showing through her lips.

Behind her, just inside the entrance to the butcher's, giant cattle thighs teetered from hooks, swaying in the breeze. Wooden counters were strewn with chicken carcasses. Bits of rump meat, brisket, fore rib, shoulder. Pink-and-white flesh glistened bright against green tables. A sheep's head stared, tongue lolling, from a high shelf.

Jane replaced the lid on the kettle and leaned forward, her eyes serious suddenly. "I heard they found a dead body by the river today?"

Mustafa set down his plastic bags and wedged the glasses on top of his head. "Some herdsmen found it," he said. "They brought it to the compound this afternoon."

The men around Jane leaned in, full of questions. He puffed up, an arm on Jane's shoulder, ashy knees peeking from beneath the hem of his shorts, eyebrows, nose, mouth bobbing in his narrow face as he told them about the corpse, about the terrible, sweet smell that rose from it, about how it was impossible to tell even if it was a man or a woman. Just a burnt pile of flesh, like a scorched tree trunk.

"God help us," said Jane. "It's not a good omen, a dead body out of nowhere." She picked up a straw fan lying on the ground beside her and fanned briskly at the coal stove.

Mahmood, the butcher, spoke. "There's trouble coming," he said. "They're arming again."

Jane's eyes widened. She pressed the fan to her chest. "Haven't we had enough already?"

Mustafa lingered, listening. A Nilot herdsman said that the rebels were south of the swamps. Another man said no, they were as far north as the River Kinu. Yet another person said that five hundred soldiers were being sent from Khartoum, for reinforcement. They interrupted one another, disagreeing about when the fighting would erupt, whether the dead body had anything to do with it, and whether they would have to pack up and run once the clashes got going.

A shadow fell on the roped handle of the teakettle. It was getting late—he still had to set up shop and look for Layla later. He picked up his bags and waved to Jane, flip-flops smacking against his heels as he hurried north, his eyes flitting over merchandise displayed on rickety tables and shelves—secondhand radios and woven baskets and guava and watermelon and glass jars full of beads like hundreds of tiny eyes.

It was the time of day when returning from the fields, or from grazing cattle, people gathered in the market to rest, to gossip, to buy supplies for the evening meal. Now half the crowd lounged lazily under the shade of a neem tree or a tattered canopy, sitting in chairs or on their haunches, clustered mostly around the tea ladies, and the other half was busy selling and buying, laying out wares, haggling over prices, exchanging money. Here and there he caught snatches of conversation, news already flitting from mouth to mouth about the body.

He walked past a clandestine shop fronting as a mechanic's that sold Kalashnikovs and other small arms to Nilot and nomad herders alike, doing brisk business during the dry season, that tense time of year when the nomads arrived. At the stall next door, a fishmonger—neck smeared with batter—stood over a huge pan full of bubbling oil, frying tilapia. Farther down a vegetable seller sat with a straw hat drooping on his head, behind a table piled with tomatoes, cucumbers, limes, carrots—flies buzzing and spinning, scaling the vegetable skins.

He arrived at the spot he'd staked out with stones the day before, across the road from Hassan's clothes shop. Dresses, blouses, and skirts dangled from hangers hooked to the shop doorway. To his left was a battered Toyota van, its axles propped up on bricks. Beyond the van, on the other side, was a market woman selling toasted watermelon seeds packed in clear plastic bags. To his right was a boy a little older than himself, arranging hurricane lanterns into a pyramid on a low table.

His eyes flitted up and down the road as he unpacked his things, already on the lookout for customers. He hauled flattened cardboard boxes from beneath the rocks, folded them into shape, arranged them side by side so he had two makeshift tables next to the van. The van would provide shade, and privacy for more modest customers. From the rest of the bags he pulled out knickers, frilly undershirts, slips, bras, spreading out his merchandise on the surface of the cardboard.

He wanted to raise enough money for school fees. He had staked all of his savings, and hopes, on underwear to get him there. He had quit school three years before, after his father dropped dead while out tilling a field one morning, to help his mother. Without school he had no future. Just a lifetime of taking out rubbish. Washing other people's laundry. Sweeping courtyards. He had bigger plans: not just a school diploma but university, in the capital, a thousand kilometers away from this small, dingy, useless town. Now, out of school, he worked hard to learn whatever English he could from the foreigners who passed through the compound. He threw around the English phrases that he picked up, casually peppering his Arabic with them until a whole gaggle of twelve-year-olds now went about the streets interjecting strange words into their sentences—"I swear on the prophet, *cheers*, I saw it with my own two eyes!"

Hanan, a neighbor girl, had given him the idea. Women needed nice underwear, she said, and it was hard to find. Hanan was sixteen and suitors were already knocking at the door. She and her friends spent long afternoons braiding each other's hair, rubbing bread dough into their skin to make it glow, restitching old trousers into skirts, scarves into blouses. Mustafa had spent his savings on wholesale polyester and cotton goods that he'd found with Hanan's help in the large market in Hasaniya, a town two hundred kilometers away. It was cheap underwear—hems already fraying and stitches coming apart—but it was pretty, and there was nothing like it in Saraaya.

Before he had finished laying out the goods, women were already stopping to look.

"What are you up to now, you little imp?" said a grandmother, a basket piled high with wood on her head.

"You've turned into a little man before your time, haven't you!" said one of the tea ladies he was friendly with, picking up a slip and laughing.

A friend of Hanan's came up, her eyes taking in the feast of red and white and blue and yellow underwear, striped, flowered, plain, spotted, laced, silky.

"How much is this?" she asked. She held up a blue bra.

"Four hundred," said Mustafa.

"Do you have something more . . ." She made a lifting motion beneath her chest.

He ferreted through the garments and picked up a green bra with black polka dots.

"Here." He held out the bra, squeezed the cups with his fingers, then pulled it around his skinny ribs. "Wire cups. I'll give it to you for seven hundred. Look at how pretty it is." He pulled the bra tighter around his chest.

"Seven hundred? Do you think I'm a millionaire? Three hundred." But she took the bra from his hands, turning it in the light. Stepping behind the van so that she was hidden from the street, she adjusted it over her T-shirt. It was too big.

"It fits just right," he said.

"Really?"

"Yes."

"It feels big."

"I'll give it to you for five."

"Four," she said.

"All right, four." He took the blue notes, ragged with sweat and dirt, and stuffed them into a bag.

Alice, the bootlegger, bought a shiny black polyester slip for six hundred pounds. Mary and Nadia, who lived in a house on the edges of the market district, each paid him five hundred for a set of blue underwear. Jane came and sifted through the merchandise. The women joked with him, pinched his cheeks and ruffled his hair, picked up garments and haggled with him. An hour after he had set up shop, the plastic bag in which he kept the money was already filling with notes.

During a lull he looked up, surveying the street for more customers, when he saw, beyond cars parked on the other side of the road, a familiar yellow thoub. The woman was speaking to someone who walked beside her, and the thoub was pulled over her hair, hiding her face, so he couldn't be sure if it was Layla; but he called out her name, cupping his mouth and shouting over the broad dirt road. She didn't turn. He called again, louder this time, but by now she and her friend were farther along the street, heading north toward the Baynabi District, and he could only see the back of her. He moved to cross the street and catch up with them, but, glancing at the spread of underwear before him—his short life's savings—he changed his mind.

Two sisters, one plump and tall and one thin and short, came up, and soon he was busy showing them his things. When he searched the road again the yellow thoub was gone, and he turned back to the underwear, telling himself he'd go look for her after he was done.

He was in the middle of negotiating the price of a pair of pink knickers with black trimming, urging the sisters to feel the smoothness of the polyester, when he saw Hassan—folds of fat bulging along his middle, bald crown glowing like a bulb under the sunlight—marching toward him from his shop across the street.

The shopkeeper pushed the two sisters aside and stood wide as a barricade before Mustafa. "What do you think you're doing?"

"Selling underwear," said Mustafa, planting his hands on his hips. "What's the problem?"

"You can't just set up shop anywhere," said Hassan.

"Who says?"

He had set up his stall exactly in this corner of the market, of course, because it was across from Hassan's. Women going into or coming out of the clothes shop were bound to see his underwear table.

"You think you can steal my customers, you little brat?" said Hassan. "Out of here. Now!" He swept garments toward the edge of the cardboard. Mustafa dragged them back.

A knee surged up, hairy calf exposed for a moment, leopard-skin shoe floating in the air, angling, before the shoe crashed into the cardboard. Both boxes crumpled. Knickers, bras, slips tumbled to the ground. Mustafa dropped to his knees, picking up the underwear before it was trampled.

"Leave him alone!" The two sisters pulled at Hassan's jellabiya.

Mustafa—bra straps and leg holes looped around his arms,

the plastic bag full of money dangling from one hand—jumped up, trying to reach the flattened boxes that Hassan had snatched and now held high above his head. "Give it back!"

"Get out of here." Hassan elbowed him away. "If I see you again, you'll be in trouble, understood?"

The folds of his chin flapped. Drops of sweat clung, dancing, to the tip of his carrot nose. Cardboard gripped under his arm, he turned and waddled across the street, vanishing into the shadow of his shop.

"Bastard," said Mustafa.

"Don't mind him," said the younger sister. "Just set up somewhere else in the market tomorrow, away from him."

They leaned down to help him pick up the rest of the underwear scattered on the ground.

"What about the underpants?" said Mustafa, straightening and digging through the mess of things dangling from his arms and shoulders to find the pink pair he had been showing the sisters before Hassan arrived. He pulled them off his arm, held them up again. The black lace trimming was chalky with dust. The rubber waistband had stretched so that now it sagged, gaping, from his hand. The knickers seemed twice as big as they had been fifteen minutes ago.

The older sister blinked.

"I don't think so . . ."

"Why? What's the matter?" He glanced from one to the other.

"Look at them," said the younger one.

"You can wash them."

He dusted the knickers against his shorts, but stopped, afraid the waistband would stretch more.

"And they're too big now."

"I'll give them to you for three hundred."

"Next time maybe."

"One hundred then."

They began walking away.

"Fifty!" He trotted after them, holding out the underpants. But they turned into an alleyway and were soon lost in the crowd.

ſ

THE FIRST TIME he stepped out in the town it occurred to Alex that he had been transformed into some kind of fantastic beast. Feathers waving from his head. A black-rimmed beak spiking from his jaw. Scaly wings sprouting from his back. A long, hairy tail lashing left and right behind him. He saw it in the faces around him. Chattering mouths fell silent as eyes fell on him. Necks craned and heads pivoted, following him down the road. People called friends from shops to come and look. Little girls tugged at their mothers' skirts and pointed. A crowd gathered, thickening, along both sides of the street. It was a shock, the way everyone stared at him, unblinking, mouths agape. He had looked down at himself, checking his arms, his torso. Touched his blue Bermuda shorts. Peered at his toes in the open-toe sandals.

It was his second day in Saraaya, and William was taking him on a tour of the town. His arrival, William explained, was something of an event. The only other foreigners in the vicinity were the Chinese oil workers who lived in little encampments out in the plains, by the oil fields, having arrived all the way from villages in China to dig up the oil. They kept to themselves, these workers, clusters of leather-visaged men in dirty clothes, only occasionally coming to town for a night of love in the unofficial brothel on the edges of the market district. One or two half-Chinese babies had already appeared among the stalls, crawling in the dirt.

"So you see, you're an attraction," said William, floating on his long limbs high up above Alex. His feet didn't seem to touch the ground so much as tread on air. Each knee rose for half a minute, each hand wafted through the atmosphere in a long, pendulous motion by his side.

Next to him Alex stumbled on rocks and depressions in the ground. Strange parts of his body tingled with sunburn. His lips. The skin around his toenails. The small circle of exposed scalp in the middle of his crown. Pebbles rolled into his sandals and pricked his heels. He felt especially clumsy when he found the whole market gathering to stare at him. As he walked he looked back boldly at those who stopped to stare: the water seller with the skullcap who had halted a donkey with two giant barrels strapped to its side; a string of old men telling rosaries; a group of teenage girls who said something to him as he stepped past.

"Hi," he said. "Hello." He waved and smiled like a celebrity. He nodded. "Good afternoon." He threw in the Arabic and Nilotic greetings William had taught him, sprinkling them like sacred offerings on everyone he passed. Some of the onlookers laughed at him. Others answered back, gesturing with their hands. Intrepid boys detached themselves from the crowd. One grabbed the hem of his T-shirt, trotting after him and giggling. Another, taking courage, reached for the giant black watch around his wrist. Small, dry fingers dug into his flesh, boldly pressing and squeezing.

Here and there William pointed out important landmarks. There weren't many: a mosque, a church, a police station, the small, dusty market. Army barracks somewhere by the highway that led to Khartoum. Alleyways careening and twisting at random angles. Huts that didn't look like houses so much as giant mushrooms that had sprouted from the earth. Big-horned cattle everywhere. Goats that liked to perch high up in trees, snipping at leaves. A brown-green landscape, interrupted by the women's bright-colored dresses in bursts of red and saffron yellow and rippling blue and orange.

"This is the local drinking establishment," William said, leading him through a doorway in an alley off the main road.

It was more like a dungeon. Low, dark walls, no windows. Benches along two sides of the room. A narrow passageway led between stools on which groups of men sat with their knees and elbows pointing. Glittering eyes, sweat-sheened shoulders, calves blended into shadow and light. People paused with their cups in midair. Spoons tinkled against plates. In the quiet, flies buzzed and zipped from one sticky teacup to another. It was close and hot, drops of sweat trickling down Alex's jaw and into the hollow at the base of his throat, the tip of his nose gleaming.

Over the course of those first two weeks he'd slowly begun to get used to the place, adjusting to its rugged edges, people becoming familiar with him, he with them. He learned names. When he walked through town, fruit vendors pressed oranges and guavas into his hand. He'd gotten up the courage to go out on his own, without William, communicating in a mixture of sign language and English and the few words of Nilotic and Arabic that he knew.

He had accustomed himself to using the pit latrines. They had terrified him at first, especially at night, when the roving beam of his flashlight exposed all the creeping, scurrying, buzzing creatures that had made a colony of the bathroom in the compound. Cockroach antennae poking up from the pit. Mosquitoes looping in the air, angling to dig proboscises into his exposed behind. Flies clustering on walls, gleefully rubbing their hands together. It had taken him days to perfect the precarious procedure of maneuvering himself over the pit, his feet—constrained by shorts at his ankles—propped on either side on two crumbling bricks, his butt hauled up in the air, his leg muscles trembling at the thought of cockroaches darting up his ankles.

Now he paced back and forth in the cramped office in the

compound, restless. His stomach had been queasy ever since the burial the day before, his body tipping between hot and cold despite the heat. He remembered dirt piling up as they'd shoveled onto the flesh, teeth screeching through the grime even as the eyes, the cheekbones, the hollow of the nose disappeared. On the way back from the burial they had stopped in the market to drop off the herdsmen. They had been accosted by a crowd, full of questions about the corpse. Bodies pressed in and suffocated him, hands reached for him, tongues jabbered. A fight had almost broken out over whether the corpse belonged to the nomads or the Nilotes. Burial rites, ablutions.

He'd grown too comfortable in the town, forgetting that he was a stranger here, alone. Up until the appearance of the corpse the war had been a distant idea, despite rumors of Southern rebels converging beyond the swamps, men with guns demanding rights, resources, autonomy. The town and its oil fields had been captured by the government five years before; the rebels wanted it back. He'd heard, not long after he'd landed—just his luck of course—that clashes might be erupting again.

He paused in front of the poster of the raised hands, the floating globe. What was he doing here? It was a long way from the easy, stable life he had known as a child. His father was a tax lawyer who had a practice in the suburbs of Cleveland—where the family lived—and his two older brothers had followed in his footsteps, but Alex had always known that a job in an office, and a suit, and a house in the suburbs somewhere, were not meant for him. Instead of going to law school like his brothers, he'd opted for graduate studies in geography, an outgrowth of a childhood love of maps, which he'd collected ever since his school days: geologic maps, antique maps, topographic maps, of places far and near. They had given him, those maps, a desire for the world beyond the suburbs, away from his family's house, identical to every other house on the street, in a planned development itself indistinguishable from a dozen other planned developments on the outskirts of Cleveland.

Music was the other love that had marked his childhood back at home. When he was still in school he went to N.W.A. and Public Enemy concerts—on the rare occasion when these, among others of his favorite bands, purveyors of a new music called hip-hop, made an appearance in Cleveland. There, his father—who insisted on accompanying him to the concerts because he was still in middle school—would spend half the time trying to clap his palms to Alex's ears when the more explicit lyrics burst forth from the loudspeakers.

Rotund of belly, bespectacled, in starched khakis and shirt, and white and middle-aged, his father was an eyesore in that crowd—and it was often a tussle Alex went through, when one of the bands came to Cleveland, over whether the delight of seeing them in person outweighed the embarrassment of appearing at the concert with his dad, especially amongst that cool crowd of jelly-curled, flat-topped kids, into which his three best friends, Steven, Daniel, and Nandan (Black, Dominican, and Indian—an anomalous group of friends in a suburban-school sea of white) melted with ease, keeping, in fact, a distance from him and his father when they, too, were in the audience.

After finishing graduate school he worked for the National Park Service, then applied to jobs abroad—it was time, he'd decided, to escape his familiar life altogether. Among them was the job here: *Mapping and Surveying Field Officer, Saraaya, Sudan.* Except for summers in between his studies spent volunteering in Central America, he'd had no experience working abroad. He was too innocent to wonder, when he was offered the job, why they were giving it to a twenty-seven-year-old with little experience either in development or international work—even if, technically, he had the surveying skills that the organization was looking for. He didn't know much about Sudan, and even less about the town where he would be stationed, but it was as distant and exotic a place as he could think to go. What drew him to the job was that he would be out and about. *Fieldwork*. He had a vision of himself running naked through a plain.

It was only after he had been plonked down in Saraaya, tumbling out of a tiny UN plane one morning in mid-November, tripping down the narrow steps to the dirt runway, his legs unsteady after the turbulent flight, that it began to dawn on him: No expat was naïve enough to agree to be stationed in that remote region, in that blip of a town with no electricity, few roads, and crucially, no other expats (they only flitted by, he'd learned when he was doing his training in Khartoum, for a few days every four or five months).

No one wanted to work in Saraaya. It was why he had been offered the job. Still it was an adventure, and a worthwhile one at that. He would make a map, and the map would be a first step leading the way to better things for people who needed it: improved development planning, a more efficient distribution of aid resources. It was rewarding work, meaningful work, and it filled him with a sense of purpose and mission. He'd been exhilarated by the challenge and had been looking forward to it all. Until the corpse had appeared and thrown everything out of balance, making him question, for the first time, what exactly he was doing here.

He blinked at the poster, suddenly weary of his own company, of the thoughts scuttling around his head. He felt caged in the small office. William, who'd gone to the police station to find out if there was any more information about the body, wasn't back.

Looking through the office door, he was relieved to see Dena. She was bent over a table in the yard packing her camera bag. Her short hair was hidden beneath a checkered red and yellow bandanna. The crisp, expensive linen shirt that hung loosely on her shallow frame marked her as an outsider in this land of ragged T-shirts, ill-fitting dresses, and hole-ridden shoes. Though they'd been sharing the compound for a couple of weeks he still knew only basic facts about her. Her family was from Khartoum. She had grown up in Seattle. She was staying in the compound for a few months while making a film—had made some kind of an arrangement with the organization in the capital.

She glanced up at him as he approached.

"You're going out?" he asked.

"Yes," she said. She zipped up the bag, then began wrestling the tripod into a side pocket.

"Where?"

"Outside of town, to shoot."

"Alone?"

She nodded.

"Is that a good idea?"

She stopped, the tripod half in its pocket.

"Why wouldn't it be?"

He gestured to the spot where the corpse had lain. "The dead body that turned up yesterday," he said. "Doesn't it worry you?"

She shrugged. "We don't know what it's about yet."

"There might be fighting soon," he said. "William says so. Some kind of attack, maybe, on the police, or the security."

"Until that happens—*if* it happens—I have to get on with filming," she said. "Anyway, there's always a chance that something might happen here."

He looked away, scanning the courtyard. The office, at the front of the compound, faced out onto the main road that traversed the town from south to north. Beside it was his bedroom. To his right was the kitchen—a long, rectangular room with blue shutters. In front of it sat a greasy red generator on deflated wheels, which was switched on for four hours every evening, between seven and eleven p.m. The gazebo was at the back. To his left, opposite the kitchen, was the storage room. Then Dena's bedroom, the bathroom, and on the other side of the bathroom the room that William and Mustafa shared, though both preferred to sleep in the fresh air under the gazebo.

All of this was hemmed in by a brick wall. It would do little to keep danger out.

Dena lifted the bag onto her shoulders. A sign that the conversation was at an end.

"How come you always do that?" he asked.

"Do what?" she asked, thumbs hooked into the straps of the bag.

"Cut things short. Talking. With me."

His mood, his fear, made him reckless.

"I was on my way out."

"You don't like me," he said. "Is that what it is?"

She stared at him, taken aback. Then, collecting herself, she shrugged again. "We're here for different reasons, doing different things. Let's just try to get along. While we're living together anyway."

"But why *aren't* we getting along?" he said.

That was it: He felt, around her, that he was guilty of some offense he couldn't identify or name.

"Maybe if you weren't so eager," she said.

He stared blankly.

"To be friends, to talk all the time."

"That bothers you?"

She didn't answer, just stood there, arms crossed.

"Fine." He raised a hand to his forehead in a mock-salute. "Good luck filming."

She glared at him, then turned. He watched as she walked toward the gate, each step a rebuke silently delivered.

ſ

DENA CLOSED THE GATE behind her and marched down the street, past more homesteads and compounds, past a boy leading two cows, past rubbish floated up by a dusty breeze, stepping quickly, impatiently, despite the camera bag—which in the afternoon heat felt twice as heavy—pressing down on her shoulders and back. Yes, she didn't like Alex. Why did he insist on being friends? She frowned. They weren't.

If she had to put a finger on it, it was his righteousness that bothered her. He was smug about his map. And condescending toward her own work. He'd wanted her to affirm his fear, just now, about the corpse. He was afraid for himself, and he was ready to run, and he had wanted her to make him feel better about it. She wouldn't. Typical of people like Alex, she thought, those types who popped up here. Full of their own heroism until the first whiff of danger. They were all over Khartoum, in their SUVs, in their "expat-only" clubs and parties and their monthly "rest & recuperation" vacations to safaris in Kenya, because it was such a hardship, to work in such a country, so unbearable—the weather, the boredom, the landscape. He was one of them.

She slowed, suddenly breathless, blood pulsing through her temples. She'd been walking too fast, and it was too hot. She reached for a water bottle in the side pocket of the bag. The water was warm, unpleasant in her throat, with a plasticky taste to it—as if the bottle itself were melting in the heat.

Time to put him out of her mind. She looked around, focusing instead on the filming ahead. Children's voices, repeating something, filtered from nearby. She remembered that up the road was an elementary school and walked, slower now, toward it. A large section of the wall had collapsed, and as she passed she could see twenty or thirty children in the yard, crowded in a circle around a teacher sitting on a chair. She stopped, drawn by the image.

One of the children looked up and saw her.

He pointed. "Is it a boy or a girl?" he said.

The whole class—a crowd of heads and eyes and teeth, bare feet bundled close to their bodies in the squashed circle—turned to stare. Chalk slabs sat idle on their laps. The teacher, a young man in dark trousers and a neat white shirt, lowered the open book in his hand.

A child rose. Then they all flooded, tumbling, elbowing one another, hurrying toward the gap in the wall.

How strange she must look to them. She forgot it sometimes. She'd shaved her hair down to the scalp back in Boston. Now it had grown out into short, shiny curls around the dome of her head. Her short hair and trousers confused everyone. Some women wore their hair short in Saraaya, but usually in tightly plaited braids. Women never wore trousers. And Dena's narrowness and her prettiness had about it the angled quality of boyhood. Broad shoulders and spare, bony hips, small breasts gone missing in the loose Nehru-collared shirts she liked to wear when she was filming. Something boyish, too, about the jutting triangle of her jaw. Her earrings—two flower-etched jade medallions dropping from each ear—confused matters more.

Not wanting to disrupt the lesson, she continued on her way, but a small group of unzippered and unbuttoned children clambered over the rubbled wall and trailed behind her down the road, deliberating.

"But he's wearing trousers!" called out one child.

"What about the earrings? A boy doesn't wear earrings!"

"But his hair's short!"

They went back and forth as if discussing a strange animal that had materialized out of the heat-mirage of the midday sun. She smiled to herself, listening to the conversation. Occasionally glanced back at the group of boys and girls who took the chance to peer at her face more closely. They weren't interested in her own opinion. They walked on for a few minutes more beyond the schoolhouse when she stopped. The children came to a halt behind her.

"Don't you have to get back to your lesson?" she asked in Arabic.

"She sounds like a girl!" a tiny boy with two missing front teeth said.

"I am a girl," said Dena. Those who had insisted she was a boy gasped in disbelief. An excited rumble went through the group.

"Why's your hair so short then?" asked a girl in a dirty yellow dress with puffy sleeves.

"Because I don't want to bother with brushing it all the time," said Dena. She'd walked into a barbershop in Boston two years earlier, determined never to comb or braid or blow-dry her hair again, and asked the barber to shave it all off. A group of teenage boys across the street watched the whole scene through the glass window, their movements miming shock and disbelief as the long strands of thick, wavy hair fell to the floor, collecting in a lifeless mass at the barber's feet.

"But you're a girl, you *have* to brush your hair!" a boy called out.

"Not if I've cut it all off," she said, running her hand over the short, glossy curls. The children stared, stupefied.

"You won't find a husband if you look like that," said a girl, bigger than the rest, with two pigtails bent outward and suspended in the air as if with their own stubborn willfulness.

"That's fine by me. Who needs a husband?" said Dena.

"Every woman needs a husband," countered another boy. "Otherwise, you'll end up a . . . a *spinster*."

Giggles rose up in the crowd.

"That's good. It means I won't have to cook and clean and look after some ugly old man."

The children didn't know whether to approve or disapprove of this blasphemy, but it thrilled them. They pressed closer around her.

"What's your name?" one of them asked.

"Dena," she said, crouching down. "And what are yours?"

They went around the circle telling her their names, shy and excited.

"Where are you going?" asked Daoud, a boy of about eight or nine who wore the child version of the long robes that the nomads wore.

"I'm going to take pictures."

"Can we come with you?"

She saw the teacher hurrying toward them. "I think you should get back to school," she said.

Before the children could scatter the teacher bore down on them, shouting, his white shirt flapping. They swept around him and ran back toward the schoolhouse. He trotted after them heavily. Daoud waved to Dena as he fled. "See you around!" he called, and she waved back.

Thatched roofs peeked up above the mud walls of the homesteads. Every now and again a cattle byre—much larger than the small huts in which the townspeople lived—loomed over the houses. The chatter of chickens clucking in a hidden courtyard mingled with the wind echoing dryly in her ears. Toward the end of the road there were fewer homesteads, and then the track spilled abruptly into a dusty clearing with two large stones—makeshift goalposts—set wide apart at either end. In the stillness, she remembered the corpse. Maybe Alex was right. Was it wise to be going out on her own? She hesitated, glancing around. It was quiet, empty. Annoyed at herself for thinking of Alex, she walked on, resolute, and crossed the dirt road that marked the end of the town's living quarters.

The wet season was ending. Sunlight cast a warm glow over the scene in front of her: the sprawling clay plain north of town, grass already fading into patches of brown and pale green and yellow, stretching for miles and miles on end, flat, open, broken only at the horizon by a line of trees and shrubs that seemed black in the distance, behind which was the river, hidden from view. Above the trees cumulus clouds rose up into the sky, their soft, spreading bulk casting huge pools of shadow over the grass. It was what she'd come for: to capture this broad sweep of the land that lay around her, around the town. She forgot about the corpse, swept up by the scene. She pulled the tripod out of the bag and loosened its locks. The legs lengthened with a heavy jerk. Peering down at the green water bubble set in the tripod head, she shifted the legs carefully, lengthening one and shortening another until the bubble settled where it should and the tripod head was balanced, then locked the camera on top.

She leaned forward and pressed her face against the eyecup, flicking on the power button. The camera whirred beneath her fingers. The picture blurred and sharpened and blurred again as she adjusted the lens and focused on the view in front of her.

Refracting the light, the lens miniaturized the landscape, flattening the soft upsurge of white clouds, the trees undulating in the distance, the rough bristle of November grass. When she homed in with the zoom lens the silhouette of trees grew clearer, the tendrils of grass sharper, but then she lost the openness of the sky. For half an hour she played with the toggle control, zoomed in and out, moved forward and backward, readjusting the tripod each time, but still the image fell flat.

She looked up and rubbed the back of her neck, watching cloud shadows shift slowly over the plain. Frustrated by the smallness of her body. The meagerness of the device latched to the tripod. She didn't know how to approach this landscape with the lens of a camera. There was nothing to focus on, nothing to draw the eye to a point. It was all planes and lines and blocks of pale color extending outward and upward, defying containment.

Looking through the lens again, she tilted the tripod head higher so that there was only a strip of grass at the bottom of the frame, then trees, then clouds above. An image floated up from the recesses of her memory, a panning shot of a savannah in a David MacDougall film she'd seen in film class in college. Now her hands traced the outline of the shot as she remembered it, slowly moving the tripod arm in a 180-degree angle beginning to her right and unfurling in a steady sweep to the left. Halfway through the glide her arm muscle slackened and the camera jerked, slowing, then lurched forward. She tried again. Her arm was steadier this time, but in her rush to avoid another lurch she moved too fast. The lens zipped recklessly, impatiently, across the landscape.

She straightened and rubbed her damp palms against her trousers. She clenched her jaw muscles, whether in despair or determination even she didn't know. How had MacDougall done it? It had seemed so easy, so effortless. There had been something of it the morning before, when she had filmed Mustafa sweeping the courtyard. An alchemy of light, luck, perspective, and positioning. She'd filmed him for hours at the compound, striving and straining day after day, taking up one position, then another, hand-holding the camera, balancing it on the tripod, capturing him under the shade, in the sun, washing, sweeping, resting, talking, laughing—and yet yesterday was the first time that that mysterious conjunction had materialized out of nowhere and there was magic in the moving picture of the boy.

Still, she put her hope in effort. In her mind she had a dim vision of the film she wanted to make, and the promise of it made her push on. What drew her was the possibility of lacing together the pieces of this place into something whole. It would be a mosaic, made up of shards of images arranged to create a wider portrait, each fragment deriving meaning from its neighbors to give a picture of the land and its people.

She stroked the buttons on the right side of the camera—the ND filter switch, the gain, the white-balance toggle that calibrated light and color. She'd learned all the nooks and crannies of the device, an obsession that had taken hold when she'd stumbled into a documentary film class during her third year of university in Massachusetts. After graduating she took out a loan to buy a camera, tapes, microphones, and—to the dismay of her parents, who worried about her returning alone to the country they'd fled fifteen years before—a one-way ticket to Sudan.

All she had known of the country until then was Khartoum, glimpsed on summer vacations she'd spent there as a child. Full of so many relatives she couldn't keep track of names. Plump aunts and chain-smoking uncles. Cousins and second cousins who multiplied in number every year. Weddings, funerals, naming ceremonies. She had avoided Khartoum. It was her parents' city. And her parents refused to understand anything about her filmmaking, or her lack of interest in boys. So she had gone as far away from them, and from Khartoum, as she could.

Looking up, she saw that the sun had descended into the trees and the light was softening. A day moon hung over the horizon. Faint sounds filled the air. The distant croak of frogs calling for mates in pools of warm water, cricket trills, and then the rise and fall of the muezzin's voice announcing the call to prayer from the minaret, wafting over the town and the plain and the hidden river. The camera stared blindly at the horizon. She capped it finally and packed up her things, telling herself that she would try again tomorrow.

s

"LAYLA?"

Dena turned. William's shadow hurried ahead of him across the doorway, then he himself appeared, halting just inside the kitchen. His face dropped. Lips came together, frustrated.

"Oh. I thought you were Layla," he said in English.

"Sorry," she said in Arabic.

His gaze darted to the corners of the kitchen, as if Layla might step out of the refrigerator or unfold herself from the onion basket by the stove, and then he looked at Dena again. She saw herself, the Not-Layla, her thin frame so different from Layla's voluptuous one. An absence of long, thick plaits that refused to hide coyly under the hood of her thoub, as they were supposed to do, preferring, instead, to parade their loveliness for all to see. And none of Layla's finesse in the kitchen. Dena stood clutching a carrot in her hand like a microphone. Everything turned into some variation of camera equipment in her hands. She set the carrot down on the countertop.

"She didn't show up today," she said.

"Where is Mustafa?"

It frustrated her, William's tendency to address her in English.

"Haven't seen him," she said in Arabic. "Any news about the body?"

He shook his head. He stood there, filling the kitchen with his long, floating presence, and she found herself absorbing the details of his appearance. Rectangular jaw framing soft plump lips. Scraped planes of cheekbones interrupted by a boldly sprawling nose. Severe brow bones set against the gentle, friendly flicker of curious eyes. Narrow khakis tunneled the long length of legs down to the sandals. The sleeves of his blue shirt were buttoned just above his wrist bones. She could see the silhouette of his white undershirt beneath the blue shirt, which pointed to another William, a less formal, more intimate William. She searched in herself, casting about like some fisherman, for some romantic response—a reflex from the days when she'd still hoped, for her mother's sake, if not for her own, that she was attracted to the opposite sex—but found none. Her appreciation was visual: She wanted to film him.

More than that, she wanted William's friendship. But there was this strange awkwardness between them. For instance, this English thing. He always spoke to Mustafa in Arabic, but, for some reason, never to her.

"How was the burial?" she asked. "Did it go all right?"

"It's done," he said. "The police have to investigate now."

"Why do you always speak to me in English, William?" she asked.

He looked at her, surprised. He was anxious, hectic today. His face was shinier than usual, a glint of sweat high on his cheeks.

His shoulders hiccupped. "I thought—" He stopped and began again in Arabic. "I just thought maybe it was easier for you." He paused. "Your Arabic is a little—" A hand floated up, palm downward, fingers spread, and wavered in the air like a rickety Sudan Airways craft on the brink of crash-landing.

She blinked at him. "My Arabic is good," she said. "Not bad, anyway."

"You're right. Sorry," he said. His eyes kept darting around the kitchen. "I really need to find Mustafa."

Dena's professional relationship to William was unclear. She was in the compound as a guest, had made the arrangement through a family friend who worked for the organization in Khartoum. William wasn't obligated toward her in any way, but when she arrived she'd discovered that he had an interest in film— Bollywood films—and because of it he was enthusiastic about her work, though at first he couldn't grasp what there was to film in the dusty, sleepy town that was Saraaya. But he'd been helpful, suggesting places she could shoot, introducing her to people in the town, and always curious about her progress.

The gate squeaked open and shut. William turned and stepped out of the kitchen.

"Mustafa!" He disappeared toward the gate.

A minute later Mustafa came in, stick arms struggling with

the weight of two large plastic sacks, followed by William. Mustafa's sunglasses, low on his nose, gave him the allure of a cool mosquito. He said hello to Dena and dropped the bags on the floor,
then, standing in the middle of the kitchen, rotated his shoulders
like an athlete warming up. He clasped his hands behind his back
and stretched his arms.

"You *saw* Layla?" asked William. He leaned down, hands
propped on his knees, to stare Mustafa in the face as he stretched.

"Yes," he said.

"Where?"

"In the market. Or I *thought* I saw her. It looked like her. But
I couldn't see her properly. She was across the street—"

"So you *didn't* see her," said William.

"I did."

"But you just said—"

"I saw her again later."

"You mean, after the market?"

"Yes."

"Why didn't you come back last night? I was waiting for you."

"The football championship. I watched it with my friend
Ibrahim and stayed over at his after."

Mustafa went to the water cooler, reaching on tiptoes for a
cup on the shelf above.

William went up to him, breathless. He put a hand on his
shoulder. "Look at me." Mustafa turned. "So you *found* her?"

"Yes."

"Where? Tell me everything."

"I went to her house. I had to ask a million people in the
market before anyone could tell me where she lived; then it took
me an hour to walk there. I got to one village but I couldn't find
the house, and then someone told me I was in the wrong village.
So then I had to walk another four kilometers to the *right* village.

The one by the wadi, the new one where all the nomads have settled. Then it turned out her house wasn't exactly in the village—"

"Cut it short. Did you *speak* to her?"

"You want to hear everything. I'm telling you everything."

Watching this back-and-forth between William and Mustafa,
Dena tried, once again, to pin down the quality of their relationship, which was something like a father and a son, but more
or less than that, she wasn't quite sure which. Mustafa, whose
head just reached William's elbow, was about a third of William's
age, and his livelihood depended on William. But he seemed to
think that he was his equal. He wasn't afraid of him, knew William went out of his way to look after him. Mustafa had told her
he'd been working at the compound for three years, since he was
nine. In the first week, Alex had huffed about this, lecturing William under the gazebo. How could a humanitarian organization
working to lift people out of poverty employ an underage child?
Shouldn't Mustafa be in school? Did the office in Khartoum know
about this?

William had rolled his eyes at Alex and turned to Mustafa,
who was busy slopping the courtyard with water.

"He says you're too young to be working here," William said
in Arabic.

Mustafa had looked pointedly at Alex. "No," he said in English. He turned to William. "Tell him: I need the money." He continued to slop water. That was the end of it. Alex didn't bring
it up again.

Now Mustafa, displeased with William's questioning, had
turned his back and was calmly rummaging through his bags.

"Just tell me," said William in a softer voice. "You found
her house?"

"Yes," said Mustafa.

"And she was there?"

"Yes," said Mustafa.

"When is she coming back?"

"In a week or two. Her father's very sick—she's looking after him."

"You saw her?" said William. "You spoke to her?"

Mustafa peered up at him like he was crazy. "*Yes*. I *spoke* to her."

"She's fine?"

"*Yes*."

William was silent. He looked at the ground, watching this news anchor there, solid. He closed his eyes. A shudder went through his body, a ripple of tensing and loosening muscle, so that his hands and his arms and his shoulders clenched and unclenched, and when he opened his eyes again it was as though his body were longer somehow, freer. Dena understood: the gruffness, the distraction. He'd connected the corpse with Layla's absence, and he had been worried.

When he looked up, he was suddenly interested in their affairs. "What's in the bags?" he asked Mustafa. Mustafa told him about the underwear, and his run-in with Hassan. "Avoid trouble with Hassan," said William. "He has a cousin in the police. Just move to another spot in the market."

He asked Dena what she was making. Could he try a little bit of salad? He picked up a slice of carrot from the chopping board and crunched it, jaw muscles rippling. He stepped about the kitchen—tall, relaxed, friendly, the room suddenly suffused with his energy. He inquired about the film. Where did she go today? What did she shoot? She answered; she couldn't help feeling happy, too, telling him about her day.

"Where's Alex?" he asked.

"In the office," said Dena. He had kept to the office ever since she'd returned from filming. It was their conversation earlier, she knew. He was avoiding her. For the best, probably. She squeezed half a lime into the bowl of chopped salad. "Is it true," she said, "that there are rebels in the area? Alex was worried earlier."

William waved him away. "Alex is worried about everything," he said, as though he himself hadn't been fretting only minutes ago. "Who knows? It's just rumors."

Mustafa, broom in hand, straightened. "Everyone was talking about it in the market. They're saying the corpse has something to do with it."

"Maybe. Maybe not," said William. His face suddenly grew serious. "When did you say Layla is coming back?"

"She didn't say exactly. Just that she'd be away for a week, maybe two. She said she'd send word."

"When? Will she send word?"

Mustafa blew out a breath. "How am I supposed to know?"

"Well." William paused. "She will be back." He smiled. "That's the important thing."

He surged forward and, hooking one arm under Mustafa's knees and the other under his shoulders, swept him off his feet and went circling and dipping with him around the kitchen. Mustafa, squealing, legs flailing, dropped the broom, clinging to William's shirt.

Dena felt laughter bubbling up. She liked these two. She liked watching them together. Suddenly she missed her camera. It was in her room. She moved to get it, then stopped. Sometimes, she scolded herself, you just have to enjoy the moment. Forget the camera. It was the first time she'd seen them laugh since the corpse. She leaned back against the counter as William swung Mustafa in the air.

THE PAST TWO WEEKS HAD BLENDED, IT SEEMED TO Alex, into one endless day of sitting in a waiting room whose details varied only slightly, depending on which office—police, military, security—they happened to be confined to that afternoon. Today the walls were blue instead of mint green. He and William were waiting at the security office instead of the army barracks. But here was the same oversized waiting-room furniture that looked like it might burst out of its seams and drown him in foam stuffing. On the wall opposite the armchairs in which they sat was framed the requisite verse from the Koran, emblazoned in kitschy, glittering gold against a black backdrop. The wheeze of a fan completed the picture, as well as the synthetic rustle of a plastic plant positioned in the corner.

Before Saraaya, he'd spent a month in Khartoum running in a maze of paperwork. From the organization's office to the Ministry of Humanitarian Affairs. From there to the American embassy. Back to the office. Then to the ministry again. Fingerprints. Passport pictures. Description of the project. Sources of funding. Visa applications. They were lovers of visas here. You needed a visa not only to enter but a visa to leave the country. He even needed a permit to travel inside the country—between Khartoum and Saraaya.

For two weeks now he had been trailing William from office to office. He'd received authorization in Khartoum to carry out work in the town. But he'd discovered upon arrival that he also needed to be vetted by the authorities in Saraaya.

He turned to William, whose elbow was propped on the armchair next to his, chin cradled between thumb and forefinger, legs crossed at the ankles reaching halfway into the room. A smile played on his lips as he stared at the plastic plant. There had been a shift in William's mood over these past few days. Bursts of manic energy that alternated with quiet, languorous stupors, such as the one he was sunk in now, in which he sat or stood for minutes at a time rapt in mysterious daydreams. It puzzled Alex. He was the only one still bothered over the body. Dena was going about business as usual. William, it seemed, had become happier since the body had appeared. Alex could make neither heads nor tails of it.

He tapped him on the shoulder now.

"How long do we have to wait?"

William, startled out of his daydream, glanced at him "I don't know. Until they call us."

"And once they call us, what happens?"

"They'll look over the papers we have. If everything is in order, they'll stamp the security authorization today."

"And then? Can I start?"

"No. Then we have to take the authorization to the district office."

"And what do they do?"

"They also have to stamp it. After interviewing you."

"And that's it?"

"No. Then they fax the authorization back to Khartoum. We have to wait for a signature from the ministry. And then you can start working."

Alex gripped the armrests of his chair. Blew out a breath, cheeks puffing. He'd been receiving calls on the satellite phone from Greg, his boss in Khartoum, asking about the map. State

Department money for aid projects in the district—a whole two million dollars of it—depended on the map, and Alex was expected to have something to show in six months, by mid-June.

"I'm waiting on authorization," Alex had explained to Greg over the echo of his own voice on the sat phone.

"What authorization?" said Greg. "You were authorized in Khartoum."

"I need permission from the local authorities."

"You've been there for weeks now. We need this money, Alex. Find a way to get going."

Alex was beginning to rethink his liking for his boss, a burly American who, in the days Alex had spent with him, had kept complaining about how awful Khartoum was. Especially compared to Kinshasa, where he'd been stationed for two years prior to arriving in the dusty nonentity—more like a big, sleepy village than a city—that was the Sudanese capital. In Kinshasa you could drink. You could party. You could *fuck*, freely and openly. In Khartoum you could be thrown in jail if you were caught with so much as a beer bottle in your hand. Alcohol had to be smuggled in through the embassies, wrapped up in towels and shirts and tucked into diplomats' suitcases—not subject to search at the airport—and then clandestinely distributed to the Americans and Europeans famished for a drop of Jack Daniel's, or Merlot, or Budweiser, in that city in the middle of the desert. Greg's pastime, to which Alex had been inducted upon arrival in Khartoum, consisted of chasing down alcohol wherever it might be found—at a Danish embassy reception, a UN gathering, the fortified American Club on the Nile.

The one use to Alex's long waiting sessions was that William filled him in on things. About the town. About the war. Alex had arrived with only a sketchy understanding of the background. Southern rebels on one side. Northern regime on the other. A war that had been ongoing in one form or another since independence in 1956. The South wanted development, education, healthcare, equal representation in government. The North wanted to keep them poor, illiterate, while digging up the oil. Saraaya was in the middle of the country, right in the middle of the oil fields. A mixed population: Southern Nilotes and Northern nomads, who spent half the year grazing their cattle here. Whoever controlled Saraaya controlled the oil. Right now it was the government. William explained to him how things played out on the ground, who was who in the town.

"The police. They *look* important. But actually they're not," he told Alex. "The ones you need to watch out for are the security men. They're the ones in charge here. They're hard to spot, since they wear civilian clothes. But you'll learn to recognize them. They act like they own the place."

"And the rebels?"

"You never see them. They're in the bush. That's where the Nilot boys go to join up."

On his first day in Saraaya, barely out of his traveling clothes, Alex had been led by William to a meeting with the second-in-charge of security, Ahmed. He was bean-poled, famished-looking. White short-sleeved shirt, black trousers, black leather shoes. Thin lips more expressive than the eyes. Twisted down. Disdain. Firmly set. Threat. Teeth bared. Amusement.

The second deputy was also there. As fat as Ahmed was skinny. Legs as thick as tree trunks. Khakis riding up his thighs. Shirt buttons straining to hold on. Arms whose plump elbows pointed sideways to accommodate his torso. Stone eyes lost in the flesh of his face. Always standing behind Ahmed, as a warning.

Then a string of other anonymous security men. William nudged him whenever they came across them in town. Usually young, well turned out: nice shoes, well-fitting clothes. They had the air of city men. Not the sunburnt complexions of the nomads, hair tinged with gold, foreheads prematurely wrinkled by the sun, but the faces of men who spent time in dark rooms and offices. You'd find them sitting at the tea ladies', at the mosque, at the barber's. Places where you could pick up gossip.

Then there were the militiamen. "The government's unofficial army," William said. "When things first blew up here fifteen years ago, they were the ones doing all the killing and pillaging. And running off with whatever they could lay their hands on." These were ordinary nomads, William explained, going up and down the plains with their cattle, sipping tea with Nilotes during peace-time, exchanging pleasantries, from time to time even letting their daughters marry them, but when wartime came, out came the AK-47s. Cattle raids, burnt villages, killings, plunder. They took orders from Hilal, son of a famous nomad chief. William pointed him out in the market. High turban with a little tail poking up at the back, a length of it draped around his chin—a frame for his handsome face. Long-lashed liquid eyes. Flat-angled planes of cheekbones. A solid knob of a nose, mountainous. Beneath it a glistening mustache; thin, dark lips; and a row of small, perfectly white teeth. He moved with a swagger, jellabiya flailing behind him. His eyes, Alex was surprised to see, were lined with kohl.

"Like the prophet," William told him. "Or so they say. He does it because he's vain as a parrot."

"Peacock," Alex corrected.

Hilal, in turn, took orders from Farook, head of security. That was whom they had come to meet today.

A taste of rubber on his tongue. Alex looked down. He was biting the eraser end of the pencil he'd brought with him to mark up "Topographic Variations in White Nile Delta Swamplands," open on his lap. He looked at the clock ticking next to the Koran verse. A familiar restlessness was spreading, tingling, from the tips of his toes to his stomach, his fingers. He returned to the report:

Beneath the plains that stretch across central Sudan—
traversing the states of Darfur, Kordofan, and Upper Nile—
a basin of wetlands and river systems feed into the White
Nile. The river moves north between the Nuba Mountains
to the west and the Ethiopian border to the east. Main trib-
utaries to the west are the Bahr al-Ghazal River, in turn fed
by the Bahr al-Arab, whose confluence with the Lol and Jur
rivers in . . .

A door opened. He looked up hopefully. An errand boy
stepped out with a tray of empty teacups. Alex got up and paced
back and forth. Already one p.m. William was now dozing. He
nudged him.

"When are they letting us in?"

William opened his eyes. "I told you, when they call us."

"Can't you ask somebody?"

"I've asked already."

"Ask again."

"Just relax. This isn't America," said William, and closed
his eyes. Alex stared at the fake gold watch gleaming against his
wrist, the neatly trimmed nails. He was nearing that point he had
often reached during the past week: despising William.

A door to the waiting room opened and a young man spoke in
Arabic. They were being called in. Alex picked up his report and
followed William, who followed the man, down a narrow hallway
rippling with the shadows of spinning fan blades. They were led
into a spacious office. Shutters were drawn over the grilled window to the left. They passed through a sitting area—a sofa and
chairs—to a desk and two armchairs beyond.

It was strange, finally coming face-to-face with Farook. The
government's muscle in the town. Also the highest authority,
higher even than the military commander. So Alex was surprised

to find that the person who rose to greet them was rather young, despite the pools of baldness creeping up over his temples. He was well built, with strong shoulders and a straight back, but not very tall. His hand was dry and cool in Alex's grasp. He motioned to them to sit down in the chairs opposite.

"So, Mr. Alex, I hear that you are in Saraaya to make a map," he said, *r*'s rolling off his tongue as he leaned back into his leather chair.

"Yes," said Alex, suddenly unnerved by Farook's cool, direct gaze. It was there—something in the eyes. A little less harmless than a schoolmaster's gaze. He looked at William, who nodded at him to continue. "The idea is to update the map of the district, so we can plan and carry out aid work more effectively."

He checked an impulse to say more, sensing that he should be careful with his words.

"A map is not an easy thing," Farook said. "Here, especially. How long do you plan to stay?"

"Six months," said Alex. "I'd like to start as soon possible." He hesitated, wondering whether to ask about the body. William had been brushing aside all his questions, telling him there was nothing to worry about. But here was a chance to ask the one person who might have a clue. "Also," he ventured, "the security situation seems a little uncertain. With this body and all?" There had been a body. It wasn't a question. But uncertainty made his voice waver.

"You're not worried just because of one body, are you, Mr. Alex?"

"Is there anything new? With the police investigation?"

"The body has been buried. The police shouldn't have let you do that. There can be no investigation. But it was probably nothing—an argument over cattle, or a woman." He paused, studying Alex's reaction. "When there are many bodies, then you can worry. Then we all worry. One body, nothing." He turned to William. "What do you say, William?"

"Yes." William sat up.

Alex pressed on. "And is it true that there are rebels in the area?"

"There are always rebels in the area."

"But is there a risk of an attack or something?"

"There is always the risk of an attack," said Farook. "Or something. This is Saraaya. But we have things under control. If anything changes, we will let you know." There was a pause. "Now," he said. "You have some paperwork for me?"

William handed a manila folder to Farook. "We have the military signature, the police authorization, and also the authorization from Khartoum."

Farook opened the folder and went through papers. He leafed back, more slowly.

"The registration."

Alex waited for him to elaborate. "The registration . . . ?"

"The registration of the organization at the Ministry of Humanitarian Affairs. It isn't here."

Alex mentally went through the file.

"It should be there," said William, indicating to Farook to go through the papers again.

"May I?" asked Alex. He was out of his seat, reaching for the folder. "I just think, there are so many papers in there, that maybe you've missed it."

"Mr. Alex, sit back down."

Alex looked to William for help. William, mouth open, half out of his seat, seemed unsure how to intervene: whether to take Alex's side and force Farook to hand over the folder, or whether to force Alex to sit back down. His eyes flashed defiance at Alex. He pinched a mound of invisible salt between the fingers of his right hand. Alex had become intimately familiar with that gesture. It summed up the spirit of the town. Wait.

He was done waiting. He got a hold of the folder and drew back before Farook could stop him. He went through the papers once, twice. Nothing. A sinking feeling in his stomach as he glanced up at Farook, now standing, lips pressed in a thin line, shoulders rigid.

"It's here," said William, digging through another folder on his lap. He brandished the registration. Relieved, Alex watched as Farook's eyes flitted over the paper.

"Where's the authorization form?"

William handed that to him too.

Farook opened a drawer, pulled out a rubber stamp, pressed it into the ink, then crushed the stamp against the form. He thrust the paper back at Alex.

"Thank you," said Alex, trying to subdue his face into an expression reflecting an adequate degree of gratitude. He held the stamped authorization like a prize in his hands. Farook nodded at them curtly as they headed toward the door.

Outside, William stopped him just beyond the porch of the security office.

"You were rude in there."

"We got the stamp, didn't we?"

"*Don't* get on the wrong side of the authorities."

"We need to get started on this map. I don't have time to waste. District office, first thing tomorrow."

Ahead, he saw a group of old men sitting by the mosque. A crowd around them, in the midst of which he spotted jeans, a tripod.

"There's Dena," he said. "I'll say hi. Coming?"

Clearly annoyed, William said no, he had things to do.

They parted. William marched away in the direction of the compound and Alex turned to the mosque.

ſ

THE OLD MEN had frozen. Five of them still as the brick wall of the mosque in front of which they sat. Stony as figures in a chromophotograph—canes held stiffly upright, rosaries dangling from fingers, feet tucked neatly under the bench, necks rigid and eyes staring straight ahead. Jellabiyas motionless as marble, in the absence of a breeze. Faces set into expressions of carved gravity. Turbans piled on top of wrinkled foreheads and cheeks embellished with scraggly beards and mustaches. Not a hair moved. A fly landed on an old man's face. His nose twitched, but he refused to raise a hand to swat it away.

Dena was aware of keeping as still as her subjects, hardly breathing as she bent behind the camera, everything there in the picture—soft light cast by the mosque's shadow, contrast of white against brick, the symmetry of five bodies, like duplicates of one another with small variations—an image that, given her careful framing, was technically perfect but which lacked motion, which lacked life. And so she waited for the veil to fall, for someone to sneeze, or to start a conversation. But nothing happened. Nothing was going to happen. The men seemed willing, and able, to sit unmoving forever.

A little earlier she'd walked up to them and asked, "Can I film you?" Though, as was always the case when she approached new subjects, she'd asked with some trepidation, because no matter how often she posed that question, she could never overcome the feeling—being reserved herself, and tending to project that quality onto anyone whose cooperation she needed, or relied upon—that pointing a giant camera into someone's face was an intrusion.

But she found that everyone wanted to be filmed. Old men, young herdsmen, husbands and wives, children, tea ladies, Nilotes, nomads. Most of them had never seen such a camera before, let alone a woman with a camera, and so they let her film them, if for no better reason than to watch her doing it.

So the old men, adjusting skullcaps and turbans over their heads, had assented. As she set up her equipment, a couple of girls walking down the street slowed. They came to watch. A pregnant woman with wood stacked on her head joined them. Two young men from a nearby tea stall left their spot under the shade and came to stand behind the women. They murmured to one another. Now a crowd of ten or fifteen people, clustered to the side or behind her, had gathered, watching as she looked through the lens.

But the old men hadn't moved since she'd switched on the device. This was her problem. It wasn't getting people to allow her to film. It was this paralysis in front of the camera, or, if not paralysis then flamboyance. Like a group of teenage boys she'd spent the afternoon with yesterday. At the end of two hours she had footage of them making peace signs in one shot, in others doing gangster-rap-inspired poses, feet wide apart, arms crossed, chins raised arrogantly, in still others engaging in mock combat, sawing each other's heads off with arms transformed into deadly swords.

When she explained to people that she wanted them just to *be*, to pretend she wasn't there, and to continue talking, or drinking tea, or whatever they were doing, they looked at her, puzzled. "Pretend you're not there?" they asked. "But you are there." The more she sought invisibility, the more visible she became. Word had gotten round that there was a woman from Khartoum—or from America? or from America *and* Khartoum?—filming people. They came out to watch her film, and to resolve the mystery of her origins, only to find themselves confronted with another mystery. She was a woman who looked and dressed like a boy. It had become a pastime to track her down. Even when she went out into the fields beyond town gangs of people trailed her, some coming from faraway villages for an afternoon's entertainment.

∫

IN THE PAST couple of weeks, she had managed only one day of successful filming. Early on a Friday morning, she had walked with Mustafa to the river south of town, where herdsmen took their cattle to drink and graze.

The light had been especially good that day, sun filtering through a sheen of cloud cover, deepening the color of the grass and the shrubs, the pitted brown rocks. They reached clusters of talh and acacia trees, and she followed Mustafa's small figure as he made his way nimbly down a narrow path that led into vegetation, then broadened out. The wind was quieter there, broken by the surrounding wall of trees. Bulbuls and larks warbled. The scent of moist mud came to her and then the harsh white glint of water through the tree branches.

The path opened out onto the riverbank: the sun huge, bare-limbed trees lining the bank opposite, the silhouette of cattle stretching along the nearer bank, hundreds upon hundreds, jostling by the water and raising a cloud of dust that made everything vague, amorphous, blending into sun and sky, so that the herd of animals seemed to be made not of meat and bone but of air and dust, a flock of ghosts.

"Let's stop here," she said.

She unlaced her sneakers, took off her socks, and rolled up her linen trousers, then waded in. The mud squished up between her toes. Mustafa watched with interest as she set up the camera, two of the tripod legs sunk into river mud.

"How much did it cost?"

"What?"

"Your camera."

Mustafa was always curious about the cost of things. How much was an airplane ticket to America? How much was a bicycle in America? How much was a house?

"Around two thousand," she answered. "Dollars."

He calculated. "William says there's five hundred pounds in a dollar. That makes . . ."

"One million Sudanese pounds," she said.

His eyes widened.

"Where did you get all that money from?"

"I worked."

"Doing what?"

"I was a waitress in a restaurant."

"You can earn that much working in a restaurant?"

"Well, yes. But everything is more expensive there. You're paid more, but you spend more."

She shot the river for half an hour, then surveyed the scene, looking for what else to shoot. Farther down the bank she noticed three herdsmen sitting under a tree.

"Let's go say hello."

As she drew closer, she saw that they were the same three herdsmen who'd brought the corpse to the compound almost two weeks before. The older man saw Dena first, eyes in his ash-smeared face lighting with recognition as she picked her way toward them. Under the tree they all rose, river behind them flecked with light, haunches and horns and flanks of cattle hazy amidst the smoke of fires crackling to keep insects away. The older man gave her his wrist to shake because his fingers were soiled with beans, while the other two—the young one with the high cheekbones, and the one with the jersey—went to wash their hands in the river before coming back to greet her.

The eldest of them was called Abel. The one with the high cheekbones, a sinewy man with quick movements and lively eyes who had done most of the talking at the compound when they'd brought the body, was named Riek, and the large-boned one, slow and retreating in his movements, was Machar. She made out in the white faces a resemblance around the mouth and gathered that they were related.

Abel invited her and Mustafa to join their meal, and, though she'd just had lunch, she accepted the loaf of bread he held out to her. It was the price to be paid for access: submitting to the hospitality of the townspeople.

They agreed to let her film, and so, after the meal, she brought out her brace, a contraption that could be suspended from the shoulder and to which the camera was attached.

With the device always on her they couldn't tell when she was filming and when she wasn't. This meant, at first, that they were uneasy. Machar ran away when she was nearby. Abel spoke nonstop, lecturing for minutes whenever the camera was pointed at him, solemn and grave as a newscaster. Riek struck poses with the cattle. He led her around, directing her to film this or that animal while he leaned ostentatiously against a massive horn, or draped himself along the back of an ox, or explained (so she thought) some special markings on a cow's hide.

But after a few hours, with the camera always on her shoulder, they no longer seemed to notice it. Light conspired to gift her images. She framed the cattle in front of her: a collage of flicking tails and rear ends and horns and mottled fur, sunlight streaming down in dusty ribbons, patterns of color and light, cow markings and spots of moving shadow. The slow shifting of the cattle as they tore at grass gave the picture an undulating quality, light and dust and color altering from one moment to the next. The animals moved against the fray of the land and the deep orange of the sky, a hundred crescents in silhouette. With her index finger she reached for the filter switch, the picture flickering lighter and lighter. The adjustment of the aperture, the steadiness of the device in her hand, framing and panning, came to her without forethought.

How could she explain this feeling, this flow, to others? It was difficult to explain it. It was the source of her friction with Alex, with his impulse to scale and measure and order. What she was interested in was a gesture, a quality of light, the motion of a herd of cattle—things that eluded measurement.

Even William, whose only notion of film came from the Bollywood melodramas he'd watched in the Khartoum cinemas, was puzzled by her film. One day, as she stood shooting a goat by a doorway, he came to stand beside her. He watched, trying to see what she was seeing.

The goat moved on, ears flopping as it went up the road. William looked at her gravely then. He motioned at the animal.

"Dena. Explain to me. What are you doing?"

To him, she seemed to be filming meaningless scenes. What was there to see in an empty street, or a stray goat?

"I've told you. It's a picture of the town. Like a painting, but on film."

"But why a picture of here?"

"Why not?"

He looked around, gesturing at the desolate street, the haphazard houses, the plastic bags and rubbish twirling in the air. Was it that people in America liked films of dusty streets and goats and thatched houses because such things did not exist in America?

"No, it's not that. It's that I'm trying to make . . . an artwork."

In high school, her art teacher had given her an *Encyclopedia of Great Artists*. Michelangelo, Picasso, Klimt. She had gone through the book, staring at the paintings, lost in the brushstrokes, rust-colored skies, shadowed faces, fog hanging over ships at port that seemed to lift from the page and suffuse the atmosphere around her, and thought that this was what she wanted to do. But she had no talent for drawing or painting, in spite of hours spent with charcoal and oils in art class.

Her first film class in college changed everything. She didn't need to paint—she could film. And she discovered she had a talent for picking up images through the lens. Shooting a portrait, she saw that the long, thin nervous fingers of a hand told a story in themselves. An unremarkable snowy meadow, when shot from a certain low angle, evoked the epic atmosphere of an arctic tundra.

The thought of a giant film set, with actors and producers and gaffers and lighting designers, didn't appeal to her solitary nature. Documentary was the genre that suited her best. All she needed were her own two eyes and a camera. She began traveling to obscure film festivals, scavenged libraries and film archives for works of documentary. It was the world she wanted to belong to; to have her work shown up on the screen to a cult of devoted enthusiasts.

But she doubted herself. William's question troubled her. What was she doing? She had a collection of random images— landscapes, people, animals, roads, houses, sunsets, sunrises. A very few were beautiful; some passable, most terrible. The footage needed culling. But what was her subject, her theme? Despite her best efforts, she was still lost. She didn't dare call herself an artist; the gulf between her ambitions and her abilities was too wide.

∫

NOW SHE WAS AWARE of bodies pressing in on her, stifled giggles, shuffling feet. Odors of dust and sweat wafted into her nostrils. Someone's stomach rumbled close to her ear. Myriad eyes hovered over her shoulder at the camera's viewfinder, screen flipped open a few inches away from the lens into which she squinted. An ache began to throb at the base of her spine, spreading up to her shoulders, lodging at the back of her neck. And still the men sat motionless in front of the mosque.

She looked up from behind the lens.

"Talk, if you want."

There was a pause, some hesitation.

"But then we'll ruin the picture," said one of the men, who, shrunken in his jellabiya, looked to be the oldest. His face was crisscrossed with wrinkles. Giant bags hung beneath his eyes. His skeleton had retreated to the size of a child's. His friends—whom Dena guessed to be in their sixties and seventies—seemed youthful beside him.

"Just . . ." She was about to say *pretend I'm not here*, but stopped. Not only was she here, there was a crowd big enough to fill a small theater behind her.

"Just try to be comfortable."

The men looked at one another. A movement of feet, exhaled breaths, a readjustment of posteriors. More embarrassed silence.

"They're shy," someone said behind her.

"What should we talk about?" asked another man on the bench, this one with a luxurious white mustache. His eyebrows, equally luxurious, were completely black. He sat at the edge of the bench, the tail of his turban fanning out by his right ear. He shifted a cane from one hand to the other.

"Anything. The weather," came a response from off-screen.

"What's there to say about the weather?" said the shrunken old man. He looked up at the sky. "It will kill us all."'

A back-and-forth ensued between the elders on the bench and the audience behind her. It was not, quite, what she had wanted, but now at least the men were talking, eyes and mouths vivified as they waved aside proposed topics or defended others, and she couldn't help being moved by the way the brick background framed their faces, which, in their sudden wrinkled animation, were like fragments of the patterned wall come alive.

A woman said, "What about the body that showed up two weeks ago?"

"There's trouble on the way," said one of the men on the

bench. This one sat on the other side, a skullcap on his head. "No end to the problems we have."

"It was all burnt up, did you hear?" said the man with the extravagant mustache.

"Have the authorities said anything new?" another woman in the crowd asked.

"No," a man answered offscreen. "Why would they? They probably had a hand in it themselves."

At which point there was a loud "*Shhhh*" as someone called, "You're being recorded. Don't get us in trouble."

The man who had faulted the authorities, suddenly aware that his voice, if not his face, had been recorded, went silent. Everyone grew self-conscious.

"Who are you going to show this film to?" A young man standing next to Dena asked. An edge of suspicious acrimony to the question, enough to make her look up, realizing, suddenly, that she had to tread carefully.

"I won't show it to the authorities."

"How do we know that?"

He wasn't the only one suddenly hostile. A companion who stood beside him spat in the dirt. Others were eyeing her now too.

"I have nothing to do with the authorities."

Still, for the next few minutes a chill fell over the conversation. The old men looked at their hands or told their rosaries. The audience behind her went quiet. Someone made a joke—something about the sudden silence—but no one laughed.

The oldest man on the bench finally spoke up, asking her how long she planned to stay in Saraaya. And where was she going to show the film? Surely she would have a showing for them? One to which the authorities weren't invited, he added. The hostility passed. She tried to explain about editing—what was the word for it in Arabic?—she had forgotten; but said that she had to piece the film together first, before it could be shown in its completeness.

But yes, she would show some of it before she left. And when she had finished piecing it together in America, she would come back, so they could see it in full.

Everyone found their tongues again: Where was she born? Where did she grow up? Was she married engaged promised to someone? One question after another. She gave short answers and didn't look up from behind the lens, but the old men's gaze in the electric square of the viewfinder was as unrelenting as their questions.

So engrossed was she in filming and trying to direct conversation away from herself that she didn't notice Alex saunter into the crowd until someone said in Arabic, "Here's the white man too."

She looked up to find him standing with his hands in the pockets of his shorts, T-shirt spelling out the words "People Power" in a cheerful yellow, that direct, overbearing look in his eyes, oblivious, it seemed, to the fact that the group of people he had joined had turned to watch him now, too, and so had the old men.

"Don't mind me," he said. "Was just on my way back to the compound and saw the crowd."

He and William had gone out to secure some sort of authorization that morning, and by his satisfied glance, she guessed that it had gone well. He was in a good mood. Standing taller than usual. It was the first sign of a return to his old self. He'd been keeping a distance from her ever since their conversation in the courtyard the day after the corpse.

She didn't say anything and turned back to the old men. Perhaps it wasn't his fault, she reflected as she peered, again, into the blinking square of the lens, that she didn't like him. It was a visceral dislike. Now she found herself bothered by the fact that he stood there, amongst the crowd, watching her. She concentrated on the old men, who had gone silent again.

"Why don't you ask them questions?" said Alex.

"It's not that type of a documentary."

"Oh right. What's it again?" he said. "Observational filmmaking."

He seemed pleased at remembering the term she had used with him in one of their early conversations. But she couldn't help wondering if there wasn't a hint of sarcasm there too. In his mouth it sounded obnoxious. As probably it had in hers when she had said it. Was it really possible that he didn't understand that these comments and questions irritated her? She wasn't sure if it was just his awkward and blundering way of being friendly or whether in fact he was being slyly provocative, belligerent, trying to push her buttons.

"That's the idea," she said. "But it's hard to do that if you keep talking."

"Oh. Sorry." He raised a finger to his mouth, shushing himself.

She turned back to the old men, ready to dive behind the camera again. One of them pointed at Alex.

"We want him in the picture."

Alarmed, Dena raised her head. "Let's just film you now."

"But why not? Ask him to come," another old man said.

She tried to quash this idea, but by now people in the crowd were signaling to Alex, pointing at the bench, and when they found that he was still confused, they nudged him forward; the old men gestured to him to come over, squeezing apart to make room for him between them.

Catching on, Alex looked at Dena uncertainly. "I don't want to . . ." he said. "I mean, if I'm in the way."

But before she could say anything, someone said "Come!" in English, and he was pushed forward; one of the old men patted the space next to him, and another one reached to pull him by the hand so that he ended up sandwiched between them on the bench, the knobs of his knees pressed together, shoulders scrunched up against their shoulders, blue T-shirt with its yellow lettering a splash of color amidst their white jellabiyas. He shook hands on one side and then the other, exchanging jumbled greetings in Arabic.

An old man turned to Dena, waved his rosary at her.

"Film us!" he commanded.

Helpless, she lowered her head behind the lens, focused on the row of faces, full of grinning mirth and goodwill, the crowd behind her moving, shuffling, everyone entertained. She was frustrated at the pointlessness of the image in front of her. At herself for failing to control things better. At Alex, for showing up and interrupting. And at the old men, who refused to cooperate with the vision of the shot she had in mind.

ſ

IN THE EARLY AFTERNOON, the main road that cut along a north–south axis through town bustled. Between the police station and mosque up the street and the quieter alleyways and neighborhoods to the south, market stalls stretched along both sides of pitted asphalt. Plastic covers shaded pyramids of paprika and cumin and coriander and hot chili. Boys sat behind tall towers of red-and-white cigarette boxes balanced precariously on tables. Children played near mothers fanning flies away from fruit and vegetables. Every now and again, a car or a truck slowed for dogs scurrying across the street or shoppers passing to and fro.

William walked toward the compound hardly paying attention to his surroundings, except when a market woman, or a neighbor, or some other town acquaintance called his name. He looked up then, the frown on his brow disappearing only long enough for him to reciprocate the greeting. Left again to his own thoughts, his lips came together, and a faint scowl showed on his brow. He was vexed with Alex. Their work depended on maintaining a civil relationship with the authorities. In the security office just now, Farook had made a show of being dissatisfied with their paperwork as a way of asserting his authority, of reminding them that he was in charge. But Alex refused to play along, had to have his way and snatch papers from right under the man's nose. They were lucky that Farook had stamped the authorization instead of throwing it in the bin.

These past two weeks had been full of awkward moments. There was that time when they met the military commander and Alex didn't address him by his formal title as he was meant to do, in spite of William's nudging. The commander had noted it. There were the inappropriate comments Alex made about the "regime." The government in Khartoum was a dictatorship, but you didn't refer to it as such when speaking to its representatives. Not if you wanted something from them. In the process of translation, William often had to edit Alex—inserting long prologues of supplication or gratitude before communicating his blunt questions and demands.

William wasn't sure if it was Alex's youth—he was twenty-seven, six years younger than William—or his American innocence, or something else entirely—an entitled brashness that was particular to his person.

He looked up to find himself passing mechanics' shops and car-part vendors in the quieter end of the market. There were fewer shoppers here, only men sitting in pairs and children rolling a tire. Alleyways lined with stalls gave way to homesteads. A familiar element in this scene—an acacia that he'd passed a thousand times on his errands to and from town—caught his attention now. He slowed as his gaze paused on the tree fanning out its knuckled branches. Flat at the top, as if its green foliage had been pressed down by a cap. It wasn't the tree itself but what had been done to it that made him stop, finally, in his tracks. For bright spots of color beckoned to him from amidst its leaves. The tree had sprouted bra blossoms. Delicate knickers flowered from its branches. White slips and undershirts hung like low-lying fruit, waved this way and that by a gentle breeze. Beneath its shade Mustafa crouched, talking to someone.

William's frown melted away at the sight. He crossed the road toward the tree. He didn't recognize the young Nilot man Mustafa was talking to. A look on Mustafa's face that William knew. Calculating, planning something.

"Mustafa!"

Squatting with arms round his knees, Mustafa squinted up at him. He seemed displeased at the interruption. Seeing William, the man sitting with him said something quietly and rose.

William stopped under the tree and watched the man head into a garage.

"Who's that you were talking to?"

"Just some guy."

"Just some guy?"

"A mechanic."

"What were you talking about?"

"Just chatting."

"About what?"

"Nothing, really."

He let a silence pass, long enough to communicate that he wasn't fooled by evasive answers. Up to something, for sure. He and Mustafa had their own silent language, layers of communication that went on above and below words actually spoken. But no way to get Mustafa to talk if he didn't want to. William would find out eventually, as he always did.

He pointed at the tree. "Did it work? Get you customers?"

Mustafa stood up creakily. His arms were bruised and his face was scratched. He was missing a flip-flop. His T-shirt was a giant hole, revealing bird's ribs, navel, shoulder.

"What happened to you?"

The boy's face twisted, mouth and nose crumpling in disgust.

"The police took my things."

The underwear tree was such a success that Hassan got wind of it across the market. He'd sent his police cousin, who'd arrived with another officer. Swept Mustafa's things into a bag, took his money, told him to get lost. Mustafa tried to stop them. But they'd roughed him up, left him lying in the dirt.

"How much did they take?"

"All my money. Everything."

William surveyed the table. It was bare.

Large dollops of tears collected in Mustafa's eyes. His chin trembled. Hunched over in his torn clothes, he seemed even tinier and frailer.

A tenderness welled up for the boy. William sometimes forgot just how young Mustafa was, though he was still hardly any bigger than when he'd first arrived at the compound three years ago. That morning, William had almost tripped over the small, ragged figure crouched at the gate. Light skin and halo of soft curls told him that the boy was a nomad, though he spoke perfect Nilotic. Twig-armed and big-eyed and barefoot. Like a thousand other children in Saraaya, but something about the boy's bright, hungry eyes had arrested him.

Looking for work, Mustafa had announced then.

"Anything. I'll clean. Run errands. I'll be your security guard."

William had smiled at the prospect of such a scarecrow of a child taking on the duties of a security guard.

"How old are you?"

"Eleven."

He looked to be about seven.

"Nine," Mustafa amended, in answer to William's skeptical brow-raise. "Mustafa's my name."

"And your parents?"

"Father's dead. My mother sent me to town to find work. We live three days' walk away."

"And you don't move?"

"No. My parents lost their animals and settled down. Before I was born."

At the time, William himself had just started work in Saraaya. Bosses who'd arrived from Khartoum to establish the field site, and whom he was to assist with translation, had lasted only a week. One caught malaria. The other a bad case of diarrhea. The third—Greg—couldn't bear the heat. They returned on the next flight to Khartoum, leaving William to set up the compound on his own.

A promotion, he'd thought. But it was a promotion only in responsibilities. No job title other than "Translator." Nor more pay, because of a pay-scale hierarchy that dictated that his salary could amount only to an infinitesimal fraction of that which expatriates were paid.

Still, he'd felt that he was making his way up in the world. He'd been working in construction in Khartoum, had given up hope of anything better, when his luck had changed one afternoon. On a break that day, he fell into conversation with a man who came to sit beside him at a tea stall. Like William he was a Southerner, though younger and well-dressed, in brown slacks and a pressed shirt and polished shoes. He'd reminded William of himself when he'd first arrived in Khartoum well-groomed and full of hope. Eight years in the city had done him in. In tattered construction clothes, he'd become just another Southerner in the North struggling to eke out a living.

William learned from the man that the white SUV parked nearby was in his charge. He worked as a driver. He was waiting for his boss, whom he had just dropped off to lunch up the road. Joseph, as he was called, was employed by an American NGO. Development planning, emergency relief, humanitarian aid, that sort of thing. Most of the job consisted of driving Americans around town. During the long waiting spells between appointments, he read the paper, followed the football on the radio, or met up with friends.

To William, it sounded like heaven. He ventured to ask if there were any driving positions open at the organization. The man said one of the drivers was leaving for the UN. Did William drive, speak good English? William assured him that he did, had learned his English from missionaries at Catholic school. In that case, Joseph said, he'd put in a word. William should visit the office.

A week later, he arrived at the NGO's offices in his best clothes—clothes he hadn't worn in years. Joseph introduced him to the boss, a big-boned American with inflamed cheeks called Greg. The white man shook his hand.

"Have a license?"

"Yes, sir. And I drive very well."

"Good. Come back in a week and Joseph here will show you the ropes."

He didn't have a license, though he knew how to drive. He borrowed money from every friend in the city to bribe an official at the vehicle registration office to get him one quickly.

It was worth it. He gave up his construction rags for pressed shirts and slacks, which he could now afford, on a salary triple what he'd earned on building sites. He paid off his debts to his friends. He sent more money to his mother and sisters in Juba. He went to the movies more often. He could afford to live alone—not quite outside the shantytown in which he'd lived with his cousin, but almost.

It wasn't the office job he'd dreamed of. But it was a step up. He drove Americans to displaced persons camps on the edges of Khartoum, to ministries and government offices in the city, to embassies and consulates. It was bliss to float around the capital with closed windows, air-conditioning suffusing the car with the cool climate of America. The smoothness of a Toyota Land Cruiser's shock absorbers, which obliterated the gaping potholes of Khartoum.

And then one day, in the car, he overheard Greg and a colleague speaking about a new field site in the district of Saraaya, in the state of South Kordofan, on the border of North and South Sudan. They were hoping to get funding to run a program in the district—hardly any NGOs operated there, with the area caught up between government and rebel forces, both of whom were fighting for its oil.

It was William's hometown. He had been born in Saraaya, though after his father died in the war, his mother had taken her children south to Juba.

He mentioned to Greg that he was from the town. He hadn't intended anything to come of it—had volunteered the information simply to make small talk during a traffic jam.

But two days later Greg called him to his office. They had secured funding for the Saraaya program and needed help.

"You said you're from down there? You know the area?"

"My family left when I was a child, but we visited. I know it well enough."

"And you speak the local language, Nilotic, is that right?"

"It's my mother tongue."

"And your Arabic is good?"

"Excellent."

"And your English is not bad at all."

"Thank you."

"We need a translator down there. Also a driver, initially. You'd be based in Saraaya for the first few months and we'll see how you get on. We'll be coming and going from Khartoum. I'm offering you the job—hope you'll consider it."

The pay was triple his driver's salary, a whole three hundred thousand pounds a month. And the title, too, was something. Translator.

The thought that for the first time in his life he'd be earning enough, not just to survive but to save, decided him. Above all there was the fact that he could help his family in Juba. He'd been sending remittances ever since he'd moved to Khartoum, but measly sums. Sometimes, while working in construction, he missed meals or walked for miles instead of taking public transport, so that he could save something to send at the end of the month, knowing that his mother and sisters and nieces and nephews depended on the help. A year or two of work in Saraaya would set him up—he could even save enough to afford a bride wealth and build a house.

And so he took the job. He arrived in Saraaya and set about securing the compound. Traveled to Malakal to buy the truck, a secondhand Toyota, which would serve as the organization's official vehicle in the district.

He got used to daily life in the town. The brief snatch of early morning coolness during which flocks of children bounded to school, herdsmen drove their cattle to pasture, women tended vegetable gardens, tradesmen set out their wares. All the while, shadows lengthened so that by three o'clock the air vibrated with temperature. Feet that strode with a spring in the morning dragged in the dust, bright smiles turned into worn-out, exhausted frowns, lively conversations dwindled to monosyllabic questions and answers.

But by twilight, life returned. It was the time for rest and gossip and conversation. Mothers turned gentle with their children, and men told jokes and bounced babies on their laps. Young women braided each other's hair. The sky turned gray, and then black, and then lanterns were brought out, flickering in the darkness.

His long years living in cities—first Juba, where his mother had fled to during the war, and then Khartoum—had estranged him from seasonal rhythms. In Saraaya, he fell into them again. The beginning of the wet season in May, when the air became so dense with moisture that the heat was like a gag blocking passage to the lungs. Nilot farmers in the villages prepared their seed and cleared their fields and gazed up at the sky and waited. The first rains were always a time of celebration. Children danced in puddles and women poked their heads out of windows and doorways, and men wiped drops from their faces, laughing.

Over the next months, farmers monitored their crops closely. Kept an eye on unwanted infestations, mended fences to keep out ever-ravenous goats. Grass wafted tall and verdant. Trees blossomed. Sorghum sprouted to the height of the tallest Nilot man. If all passed well—if the rains didn't come too late, or too soon, if they didn't flood or not come at all, if an infestation didn't ruin the crops—then the villagers were busy harvesting in October. They stored their grain and were at ease, knowing that between their cattle and the harvest there was plenty to live on until the next wet season.

With the first showers Nilot herdsmen packed up their belongings and headed north to the sandy plains of the Goz, which turned green during the rainy season. They went to save their cattle from flies and parasites and worms and insects that congregated in the pools of groundwater that accumulated. In the Goz, water drained into the sand; the land was full of pastures but no pests.

The months passed. By late November skies turned bone white again. Savannahs dried out and swamps evaporated. Nilot herdsmen returned from drier pastures in the north, leading herds trundling into town. The nomads, too, arrived with their cattle. The town swelled with newcomers and animals, and nomads set up camps throughout the district. There was more traffic from larger towns farther afield. The market was busier, and a cattle market opened up beside it. During the dry season you could find things you couldn't find during the wet season—clothes and shoes and electronics that arrived by way of the roads that opened up only in the absence of rain.

For the most part newly arrived nomads kept to their allotted pastures and Nilotes to their farms and grazing fields. But troubles escalated when rains were bad, when pastures and streams didn't reappear. Cattle rustling, fights over grazing rights, violence. These were isolated disturbances at first, but over the years they'd become more regular, encouraged by the authorities, who were happy to arm nomads to keep in check villagers sympathetic to the Nilot rebel army hovering on the southern edges of the district.

It wasn't an easy place to work, but it was home, even if his family had left Saraaya so long ago that he barely remembered his early childhood there. Back in the district, he turned to his duties with enthusiasm. He began the work of establishing a relationship with the authorities. No easy task in a town under government control in which any Nilot man, including himself, automatically fell under suspicion.

He had in fact been looking for help with the compound when Mustafa turned up. He hadn't counted on a child. But the boy impressed him. During his trial week, he scrubbed and swept and wiped. Reorganized the storage room so that when William walked in, he was amazed to see neat stacks of boxes; folded newspapers; unused furniture lined below the windows. He planted cacti and bougainvillea in recycled oil drums. He found a streamer of national flags in the storage room and attached it along the compound walls for decoration. When William sent him for truck parts in the market, Mustafa haggled the mechanic down to a price below that which William himself normally paid.

William had no immediate family in Saraaya, and neither did Mustafa, whose mother lived on the far edges of the district.

And so they spent their time together. Whenever William traveled to Hasaniya, three hours away, to pick up supplies for the compound, Mustafa came along. On Fridays, their day off, they listened to football games on the radio, betting on the two opposing Khartoum teams. William always paid when he lost; Mustafa never did.

The boy was full of questions. What was Khartoum like? Could William teach him English? What was the cinema like? Mustafa was dazzled by William's diplomas, which William liked to show him. And William preferred Mustafa's company to anyone else's. Though Mustafa could be sassy, rude, and rebellious too. And though William scolded him when he misbehaved, he secretly relished his spirit.

∫

NOW, HOWEVER, Mustafa's usual chattiness was replaced by sullen silence. His shoulders drooped as he kicked the dirt. William reached a hand to his head. He wished there was something he could do. But if he went to object about Mustafa's things and money being taken, the authorities might make life difficult for him in other ways. And with pressure to finalize authorization for Alex's map, he couldn't risk it.

"Let's get what's left up there, all right?" He pointed to the tree.

Mustafa nodded.

"Hold the table."

William clambered up. He wobbled on top of the table, flailing his arms and clutching at branches as though about to tumble.

"You're silly," Mustafa said, assuming his customary attitude of superiority.

William was reassured. He reached into the tree and grabbed bras and negligées. He dropped a pair of underpants on Mustafa's face, who huffily removed them from his eyes. William could see he was beginning to smile.

He jumped down from the table. They folded it and carried it together along the market road. Every few steps someone waved hello to them, or stopped William to ask for some favor. He was one of the few people in the district whose livelihood didn't depend on rains coming and going, and given that the rains came and went more erratically with each passing year, more and more people struggled.

He shaded his eyes. His mind had been busy with the security office, with Alex, with Mustafa. But the knowledge suddenly returned to him: Layla was coming back tomorrow. She'd sent word through her brother. It was what had made waiting in office after office with Alex bearable these past days. Made him cheerful, tolerant, patient, even in the face of Alex's endless demands and provocations.

Only a fortnight since the corpse, since he had last seen her, and yet it seemed like a lifetime had passed. His mood lifted; his frustration with Alex dissipated, and as for Mustafa, he was sure he'd recover.

ſ

MUSTAFA OPENED HIS EYES to the white gauze of his mosquito net. He lay there, watching the gauze shifted by a barely perceptible breeze, sun creeping over the edge of the compound wall casting a feverish heat on his neck and forehead. Flies droned just beyond the mesh. He'd slept fitfully, sleep full of dreams whose details he couldn't grasp but whose atmosphere of anxiety clung to him.

He lay still, wishing away the feeling, but the buzzing just beyond the net and the sound of someone hacking up phlegm in a neighboring yard and the ray of sunlight that cut like a blade across his neck made him feel that, on top of his big annoyances, the world was intent on plaguing him with small ones too.

He got up and rubbed his eyes, felt for his flip-flops beneath the bed, and made his way to the kitchen. William was already seated at the table under the gazebo, dressed up in a fresh blue shirt, scribbling in account books.

"Good morning," William called. "How are you today?"

Mustafa ignored him. He felt William's eyes on him but didn't return his gaze, taking a spiteful pleasure in the fact that he was being rude, when William was being nice. And hadn't William been nice yesterday, when he'd found him under the tree? He'd cheered him up and helped him carry the table back and still Mustafa reveled in being rude.

In the kitchen he found a slab of feta in the fridge. Rather than bother with a knife, he dug into it with his fingers and crumbled it onto the loaf of bread, which, out of spite, he also tore with his fingers.

He chewed and gulped down tea, and, still chewing, went to the storage room. He shoved brooms and buckets about violently enough to disturb the small creatures that lived in the recesses of the room—a lizard dashed sideways across the wall. A spider scurried up its cobweb. So much dust rose that he stepped out coughing. Again he ignored William as he asked why he was making such a racket.

With his cleaning things in tow, he went to the latrine. Always the most unpleasant task, befitting the foul mood he was in this morning. The dank, humid stench filled his nostrils as he stepped inside. He swept around the gaping black toilet, then splashed water sloppily around the footrests, dribbles landing on his toes like misfired pee. He took his cleaning things next door to the mud room set back from the gazebo used as a shower room. A cracked mirror hung above the sink, and on the other side was a low ceramic basin with a faucet—William had rigged a watering can above it into a showerhead. Mustafa filled a bucket with soap water and plunged a brush into it and scrubbed around the basin, the movement fueling his wrath.

It was what had happened after the police yesterday that bothered him most. As he was lugging the table back with William through the market he became aware of a flurry nearby, and when he turned, he saw his mother. Her eyes were bloodshot, her jaw was set, and she moved with furious energy as she pushed people out of her way and came at him with his sister on her back and his brother running after her.

He hadn't gone home in two months. That was why she'd come to find him. Usually, William drove him home once a month to hand over his wages to her. But he'd had no money to give, because he'd spent it all buying underwear. He'd been counting on a profit from the venture, making up just enough to give her what she was waiting for. But then the police had ruined everything.

It was a three-day walk from their home village to Saraaya, unless you were lucky enough to hitch a ride, but cars were so rare in that part of the district that sometimes days passed without one showing up. And judging by the sand coating his mother's thoub up to the knees, and his brother up to his chest, they had walked most of the way.

She marched right past William, ignoring his greeting, and stopped before Mustafa. His little sister peeked over his mother's shoulder, her nose running and her hair half unbraided. The only piece of clothing his little brother had on was a T-shirt, beneath whose frayed hem a tiny, dusty penis dangled. He drew back when Mustafa reached out to greet him.

"Where's the money?" his mother asked.

There was no point in lying. He told her about the underwear business and said that the police had robbed him. In one long stride she was on him. A sharp, hot smack landed across his face.

William pulled her away and his brother and sister started to cry and people turned to stare.

It had ended only when William reached into his pocket and gave her all the money he had and arranged a ride back for her to the village. From the car she called to Mustafa to bring her money next month, or else.

And like that they vanished back to the village—a sad, poor place with fences falling down, plots of land at which villagers scratched year-round but which yielded little. His mother grew millet and maize. Some of the crop she kept for the family; the rest she sold wholesale to middlemen merchants who then sold it for triple the price.

There was a time in his early childhood when, not knowing what money was, he was free of cares. Back then he had no sense of the past beyond yesterday, no notion of the future. There was always food. His mother called him her little grasshopper, and he followed his father to the fields and played in the dirt as he tilled the soil. He remembered his mother kissing him on the cheek and his father telling him stories. He remembered the sound of his mother's laughter, but he couldn't remember when he had last heard it.

He remembered cold nights when he snuggled between them, or, on hot nights, how his mother sprinkled water on his mattress so that he might keep cool while he fell asleep. And then, when he was seven, he had started school, which he loved so much, hurrying each morning at dawn the few kilometers to the next village, with the backpack that his father had gotten him from town, and the pencils, and the sharpener, and the notebooks.

In second grade he had gotten a perfect score on a spelling test. The teacher stood him up in front of the class and patted him on the head, told all the others that Mustafa was the best. He rushed home to show his mother and father the notebook with the teacher's ticks all over it, and even though they couldn't read he could read to them that the teacher had written "EXCELLENT" in big letters on the page. And he clutched the notebook tightly in his hand and finally caught sight of the homestead. People were gathered there. His mother was on the ground. His little brother and sister, just babies then, clung to her. There was someone lying there. And only when a neighbor pulled his mother away did he see that it was his father, eyes open to the sky, dead.

Like that, his mother had pulled him out of school and sent him to work in town. And now his father was gone, and his mother was a stranger who never smiled, and his little sister and brother didn't even recognize him. He'd learned that the past was past, and the future could bring calamities.

He scrubbed beneath the faucet and scrubbed above it, soap vapor making his eyes sting, dark thoughts swirling in his head.

A knock at the gate interrupted his rumination. He peered through the bathroom door.

"Layla!" he gasped.

He dropped the brush and, in his excitement, knocked over the bucket of water standing on the rim of the basin. He splashed his way into the yard, glum thoughts suddenly vanished.

ALTHOUGH WILLIAM HAD BEEN waiting for Layla since early morning—strategically positioning his chair beneath the gazebo to allow for an unobstructed view of the gate, ears pricked for the scrape of its creaky hinges, account ledgers, receipts, supply lists open in front of him in a pretense of work—he missed her when she finally arrived. Just when he stepped out to the street to get equipment Alex wanted from the truck, she had walked past on the other side of the car, neither of them seeing the other.

When he found her in the yard with Mustafa, he stopped

abruptly, clutching boxes to his chest. She didn't see him right away. Her head was bent over Mustafa, her arm draped over his shoulder. Mustafa spoke to her excitedly. In her other hand she carried grocery bags. She couldn't reach up to fix the hood of her yellow thoub, which, as William watched, slipped from her hair, revealing a luminous coil of braid. He was confronted with the tide of her beauty—the full body, whose shapely curves were visible even beneath the loose cloth of the thoub; her feet in yellow flip-flops, which matched her dress, an air of alluring dishevelment to her, with the falling thoub and the braid of hair. A swath of neck gleamed under the sunlight. Even from a distance he could see her eyes narrowing in a smile, and the whites of her teeth. He could make out her dimples. Absorbed in conversation, she and Mustafa turned and walked to the gazebo. She placed the grocery bags on the table while Mustafa continued to talk.

She was more beautiful than he remembered, and he felt the energy rise and concentrate in his chest, a familiar flutter of excitement and fear, a sudden self-consciousness—he was sure he looked stupid with the boxes; his elbow and shoulder were raised awkwardly to stop the top one from tumbling.

She looked up and saw him then. She smiled from across the yard. He wanted to wave but couldn't. He began maneuvering clumsily, the top box was slipping, and he had to stick out his chin to keep it in place. He was aware of her eyes on him—she made a movement in his direction, as though to come to his rescue, but before she took two steps, he managed to crouch and get the boxes to the ground. He straightened, his shoulders buzzing with strange impulses. He waved. Mustafa picked up some of the shopping bags and dashed to the kitchen. William stepped toward her, then stopped as she walked toward him. Jammed his hands in his pockets, took them out, stepped forward, hesitated, then, collecting himself, crossed resolutely to her.

Under the shade of the gazebo, he could see her face clearly, the features he'd been picturing in the days of her absence—the narrow forehead, dark eyebrows, large eyes that settled on things with a warm attentiveness. But the reality of her face, close-up, was even more dazzling: a sheen of sweat on her skin now, from her long walk to the compound, probably also the hubbub of the market through which she had passed. A glow to the top of her lips, her eyelids. Light seemed to pool around her even under the shade, and suddenly it seemed ridiculous that he'd ever thought that she was dead.

"I'm sorry I was away for so long. Did Mustafa tell you? About my father?"

He'd forgotten about the voice, how resonant it was. A trace of nervousness in it now: she was worried about her long absence.

"Yes, of course," he said. "I'm so happy to see you." Words fell flat against his own ear. "Really happy. I was worried—"

"Hi!"

Alex, eyes full of delighted surprise, hurried across the yard. He must have seen her passing by the office window, and William silently cursed him for it. Soon he was parked beside William.

"You're back," he said to Layla. She beamed her dazzling smile in greeting, a quality of her expression, a warmth that made him, was making Alex now, feel special. "So nice to see you!" Alex said. "Where were you?" Then remembering she didn't speak English, he turned to William. "Where was she?"

"Looking after her father," William said curtly. He stepped forward and continued in Arabic. "How's your father? Is he better?"

"Yes, much better."

"What's the matter with her dad?" Alex asked, having reinserted himself into the conversation by also stepping forward.

"He's ill," said William, but before he could continue, Alex asked, "With what?"

And so William was forced to play his part: translating to

Layla what Alex said and translating to Alex what Layla said. A perforated ulcer. They took him to the health clinic. Yes, the doctor said it was quite serious. Her father had to have surgery. Thank you, he's well now. Had she heard about the body? Yes, terrible.

"I'm hungry," said Alex, rubbing his stomach. "We missed your cooking, Layla. What are we having for breakfast?"

William's jaw clenched.

"Ask her."

Eggs and beans and salad. She picked up the remaining groceries on the table.

"I'll go now."

She turned and walked across the courtyard, stopped for a moment to readjust the bags in her hands, then disappeared into the kitchen.

ſ

ALL MORNING he couldn't get a moment alone with her. First it was Mustafa, chattering away as he mopped the kitchen floor, recounting his fights with Hassan and the police, soliciting her advice on what to do to get his money back and revive his underwear venture.

It wasn't just him, he realized, who had felt her absence. Now that she was back some spark of life returned to the compound. She laughed a lot. She was full of lightness. Her energy in the kitchen made it the center of everyone's attention, when she was in it. He stalked in front of it this morning, finding excuses to go from one end of the yard to the other, each time looking in, waiting for Mustafa to leave. When he didn't, he thought up an errand to send him on.

"Go check if the bus from Khartoum's arrived."

"Now?" The mop drooped, dripping onto the linoleum. "It doesn't come until two."

"It comes early sometimes," said William. "Alex is expecting a delivery." Dishes clattered in the sink over which Layla stood. "*Now*."

No sooner had he gotten rid of Mustafa than Dena came in, bringing with her the whiff of exertion, a jumble of wires and camera equipment, a blade of grass stuck to her cheek. She'd gone out at dawn to film along the river. She wasn't expecting to see Layla, and when she did she went over and hugged her, so that, not for the first time that day, William was jealous. He stood helpless as Dena, insisting on helping Layla with breakfast, unloaded her camera equipment on the floor.

Half an hour later Mustafa came into the yard. "Bus isn't here."

"Which bus?"

"The bus. The one from Khartoum you sent me to check on. With Alex's things. They said it won't get here before two."

He crossed his arms, waiting for William to acknowledge his error.

"I see. Thanks."

Mustafa stalked away, cursing under his breath just loud enough for William to hear.

"Your mouth," William called. In answer Mustafa sucked his teeth, in the way that old women did when they wanted to express disapproval.

Dena and Alex—Dena coming from the kitchen with a jug of water and Alex from the shower—arrived under the gazebo, and William (could he believe his luck, given the way the day was going?) settled himself in the seat next to Layla, who had also come from the kitchen carrying plates. But then she got up, saying she'd forgotten a ladle, and Mustafa, returning from washing his hands, took her place.

"Sit over there." William nodded at the empty seat on the other side of the table.

"I want to sit here."

"Layla's sitting here."

"She can sit over there."

To make his point, Mustafa scooted his bottom back into the chair, planted his elbows on the table, cracked his knuckles, and surveyed the spread of food before him. Revenge for the pointless errand William had sent him on. And so William found himself separated from Layla by Alex and Dena to his left, Mustafa to his right.

He tried to follow the Arabic conversation across the table. But to his left Alex spoke nonstop into his ear. They were going to the district office today to finalize authorization for the map, and Alex was making plans.

"Let's start by mapping the water wells," he said, "and after that maybe the grazing routes. We can do the grazing routes now, no? And we also need to talk to the elders about the farm boundaries. Have you set up that meeting yet? We need that soon. Like, next week. William, did you hear what I said?"

William was forced to respond, between surreptitious glances across the table at Layla, who was engrossed in the conversation and never seemed to look up at him, except for once, when they both went for the bread and she was about to touch his fingers, met his eyes instead, embarrassed.

"When is the rest of the equipment arriving?"

"Today, maybe," William said.

He tried to interrupt to ask Layla more about her father, but the conversation had moved on: Mustafa had gotten up and was making Layla and Dena laugh with an impression of the policeman waddling with his belly under the tree.

BREAKFAST OVER and he'd barely said a word to her. Already she was picking up plates, helped by Dena. Mustafa was sweeping crumbs into his palm. Alex was finishing up the beans. William watched Dena and Layla walk to the kitchen, and, when Dena returned alone, he saw his chance, and rose.

Something in his face must have communicated itself to them, because Dena stopped with a plate in midair and Mustafa paused with his hand over the table, and Alex—who had been saying something about repairs to the truck—closed his mouth.

"I need to speak to Layla," he said. And in Arabic to Mustafa, "Stay here."

Dena understood.

"Yes, of course."

He trusted her to keep the other two away.

Inside the kitchen he stopped abruptly, eyes adjusting to the dimness. The room was full of blue shadow, blue laminate floor mirroring blue shutters, which were drawn shut. Dishes were stacked beside the sink. On the table, a tea tray was set out with a thermos and some biscuits. He saw Layla half-hidden behind the open leaf of a cabinet. She must have felt the light change because she looked around. Alarm on her face as he bore down on her.

He'd been deprived of time alone with her all morning, had been missing her, and now that he had a moment with her, he blurted out the first words that came to mind. "You didn't come to work that day. And there was a corpse. I was worried something had happened to you."

She shut the cabinet door and stared at him. She seemed to have trouble making sense of his words. It occurred to him that he sounded crazy—the link he'd made between the body and her absence was his projection. All the while she had been safe, at home, taking care of her father.

The silence lengthened. He thought how to backtrack, explain. But then she made a movement.

"Oh," she said. "You thought I was . . . dead."

He was quite embarrassed. "It's crazy, I know. But I was worried." He looked at her. "Really."

He heard Alex and Mustafa in the yard. She continued to gaze at him as she adjusted teacups in her hand. Slowly, a knowledge began to settle in her eyes. Her lips moved. Faint dimples as a smile showed.

"Well," she said. "I'm here."

THERE HAD BEEN A RIVER HERE THREE MONTHS BEFORE. A full-blooded river jolting over rocks, rippling with currents, swooshing around bank bends. Now there was no river. Just an arid depression, not even a hint of moisture to suggest that there had ever been water here.

"Where is it?" asked Alex.

William stood beside him, gazing at a bank that had been green when they'd first driven through shortly after Alex's arrival in Saraaya. They were sixty kilometers north of town, there to survey one of the main grazing thoroughfares through which the nomads passed on their way south.

"It's gone," said William.

"Gone?"

"I guess it dried up already."

"And when will it come back?"

"Next July maybe."

"Maybe?"

"It used to come back every wet season, but the last few years, it's so-so. Sometimes it comes, sometimes it doesn't."

Alex turned back to the landscape. A scene that overwhelmed and underwhelmed all at once with its spectacular monotony. Blank slate of a bleached sky. Flat land stretching around him. Clumps of desiccated trees to the east. In the far distance, a man sitting atop a camel wound his way from nowhere to nowhere.

After authorization for his map had finally arrived in December, he had set about his work in earnest. Trailed by William, he'd zipped around the district with his measuring rope and his surveying telescope and his satellite devices, pouncing on unsuspecting passersby in the market to ask about farms and roads and grazing routes; traveling to villages and water wells and nomads' camps in the plains on the peripheries of town. He and William had undertaken expeditions to the sandy plains of the Goz to the north, which stretched from Chad to the White Nile. Great tracts of flat semi-desert unfurling as far as the eye could see, dry shrubs dotting the landscape here and there.

They had driven south, to the enormous wetland terrain of the Sudd, a carpet of marshes and swamps and bogs with islands of floating reeds as vast as football fields, feeding into the White Nile that flowed toward Khartoum. They had explored the network of rivers between these two terrains, life source of nomads and Nilotes, irrigating crops, nourishing livestock and people.

But the more Alex studied the landscape—squinting over his maps by night and gathering information during his expeditions by day—the more confused he became. He had never dealt with a geography like this before. It confounded everything he knew about natural habitats, land formations, water systems. He was used to landscapes changing slowly, in minuscule increments, over years of soil erosion, the weathering of rock layers, the creep of vegetation.

But here, from one season to the next, the landscape changed completely. During the rainy season swamps and rivers and lakes materialized, only to disappear entirely during the dry season and reappear in different places with the following rains. A river twenty meters wide that gushed with torrential water dwindled to a pathetic dribbling stream three months later, or dried up altogether, as this one had. Desert turned into lush, rolling grassland between May and November, only to turn back into desert during the dry season. Nomadic settlements sprung up with their rickety reed houses and cattle and camels in one place only to be packed up soon after. Even the town was in a continuous state of upheaval. It had been destroyed three times during the war. Each time it was rebuilt—after people returned, dragging behind them their diminished belongings—things changed. Streets shifted. Families invaded each other's compounds. Land that belonged to one person was suddenly farmed by someone else. The market disappeared, reduced to skeletal bones of burnt stalls, only to spring up elsewhere, with all the hustle and bustle of trade. Everything—villages and rivers and grazing routes—had two names, one in Arabic and one in Nilotic, so that he found himself having to cope with the confusion not only of multiple languages but of multiple place names.

One map, he realized now, would not be enough. He had to make two. One depicting dry-season geography and one for the wet-season landscape. Even then, he knew that within six or seven years the maps would again have to be updated. Once rivers shifted their courses the meander lines would have to be redrawn; new grazing routes would have to be shaded in, new swamps, new deserts spreading south with diminishing rains.

He'd been in Saraaya since November and it was already the end of February. A little over three months left to present something to his boss, Greg, who'd been calling from Khartoum to check on his progress.

After his last phone call to Khartoum, in which Greg had exhorted him to get going quickly or else, Alex had asked William to arrange a meeting with Nilot and nomad elders. Three days later they'd arrived to find a large group collected in a clearing on the edge of town, under a tree whose branches were still verdant. Men and women and children sat on straw mats on the grass. Light darted and leapt from face to face. Alex stood nervously before the unabashed gaze of the congregation, branches above him swaying with a breeze that stirred the heat into life rather than dispersed it.

He hadn't expected so many people to show up. William had arranged for him to meet a handful of elders. But word had gotten out about the meeting, and he'd found bodies and faces packed under the shade, looking back at him expectantly. Being the only white man for miles around meant that he drew a crowd.

Turning to William, he said, "Can you ask them to introduce themselves first?"

One of the Nilot elders—a man with drooping eyelids and milky irises and wearing a red beret angled jauntily on his head—spoke. William translated. The elder wanted, first, to hear from Alex. What was America like? Did he like Saraaya?

The next ten minutes were lost to chitchat. Growing impatient, Alex told William to ask about the boundaries.

"They will answer your questions, so you must show them the same courtesy."

Again, Alex felt the precariousness of that balance of power that he shared with his translator, who was really the one in control of things, and he was compelled to oblige him by answering more questions from the crowd.

Finally they returned to the business at hand. William translated as Alex, pointing to a map pinned and fluttering against the tree, tried to explain what he wanted to know. An old woman in a blue dress yawned. Three children fidgeted at the front. A man in a jellabiya scratched his arm. A little girl sucked her thumb. He rushed on.

"Tell them I'm meeting with them to determine the boundary between Nilot farms and nomad grazing lands," he said. "Ask if any elders would like to speak to the matter."

William translated. The same Nilot elder rose, propping himself up on his stick. He pointed to the horizon. The boundary, he said, was clear. Since the time of his forefathers there had been an understanding that when the nomads arrived in Saraaya at the end of the rains each year, they could graze their cattle north of the bend of the River Kinu, at a village about one day's walk from the town. Their grazing land stretched from that bend up to the gum-tree forest. The nomads who had lost their herds in the droughts and settled in Saraaya cultivated farmland in that stretch. Down from Saraaya to Agok was Nilot grazing land, and from Saraaya to the savannahs was Nilot farmland.

Murmurs of assent rippled through the crowd. But then a nomad elder stood up. The jellabiya he wore was a bright white, brighter than those worn by the men sitting with him, a turban wrapped neatly above a high brow and small eyes and a thick, graying mustache.

It's true, he began, that back in the time of their forefathers, the nomads grazed north of the river bend. But that was long ago. Before the war. Before the droughts. Back in the time of the English. Things had changed since then. Grazing routes had shifted with lessening rains; war had scattered people. Many of the nomads had settled to farm, many of the Nilotes had moved south to join their kinsmen beyond the savannahs. The land boundaries were different now.

When he spoke again, there was an explosion of movement. People sprang to their feet. Babies crawling on the ground and little boys and girls hovering around the circle stopped what they were doing to stare at their agitated parents in surprise.

"What did he say?"

"He's saying the nomads' land stretches from Saraaya up to the gum-tree forest." William's finger traveled from the black dot of the town on the map up to a gray-shaded area, about thirty kilometers northwest, indicating the forest. "He's claiming half the land the Nilotes say is theirs as grazing pasture for the nomads."

Shoes and sticks rose in the air. Turbans unspooled to the

ground. Heads and hands and legs were suddenly locked in a jumble. From the sidelines, women urged on their menfolk. William plunged into the circle to separate people. Alex, too, pushed his way in. Immediately someone's elbow landed in his cheek, and he stumbled out, eyes watering from pain.

That was the first meeting. He arranged meetings with each group separately, but the map of nomad grazing routes then conflicted with the map of Nilot grazing routes. Same went for the farmlands. He hadn't even figured out the district boundaries yet, and there were still field trips to be taken, long days of compiling information—correlation of Arabic and Nilotic names of rivers, lakes, villages; cross-checking findings with the authorities; entering data into his blueprint map.

Each day brought more doubts and questions. It wasn't just that he was thwarted at every turn. Or that his measuring instruments were useless in the face of boundaries as difficult to grasp as smoke. The war, too, was taking its toll. The rebels inching closer to the district cast a cloud of peril over the map. He'd begun having nightmares in which he was lost in a maze of mud walls, chased by faceless armed men, unable to find his way out; in another dream he was trapped in a vault packed from floor to ceiling with maps; maps weighing on his chest and arms and legs and maps in his mouth.

And now, as though in a dream, this river that had disappeared. He stared out at the smooth parched depression at his feet.

"How long will this take?" William asked, glancing at his watch. "I promised to drive Layla home today."

Alex sighed. Another date with Layla. Alex had been clued into the romance by Dena, who'd explained, the day of Layla's return back in December—when William had abruptly marched off to the kitchen to speak to her—that Alex, Mustafa, and she needed to give William and Layla more room to be alone. A few days later, during one of their field trips, William confessed that he and Layla were "getting to know one another."

Alex was happy for William. It was sweet how he and Layla huddled together in the kitchen. The little presents that William picked up for her when he was out and about with Alex—a beaded necklace, or a silver bracelet—which Alex was invariably asked to give his opinion on, in William's quest to identify Layla's tastes and preferences, to please her by surprising her.

But the courtship interfered with work. William was slow to leave the compound when Layla was in. And when he and Alex were out on one of their expeditions, he was always impatient to return. No matter how often Alex explained to William the intricacies of mapping—yes, he had to map all the grazing routes, and yes, it was necessary to document precise coordinates of water wells in the district, which meant that they did, indeed, have to travel to all of them—William didn't get it. The long drives, the hours spent fiddling with equipment, the mindless waiting were all great chunks of time that it was clear he'd rather be spending with Layla.

"We just got here," said Alex.

They had been delayed leaving because, first, there had been a problem with the truck tire, which had to be replaced. That had taken all morning. By the time the tire was fixed, it was lunchtime. Alex had wanted to head out anyway, but William insisted on staying and having lunch at the compound. "We should have left earlier. You wanted to stay because of Layla."

It was the first time he was voicing objection to the amount of time William was spending with her.

William's eyes narrowed.

"So I'm not entitled to my lunch break?"

"I'm just saying," said Alex, "I want to finish as soon as possible, too, but I need an hour."

"It's the end of the day."

"It takes—" Alex stopped. It was pointless. They were both frustrated and getting nowhere. "Right now we're wasting time. Let me just get on with it, OK? The sooner I start, the sooner we can get back."

William folded his arms and stared imperiously out over the riverbed.

Alex walked back to the truck. A gust of wind filled his ears with noise, lashed dust against his calves. Shrubs in the distance bent their branches one way and then the other. He squinted to keep dirt out of his eyes. He pulled out surveying equipment from the bed of the truck as William crouched by the bank, whipping at sand with a supple branch he'd picked up somewhere.

"Are you coming to help or what?" Alex called, stacking boxes on top of one another.

William rose and threw the branch away. Took more time than was necessary dusting off his trousers. Finally came over to the car, lifted equipment out.

Alex walked back to the bank and dropped the boxes on the ground. He looked out at the river that had ceased to be a river, a river that might or might not become one again next year, and wondered how on earth he was to find his bearings.

TWO HOURS LATER, they were back at the compound. William kept the engine running and honked as Alex stepped out. The gate opened; Layla greeted him; Mustafa tapped an invisible wristwatch in disapproval of their tardiness. He climbed into the backseat and Layla took the front.

"See you later," called William.

Layla and Mustafa waved.

The three of them looked like a family. As he watched the car sputter up the street, he suddenly felt like a child being left behind.

In the compound, he saw Dena under the gazebo, tinkering with the camera. He closed the gate quietly and watched her. It was nice, for a change, to look at her without her noticing; she was always the one looking at others. She sat with her head bent, camera on her lap. The thatch roof cast a circle of shadow around her, around the white chairs and table, the wooden bedframe used as a sofa. Behind her, the hammock swayed faintly.

He took in her shoulders and arms. She was slender but strong; carrying the camera made her so. Once he had lifted the device and was surprised by the heft of it. The labor of filming gave her limbs an elegance—not feminine, exactly, but a grace that was athletic. Even when he wasn't looking at her, he was always drawn to her presence on the edge of his field of vision. Now as he dwelled on her neck and the lips framed by her angled chin—lips pursed as she fiddled with the camera—the sense came to him again that he was terribly, hopelessly attracted to her.

She disliked him. He knew this, which was why he resisted his infatuation. She went out of her way to keep a formal, cold distance from him, when with William she was open and famil- iar. But because of his boredom, or because of his loneliness, he felt—especially in this moment when she was oblivious to him—drawn to her. And that cozy picture of William, Layla, and Mustafa in the car just now tapped in him a desire for contact. It made him bold.

She noticed him hovering just inside the gate. As he crossed to where she sat, she looked at him warily. He pulled up a chair. She glanced around.

"Where's everyone gone?"

"William and Mustafa went to drop off Layla."

She half nodded, vaguely acknowledging this information,

then turned back to the camera. He could sense her defenses rising up. If he let her, she'd go on ignoring him. He willed her to look at him. For a few moments she pretended to be absorbed, diligently wiping at the rim of the lens with a cloth.

Finally, she leveled her gaze at him.

"What?"

A feeling of triumph flared up in him at this surrender. He sat back in his chair, elbow on armrest, fingers on temple and chin. He was strangely unafraid. He smiled.

"I like looking at you."

A small frown of irritation showed on her brow. Then she shrugged, her face emptying. She'd tolerate him out of politeness. She adjusted the camera on her lap, ready to ignore him again.

He refused to let her get away so easily.

"I've been wondering. Are you spoken for? Have a beau back home?"

At this she burst out laughing. She was laughing at him, he knew. Still, he couldn't help admiring how pretty she was when she laughed.

"Is this a come-on?"

He was unfazed. He shrugged coolly.

"Maybe."

What did he want to say, exactly? What he wanted to say was that he liked her, was attracted to her, wanted to come close. William and Layla were together. It gave him ideas. Dena made a show of despising him, but a part of him hoped that this pointed, in fact, to its opposite. He wanted to know if she felt something for him too. But just as he was formulating the thought, she cut it short.

"No hope there, Alex." She shook her head in mock regret. "Sorry."

"No hope at all?"

"Never."

"Why?"

She rolled her eyes. "There you go again."

"OK. Forget about liking me. Why do you dislike me so much?"

That was the thing. He was smart and interesting and handsome enough to have had no trouble with girls in the past. There was no harm in finding pleasure, or at least getting to know one another better, while they were stuck here. There wasn't much else to do in Saraaya.

She narrowed her eyes at him. "Do you really want to know?"

"Yes."

"Because you're smug and entitled."

He could tell that she took pleasure in saying it. That she'd been thinking it almost since the beginning, and now, because he'd openly hinted at his feelings, she felt free to be candid—brutally so.

"I mean, look at how you just ambushed me. You do it all the time. It's intrusive. It's rude." She considered him. "And the way you treat William."

"How do I treat him?"

"Like he's your lackey."

"His job is to help me. And my job is to finish this map. I'm working for everyone's benefit. What's the harm?"

"It's the way you do it. You show up knowing nothing about the place and expect everything and everyone to bend to you."

She was leaning back, her jaw angled condescendingly, a self-satisfied look on her face. Her fingers stroked the camera as though it were a cat. He was torn between his attraction and a sudden dislike.

"And you." He turned on her. "Going around town with your camera, making an art film. That's not smug and entitled?"

"That's different."

"It's not." He sat up in his chair. "You look down your nose at me because you're an *artist*." He quoted the word sarcastically with his fingers. "As if that makes you special or something. Tell me. What is this film? What's it about? As far as I can see, it's just some crappy shots of grass rustling and cows and teatime."

"You're a fucking jerk."

"And you're an arrogant, self-righteous bitch."

Her face hardened. She rose in slow motion, as though summoning up her strength to stomp him into the ground. The camera was like a rock in her hands. She lifted it. She was going to hurt him. He needed to move. Another part of him was too fascinated to react, simply sat there, wanting to see the end of it, what she would do.

He flinched as she heaved the camera down. She caught herself just in the nick of time and carefully lowered the device. For a moment, she looked like she might say something, but instead turned and marched to her room and slammed the door.

He stared helplessly at her shut door. His gaze drifted over the yard, to the sun-bleached flags flapping sadly along the compound walls, the stripped metal bedframes, the parched, drooping plants in the oil drums by the gate. It wasn't meant to go this way. He had gone too far. But so had she. Why did it always end up like this with them? He hadn't imagined that she was capable of such anger. She had really almost hit him. Had he meant to drive her to it? He wanted to kick himself. But he was also elated.

He was full of confused emotion. Suddenly he wanted to escape the compound. A walk, to clear his head. Better yet, a drink. He remembered the drinking establishment William sometimes took him to. He was thirsty for beer—even the terrible-tasting local variety. A drink was the thing. He cast one last look in her direction and, on an impulse, got up and ventured out through the gate.

∫

AS SHE SAT in the truck's passenger seat beside William, snatches of the song Mustafa was humming to himself in the back reaching her over the growl of the engine, Layla, in a momentary silence in the conversation, wondered at the strange changes that had come over her. It was as if, she thought, looking out the window at the landscape rolling past, there were two Laylas. Layla of Before and Layla of Now. Layla of Before could have never imagined feeling as content as she felt now, sitting in a car with a strange Nilot man. Layla of Now not only sat in the car with this strange man, she often daydreamed about a future with him. The old Layla spent her time confined to the homestead, whereas the new Layla thought nothing of lying to her family, as she had done today, telling them she had to work late, so she could spend time with William.

Now, contemplating his hands on the steering wheel, she said, "Teach me to drive."

A tendency the Layla of Before was beginning to recognize in the new Layla. This latter Layla had strong impulses. On which she acted.

William's eyebrows arched in surprise. She liked being in the car with him because then she could look at him in profile. From which angle beguiling features—the steep precipice of his brow bone, the mesmerizing canyon of his right ear, an Adam's apple petaled by a crisp collar—were prominent. She felt a tenderness for the long legs and arms confined by the small space of the driver's seat. They were on a stretch of road between Saraaya and the surrounding villages, sun dipping below the horizon, truck-shaped shadow rippling and shrinking and expanding over sparse shrubbery and rocks as they drove toward home. She didn't want to go home.

"Really?" said William, dubious. But even as he said it his expression changed, the possibilities unfolding in his mind. He, too, was imagining a new Layla.

He glanced at her, to confirm. The truck slowed, then trundled off the road as he steered onto an area of smooth dirt. He stopped the car. Mustafa popped up in the gap between her seat and William's.

"Why're we stopping?"

"Layla's going to drive."

Mustafa looked at her in awe. "Do you know how?"

"No," she said. "I want to learn."

She had, until recently, only ever ridden in buses, not cars, and yet here she was, this new Layla, stepping down from the passenger seat of a truck, circling around to the driver's seat, and, in a moment of fleeting intimacy, in which they were alone in the silence of the still landscape, crossing paths with William. She felt both shy and bold as he came toward her, conscious of a feeling of constraint, a tension of expectation. Admiring his broad, strong shoulders against the sky. The neat, crisp clothes that threw up the beauty of his figure. He noticed her appraisal of him and smiled.

A distance from her old life, in which there had been no surprises. Just movement: south toward Saraaya with two hundred head of cattle that the family owned, when the rains stopped. Six months in the cattle camp there. Three months traveling back up to the plains around Hasaniya. North to south, south to north. Through desert and bush and elephant grass, looking for still pools of water, only stars and endless land and cattle for company.

But that landscape she loved had been marred by her father. A squat man with heavy shoulders and bitter eyes always on the lookout for an outlet for his rage against the uncooperative elements. Not enough rain one week and her mother was sure to get a beating. Dried-up waterholes where there had been some before, and Layla might be slapped for being tardy with his afternoon tea or his breakfast. He grew harder toward her and her mother as the years passed. As the rains lessened and the pastures shrank and they had to travel farther and farther to graze the animals.

The only woman he didn't come near was his own mother, Layla's grandmother. She did what she could to protect Layla and her mother, but she was old and frail, a shriveled, barely visible figure atop the massive ox she rode when they were on the move. She cursed a stream of filthy epithets at her son whenever Layla came crying to her. It was her life's disaster, she'd say, that the only child of her seven children to survive into adulthood was a useless, heartless good-for-nothing. Just like his father, she'd add. To the extent that she despised her son, she loved her grand-daughter, and growing up Layla had been closest to her grand-mother. Adored her henna-dyed hair, gathered in a scorpion's-tail plait at the back of her neck. Her huge glasses, which magnified gray-fogged eyes and the wrinkles that surrounded them. Ancient earlobes that reached almost to her shoulders, weighed down by the heavy silver jewelry she liked to wear even into old age, like a young bride. She was the only woman Layla knew who smoked. Sometimes she let Layla have a drag of her cigarettes.

From her grandmother Layla learned two lessons. First: men were weak, much weaker than women. Second: because they were weak, they were her enemies. Her father, uncle, and brothers confirmed the truth of these lessons on a daily basis. So that Layla, grasping her stinging cheek after a slap from her father, or hot with anger after an insult from her brother, would repeat to herself: *Men are weak, and because they are weak, they are my enemies.*

Her grandmother's words made the slaps and kicks, the work that she and her mother endured as her father and her uncle and her brothers waited for their tea to be served, or their clothes to be washed, or their firewood to be brought—bearable. The words gave an order to the universe. They explained the small and large injustices she experienced in her daily life. Most important, they gave her a power that made her feel superior to the men who ruled her world. For her world was limited: it was the homestead, cattle, pastures. Sometimes when they were on the move she would go for weeks without encountering anyone outside the family. Consumed along with everyone else by the routine of rising before dawn, packing up camp, mounting oxen, herding cattle thirty, fifty, sometimes sixty kilometers that day.

And then, last year, her grandmother died. Layla cried for three days straight in a corner of the tent that she shared with her mother.

And four months later, the catastrophe of the drought, and the lost herds. Having to settle down in Saraaya with nothing to live on. Having to find work, which she'd never had to do before, to help her family.

⌠

IN THE DRIVER'S SEAT the truck seemed much larger. The steering wheel too far, the windshield too high. She had a sense of William's height, the length of his body, in the abyss between her feet and the pedals. She sat forward, toeing them.

William's eyes roved playfully over her outstretched arms as he shut the passenger door.

"First thing, you're too far back. Move forward."

"How?"

"There's a latch under your seat, by the door."

She fumbled for it but couldn't find it.

"Here," said Mustafa, ducking down behind her. Small fingers scurried over hers. A click. "You can move now."

The novelty of a smooth gliding motion floating her forward toward the steering wheel. Her new life was full of unfamiliar experiences, big and small. In the compound, for instance, she had a whole kitchen to herself, with its own gas stove and running water, whereas at home she cooked out in the open on a coal stove, or used firewood, and water had to be fetched from a well. And the people she cooked for in the compound were far less fussy about what they were fed than her own family.

It was easy work, and with it she'd discovered this new Layla. The one who spent her days with four strangers and had become a stranger to herself in the process.

"Here." William leaned toward her, a whiff of his cologne enveloping her, and pointed at the pedals. "Clutch. Brake. Gas. The clutch you need when you put the car in motion, and when you switch gears. Gas, to accelerate. Brake, to slow or stop. Use your right foot for the gas and brake. Left for the clutch."

She nodded, her feet moving between the pedals, feeling out the information.

Of the three adults in the compound, William should have been the most familiar, but from the beginning she'd been more awkward with him than around the others, and only now was she beginning to understand why. For he was different from the nomad and Nilot men she was used to. Different from her father and her brothers and her uncle. He was the first man she knew closely who wasn't a foe, and in her mind his goodness was evoked in that lemony scent that spoke to her of elsewhere, of somewhere cool and green and peaceful.

She had Nilot friends growing up, and she spoke their language. But there was a line not to be crossed with them. And with William she had crossed it. She couldn't deny to herself that he was courting her. Unthinkable to the old Layla, the one who had accepted that her father would pick a suitable husband for her, preferably a cousin or a second cousin, preferably rich, to recover, through the bride wealth that would be given for her, some of the cattle the family had lost in the drought.

But there was something about being around these four strangers that made things that had been inconceivable in her previous life seem suddenly possible.

"Now, adjust your mirrors," said William. "The side-view one first. Like this." He demonstrated on his own mirror.

She leaned out of the window, again conscious of the proportions of the truck, how large it was, and adjusted the mirror. The wide-open landscape came into view.

"And the rearview mirror," said William. "So you can see behind you."

Mustafa's blinking eyes, and the rest of the car and the back windshield.

What made her fall for William was that he made her realize that there could be more between a man and a woman than she had imagined. You could be friends with a man. That was the first revelation. The fact that she could sit and talk to him about silly things, mundane things. Memories of her grandmother. How she wanted to learn to read and write properly. Her thoughts and fears. He grasped things about her that she hadn't fully grasped herself. And that was before she took in his education, his work. He was a Nilot, it was true, and according to her family's standards, that invalidated everything else about him, but now, with these new eyes with which she looked out on the world, she knew that she was lucky that her path had crossed his.

"Here are the gears." He reached for her right hand and placed it on the stick shift. "When you start the car, you're in neutral." He spoke normally, as if nothing was different, but of course everything was different, because his hand was on hers, and it was the first time that they were touching. "Move to first gear when you want to drive." His hand was rough and warm. "When the engine begins to strain, switch to second." He pressed down on her hand and shifted the stick from neutral, to one, to two.

"Don't forget to press on the clutch when you're changing gears," said Mustafa behind her.

"All right," she said, overwhelmed more by sensations traveling up her arm than instructions. William removed his hand. A hotness coated her knuckles, and she realized that for all of his nonchalance he was nervous touching her too.

"Any questions?"

"No. I want to try now."

"Switch on the engine then." He smiled.

She reached for the key and turned it, as she'd watched him do many times over the previous days. A splutter followed by a steady purring, and she was aware of her changing relationship to the car. She was making it do things, and she was thrilled by and afraid of this all at once.

"Press on the clutch with your left foot. Then slowly release as you press on the gas."

She released the clutch and the car jerked forward, stalling.

"Too fast," said Mustafa. "Do it slowly."

"Why do you know so much about driving?" she asked over her shoulder.

"Nabil, in the market, lets me drive his car sometimes," said Mustafa, looking wistfully at the steering wheel. He eyed William.

"No. You're too small for this truck. Anyway it's not my car, it's the organization's."

"How come Layla gets to drive it then?"

"Forget it," said William. "You're not allowed."

Mustafa made a face but said nothing.

The thing was, she knew that she wasn't just any girl with a pretty face. Something had always separated her from others like her. Some yearning that extended beyond the limits of her own place. She got it from her grandmother. She liked to laugh. She liked to dance. She liked being happy, and she felt that it was her right, when she knew that it wasn't a woman's right to seek such things. William, somehow, understood this about her—that she felt entitled to happiness, and he knew how to give it to her freely, effortlessly.

That was the second revelation: that she didn't have to settle for less than what she wanted. She had never, until recently, been able to articulate these things to herself. She'd grown up resenting her father and her brothers, for that injustice she experienced in her everyday life. And when she had named it, or acted against it, she had been punished. Only now, after meeting William and working in the compound and spending time with these strangers, did she understand what it was that had bothered her all her life. It was what was taken for granted. That she deserved less than her brothers. And here was a man who was not only beautiful and kind but who actually wanted to make her happy. Him being a Nilot—when she took all of these things into consideration— suddenly didn't matter at all.

She focused on her feet, on coordinating the pressure of one foot with the slow release of the other. This time the truck heaved forward with a lightness that took her by surprise, and she gripped the steering wheel as the truck lurched ten meters, then twenty, forty.

"That's good!" said Mustafa.

At which, in her excitement, she pressed too firmly on the gas, and the truck jumped, so that in a panic she crushed her foot against the brake, and the truck came to a sudden halt that sent Mustafa—who had been standing in the back, elbows propped on front seats—careening into the gap between her seat and William's.

"I'm all right," he said, his hair in the air-conditioning vent.

"Are you sure?" she said, laughing, reaching for him. "Sorry."

William lifted him up. "*Sit* back there," he scolded.

As she switched on the engine again her thoughts returned to her family. That was where the trouble lay. Her father with his bitterness over the loss of the herds and her sly uncle and her brothers who went along with whatever her father and her uncle said.

William brushed aside all her warnings. Now that he'd won her heart he behaved as though anything were possible. What he didn't understand was that winning her over had been the easy part.

ſ

THEY WERE BACK on paved road—William behind the steering wheel, Layla in the passenger seat. Mustafa huddled in the plush cushioning of the backseat, frowning to himself behind his sunglasses, which he'd pulled over his eyes not so much to soften the glare of the setting sun but because he was sulking.

At the end of Layla's lesson he had begged William to let him drive, but again William refused. In his mind he continued to argue with William. He could drive better than Layla. And his feet could reach the pedals—he'd tried it once while waiting for William in the car—he had sat in the driver's seat and placed his bottom right on the edge and then he could just reach the pedals with his toes. William had no qualms about sending Mustafa on errands to the far corners of the district, or even to the town of Hasaniya three hours away, all on his own, like a grown-up, but now it was convenient for William to decide he was a child. He couldn't wait to get to an age when he didn't have to ask for permission to do things. But looking out at the passing scene, it seemed to him that the road to adulthood was as endless as the one along which the car now moved.

He blinked against a last ray streaking in through the windshield, silhouetting William and Layla's profiles in the front. Mustafa was spending lots of time with them these days because William wanted to take Layla out for scenic drives along the wadis, to sit under the shade of a tree and drink mango juice in the market, for walks to some of the surrounding villages. Mustafa came along as a chaperone. Having a child around protected them from gossiping townsfolk. Today was one such occasion when Mustafa was acting as chaperone.

"Three hundred per outing," Mustafa had said, when William first propositioned him.

"I'm taking you out. I shouldn't be paying you."

"Still it's extra work for me," said Mustafa. "It's my free time."

William sighed. "Fine. Three hundred then."

So Mustafa agreed, also managing to wangle, on these outings, little treats—soft drinks, sweets, a sandwich, on top of his three hundred pounds. The best he could do now that his underwear venture had been shut down by the police. He'd gone three days in a row to the station to try to get his money back, bribing guards at the front with packets of cigarettes—the only bribe he could afford—until finally, on the third day, they relented and let him loose in the hallways at the back of the station. From which he was immediately dragged out by an officer. When he returned the next day, one of the guards thwacked him over the head and warned him not to come again.

His underwear, too, was lost forever. All that was left of his things were one or two panties still clinging high up to the branches of the acacia, sad flags to his failure.

On their first outing together almost two months ago, William took him and Layla to a café in the market. A canopy hung overhead, shading customers who sat at plastic tables. Profusions of potted plants—creepers, hibiscus, cacti—were grouped in pretty configurations around the room.

As Mustafa sucked on a straw dipped in a bottle of Pepsi, he watched William and Layla across the table. Layla held a soft drink in one hand. William's eyes were riveted to hers. He talked to her in low, intense tones about Khartoum; the two Niles meeting, tall buildings, traffic, markets that were so gigantic you got lost in them.

Mustafa was interested in this conversation—Khartoum was his future home, or so he hoped. But what was just as intriguing was the way William lapped up Layla's every gesture and word. His whole body strained toward her, so that it looked like he might fall out of his chair, long limbs splashing to the floor. When she giggled or smiled he grinned so widely that his face might have split in two. If her bottle was about to be emptied, he called to the waiter for another one, whereas Mustafa had to tug on William's sleeve to get a second drink.

Since Layla's return, William was like a calf following its mother around. If she went to fill water from the outdoor tap he came along to carry buckets for her. After breakfast he sat with her under the gazebo, talking in whispers. He burst through the gate, after his long field trips with Alex, scouring the courtyard for her. He followed her into the kitchen, where he'd taken to being assistant cook, helping to chop garlic or onions while tears streamed down his cheeks.

It was strange that the clever William he admired, the William who'd lived in Khartoum, who was his role model, not only in matters of substance such as linguistic versatility, but also in matters of style—for Mustafa dreamt that when he was all grown up, he, too, might wear such lovely starched white shirts, with a pen peeking out of his breast pocket—it seemed strange that this William should turn into such a lovestruck being.

Layla fretted and fussed over William too. But that was what women were supposed to do. He liked Layla: she made his favorite dessert—dough balls dipped in sugar—at least once a week, especially for him. And sugared things, along with money, were the key to Mustafa's heart. Plunging a dough ball in a glass of tea on a morning, tearing it apart with his teeth, tea and dough melting in his mouth, at such moments Mustafa, too, felt that he loved

Layla. And he told her so, when he went to return his plate to the kitchen. But not in the way that William did.

Mustafa's own relationship to girls his age was limited to insulting them and making them cry. There was a clique, archenemies to his group of friends, of the same age or thereabouts. Mustafa called them names. He pulled their hair. He played practical jokes on them. But sometimes they made him pay. Once, a group of them ambushed him in an alleyway and pinned him to a wall—one held his legs, the other two an arm each—and, while he was thus restrained, the fourth girl, the one he'd insulted by calling her mother a hag, kissed him all over his face. They let him go, laughing. He wiped his mouth and spat into the dirt. He'd felt helpless, afraid, pinned by those lips against the wall, and ever since he'd kept his distance from the girls, more wary now, always traveling with a guard—one or another of his friends—if he was going somewhere quiet.

Anyhow his thoughts were not on love but money. The loss of his things made him bitter. Not just the loss of his things: his poverty. The week before he'd asked Alex about his salary. Alex disclosed a sum so gigantic it had boggled Mustafa's mind. Millions upon millions, each month. It would take him half a lifetime, at his current pay working at the compound, to make what Alex earned in a month.

Everything reminded him of his poverty. Innocent objects around the compound, such as Alex's beautiful wash bag hanging off a nail in the bathroom. Its luxurious gleam of blue nylon. Its see-through pouches. Its small rectangular mirror (detachable). Sometimes he stood for minutes, eyes tracing convex outlines of the wash bag, angles of fabric winking under sunlight, blue changing from metallic to almost black along its shadowed nooks. He could spend all day zipping and unzipping the wash bag's many pockets, thinking of what to store in them. His sunglasses? Coins in the side pockets? Tissue paper in the transparent pouch?

He wanted the multicolored pens and pencils that Alex marked his maps with. He wanted Dena's CD player that enveloped his ears in a river of sound. He wanted a computer like the one Alex kept in his office, on which he could learn to type. He wanted Dena's camera, which was the world's most expensive toy. And Dena's battery-powered toothbrush, which, when he secretly used it, made his skull buzz.

But these things were not his. And he had no means of going to school so that he could eventually earn a good living and be able to afford such things as Alex and Dena had. In the meantime, he could do no better than chaperone William and Layla. And all for what? For three hundred pounds an outing.

He glanced out the window. The sky was a tempest of orange and purple. Beneath the flare of the setting sun the earth darkened. On the horizon, beam pumps came into view, sucking up oil from the bowels of the plains.

As he watched them, his mind returned to the man who'd come to him under the tree after the police stole his things back in December. His name was Deng, and he said he might have work for him.

"What kind of work?" Mustafa had asked.

"I need someone to deliver things."

"What things?"

"This is between us, do you understand?"

Mustafa nodded.

Deng looked up and down the street then, to make sure no one was listening.

Then he said, "Guns, to the rebels in the bush."

Just as Deng was about to say more, William had interrupted them.

Ever since, whenever Mustafa ran into him, Deng reminded him to come and visit. Mustafa never went. But now he thought why not.

At the front, William and Layla struck up a conversation, but the wind was too loud, and he couldn't follow. A hot surge made its way up his neck and ears. He bit down bitterly on his lip, scheming in his head, thinking of money, and school, and beautiful things like Alex's computer.

If he couldn't make money the honest way, then why not the crooked way? Why not visit Deng and see what he had to offer?

⸱

THROUGH THE WINDSHIELD, William took in light pooling along the horizon, felt the truck thrum beneath his hands. They had just dropped off Layla and were on their way back to the compound. Mustafa had taken Layla's seat at the front. He sat with his arms crossed, lips pursed, sullen.

William ignored him. His eyes roamed over the road, over shadowy shrubs and undergrowth, soil darkened to a rich, tawny color, his thoughts winding back to the driving lesson. In the car with Layla earlier, he'd glanced up to the rearview mirror to find Mustafa mocking them, hugging himself and making kissing sounds. William scolded him. But Layla wasn't offended. She joined in on the joke, pouting her lips and sucking the air in a passionate kiss. William had almost swerved off the road. They had laughed, but that moment of her lips kissing the air, her eyes and face flecked with sun took his breath away.

They'd been spending time together ever since her return to the compound, over two months ago now. Bit by bit the barriers that kept them apart—the fact that he was her boss, that she was a nomad and he a Nilot, the formalities that governed relations between unmarried women and men—were crumbling. She spent time with him, enjoyed his company. He could see the warmth in her smile whenever her eyes lighted on him. But he feared that there was a limit to how far she was willing to go. Would she marry him, if he asked her to? Would she risk bringing home a Nilot suitor to her father? It wasn't easy to break ranks. And he was afraid of asking, afraid of destroying the intimacy that was growing between them.

She kept him away from her family. When he and Mustafa drove her home, she never allowed him to drop her off directly at the homestead, where he was bound to meet her father. She preferred instead to walk the last kilometer alone. She said that if her family saw her in the car with him, they'd ask too many questions.

He knew the family's story: nomads who had lost their herds in the drought, forced to stay put and to find new ways of making a living. It was why Layla had had to find work. It was happening to landless nomads everywhere in the area. Over the years they'd been settling down instead of moving on as they had always done, their herds of hundreds or thousands reduced to a handful of emaciated animals, ribs and haunch bones showing. More and more nomads were setting up permanent home in the district. It was why tensions were rife. Some of their young men joined nomad militias, fighting alongside army soldiers to beat back Nilot rebels and raiding land and cattle.

Ahead, the landscape settled into shades of orange. He thought he could see a star. On either side of the road, bushes rose vague and shadowy. Wind gusted in through the window. He drove mechanically, full of thoughts of Layla.

Mustafa moved in his seat. "What's that?"

William peered into the distance. A cluster of dark shapes at the point where the road met the horizon. As they drew closer, he made out two cars stopped in the middle of the highway. A mass of seething cattle spilled off on either side.

He shifted gears, slowing.

"Cattle crossing."

But the cattle didn't move, nor did the cars. Two men stood

at the edge of the crowd of animals, half visible in a haze of shadow and dust.

He braked and honked. Cattle jostled from the road. The men looked over their shoulders, then turned back to something happening farther beyond. He waited for them to clear the way. But they ignored him.

He switched off the engine.

"Wait here," he said to Mustafa.

He stepped out, shoes scrunching against pitted gravel, the smell of animals in his nostrils. Faint twilight revealed shapes and patterns of cowhide. The air hung motionless.

As he drew closer one of the men looked over his shoulder. He tapped his friend and they both suddenly turned and walked toward him. They wore blue jellabiyas, and their feet were clad in military boots. William stopped when he saw the boots.

"What's happening here?" he asked. "You're blocking the road."

One had a turban around his neck. He held a gun.

"We'll let you through in a few minutes," he said. "Wait in your car."

A thin face, eyes pressed deep into the skull, and a wide slit of a mouth. William looked from him to the other one—younger, scrawny, with a cold, hard gaze. He glanced at the military boots again. Armed nomads—militiamen.

The silence was interrupted by the sound of blows, rocks scattering. A retching noise—someone hacking up spit or vomit. He looked up sharply, trying to see, but the cars and cattle blocked his view.

Then a scream, piercing and desperate, rising above the noise of animals.

He moved, pushing deeper into the cattle. The men pulled him back, but not before he caught sight of two men kneeling.

One blindfolded, the other staring at the asphalt. One had wet his pants; a stain spread from his groin along his khakis. They were surrounded by a half-circle of militiamen. One of them held the butt of his gun raised, either about to give a blow or retreating from one.

A cattle raid.

"I want to know," William said, "why are these people tied up? Whose cattle is this?"

"Back to the truck."

William swallowed. "What right do you have to detain these men? What have they done?"

The man adjusted his rifle, drawing William's attention to it. A fear crept up his spine. He remembered Mustafa in the truck. Layla at home.

"Last warning," said the one with the rifle. "Back to the truck."

He looked again to the cluster of cattle and cars, then to the militiamen, their faces shadowed in the rising darkness.

ſ

"WHAT'S GOING ON?" asked Mustafa.

He shut the door.

"Militias." He didn't mention the screams, or the kneeling men. "They said to wait."

"Militias?" Mustafa stood up and leaned into the windshield. "Why are they blocking the road?"

"Sit down and be quiet."

"Cattle raid?"

"Sit down."

Hearing the edge in William's voice, Mustafa sat.

William stared, unsettled. The last time the authorities armed groups of herdless nomads looking for ways to gain back by force what they'd lost in the droughts, the town had been razed to the ground.

In the distance, one of the men gestured. They were being waved through. William switched on the engine. Animals heaved and eddied off the road. He drove slowly through the throng. The militiamen stared into the truck, and Mustafa gaped back. The two kneeling men had disappeared, only a stain on the road marking the spot where they had knelt.

ſ

ALEX'S THINGS HAD SPILLED out of the office and into the kitchen, under the gazebo, into the yard. Now, as Dena passed the gazebo, she regarded the mess of documents on the table and considered that she couldn't have her morning tea in the fresh air as she wanted to. And the kitchen would be occupied; William was there every morning with Layla. Dena didn't like to disturb them.

Beyond the table piled with papers, maps were pinned to a wooden board propped against the gazebo's ridge pole. Some were hand-drawn, showing numbered blocks of land, cattle-grazing routes marked out with dotted lines; others were printed maps of rainfall patterns, altitudes, villages.

She saw Alex step out of the office with Mustafa. They were carrying maps and folders, speaking in a mishmash of English and Arabic.

Alex stopped when he saw her. Two weeks since the fight, and the anger still lingered. What had happened between them—that moment she'd lost herself and almost smashed the camera over his head—felt private, like a secret they shared. He'd provoked her. He had belittled her most precious thing—the film. A sense of shame at her exposure, mixed with outrage. To insult her, when the minute before he'd been confessing his feelings for her.

She could have nipped their conversation in the bud by telling him the truth about herself—she wasn't interested in men. It would have been the simplest way to end it. Why didn't she? Because it would have allowed him to think that her dislike of him had to do with men, when in fact it had to do with him.

Now his gaze, under brows bleached lighter by the sun, was unabashed. There was a new quality to his look—an invasive, prying interest. As if waiting for her to let her guard down again.

"Hey," he said.

Mustafa looked from Alex to her.

"Hey," she said, and walked past him to the kitchen.

There she found William at the sink with sleeves rolled up, washing vegetables in a colander. He spoke over his shoulder to Layla, who sat at the table chopping parsley. The room was humid with steam. Shutters over the sink were drawn half-shut so that only an oblong rectangle of light fell on the floor.

Layla, sitting closest to the light, drew Dena's attention. She was brighter and more beautiful than ever; a glow, Dena knew, that had to do with the blossoming romance. From the moment William had sought her out on the day of her return to the compound, they had been inseparable, William mooning over Layla whenever he could get away from Alex, Layla blushing whenever he was around.

William was full of good humor and benevolence. Dena associated his deepening infatuation with his resplendent cologne—everywhere he went smelled of a lemon orchard bursting into bloom. Layla expressed her affection through increasingly elaborate dishes—peppers and zucchini stuffed with minced meat and rice and dill; a cardamom-spiced lamb stew; flatbread that she spent hours grinding with stone and then cooking over a coal stove.

They all looked forward to Layla's lunches. William's ecstasy over the food was such that he often lost himself in staring at

Layla in wonder as he ate, which would make her giggle, and then Mustafa, in the midst of stuffing his face, would also giggle, and then they would all fall to laughing around the table—even she and Alex forgot their tensions momentarily.

Now Layla rose with a parsley-piled chopping board and went to the stove. William dried his hands on a dishtowel and said something in her ear.

Dena hesitated in the doorway, reluctant to interrupt. But finally she stepped to the tea thermos on the table.

"Morning."

They turned.

"Morning."

They stood side by side against the counter—William broad-shouldered and handsome with his genial sparkling eyes and Layla with her shapely frame and skin the color of sandalwood and the braid that fell heavily on her shoulder.

The developing romance, with its rituals of courtship counterbalanced by elaborate observances of propriety—they had to be accompanied by an escort, Mustafa, when they went out together; and no obviously physical demonstrations of affection, even inside the compound—brought Dena back to her own strangeness. Once or twice, during their conversations in the kitchen, Layla ventured to ask her about her future. Didn't Dena want to get married, have children? Was there anyone waiting for her back in America?

Marriage dogged Dena wherever she went. She'd already received several proposals from men in the town, who were dazzled not by her trousers or her short hair or boyish figure but by her connection to America: here was a woman who might whisk one away from the dirt and narrowness of Saraaya. In the face of such a prospect, her eccentricities were easily forgiven.

She deflected these proposals, as she did Layla's questions, as tactfully as she could. She felt that there was a gulf that couldn't be bridged—she'd spent most of her life in America, and it meant that she belonged neither here nor there.

Growing up in Seattle, she'd often listened to her parents recall their youth in Khartoum. Before the dictatorship. When the streets of the capital weren't full of exhaust fumes, when the weather was cooler. When schools and universities turned out graduates who spoke English as well as Arabic. When women wore miniskirts and towering wigs. When there were parties and discos. When there were politicians who didn't stash the national wealth in Swiss bank accounts.

It had all come to an end in 1989, when a soldier with gleaming epaulettes appeared on television and announced a coup. He wore glasses and a beret. He hunched over the paper from which he read. Inflation was out of control, the civil war in the South was raging, the country was in bad shape. The army men were going to bring order. Behind the army men was another man who used the military men like puppets. He set about creating an Islamic state.

She was too young to remember the time well, but she was steeped in her parents' memories of those fretful weeks of the coup, and the months after. Power cuts and army trucks in the streets of the capital. Curfews and arrests. Suddenly Khartoum was full of convicted thieves with amputated hands, get-togethers raided by morality police, women arrested for brewing beer. Banned from selling alcohol, the women sold their bodies instead. It was the only way to feed children or pay for university fees or for falling-apart houses in the city's slums. In a show of piousness, they wore black abayas to throw off the morality police. Beneath the abayas, they went completely naked. They slipped in and out of open car doors, as stealthy as ghosts and as black as the night into which they vanished.

Exorcism parties, in which women communed with the spirits that possessed them, were forbidden as a heathen practice. Young boys were snatched from the streets of the capital and shipped south to fight in the civil war. A son sent to fetch milk from the corner store might simply vanish, leaving his mother roaming the streets half-crazed with anguish, searching for him in vain.

In his days of feverish youth activism, Dena's father had joined the Communist Party. He had long left the party and devoted himself to more capitalistic affairs, establishing a profitable accounting firm in the capital. Still, the taint of his political days made him a target. The new regime was full of Muslim Brothers, for whom communists were mortal enemies. Their fights went back to their student days—the cafeteria of the University of Khartoum had been ripped apart on several occasions over the decades, during brawls in which communists pounded Muslim Brothers over the head with chairs, and Muslim Brothers broke plates over the heads of communists.

And so, within the first month of the coup, her father was picked up by security men. He spent five months in jail. Her mother was allowed to visit him once—Dena was just a child then. The prison yard was a casual and disordered melee of thieves and murderers and fraudsters and political prisoners. She sat on her father's lap. Prisoners gathered around them. Her father beamed proudly as his fellow inmates gushed over his daughter. Her mother had been horrified but was too afraid to speak.

When her father was released from prison, he found his lucrative business shut down by the new regime. There was nothing for her parents to stay for. Any family with connections abroad left. Entire clans boarded up their multigenerational homes. Grandmothers who'd grown up in desert villages found themselves at the end of their lives shivering in the snowdrifts of Missouri, or contemplating kangaroos in Australia. Dena's mother had a brother in Seattle. Through him her parents got a holiday visa. When they arrived they declared asylum. Within a couple of years, the family were permanent residents, and soon after Americans.

The exile in which they lived was punctuated by annual trips to Khartoum, which were the highlight of her parents' year. Going to Sudan was like stepping through a porthole. A different world entirely from her sanitized Seattle life. An only child used to spending her time alone, she was taken aback by sudden communal living. Bedrooms shared with five others, doors always open, people coming and going. She hardly saw her mother and father—her father disappeared into the men's quarters, her mother disappeared with her sisters-in-law, mostly in the kitchen. Dena was grouped with her girl cousins, a gaggle of tinkly-voiced, sweet smelling, bejeweled teenagers on the brink of womanhood.

Her girl cousins thought only of marriage. They spent time perfecting arts of femininity that were entirely uninteresting to Dena. She was not into henna; it was boring to sit for half a day, incapacitated, with wet black goo on her palms and fingers. As were the long visits to the hair salons, in which her mane of long curls was wrestled into shape by hot tongs and hair-dryer caps that set her scalp aflame. Sugar waxing was a torture—it felt as though the skin was being ripped from her legs and arms. The country was under Islamic law, you couldn't reveal flawlessly soft, hairless arms and legs anywhere but in private, and so she didn't see the point.

She was not interested in learning the bridal dances that her cousins spent hours practicing. Her thin, gangly frame was useless for such dances—she had no budding breasts and hips to wiggle alluringly before an imagined groom. Only her cousins had such assets. At wedding parties, they placed themselves in front of the camera, coyly fluttering their eyelashes in the hope that some well-to-do Gulf expatriate might see them and whisk them away to be his bride.

The world of the girl cousins was lived in windowless henna salons and disused living rooms transformed into dance rehearsal spaces, and bedrooms, where eye shadow and blush and nail polish and hairbrushes were spread out on beds. It was spent in front of the television, watching Egyptian and Lebanese and Turkish soap operas in which astoundingly beautiful women married astoundingly beautiful men and lived in waterfront villas decorated with golden furniture.

It seemed wrong to Dena, after the gray days of Seattle, to spend her time in the dark when there was so much sun outside. And yet her girl cousins shunned the sun like the plague. It darkened the skin, and dark skin was to be avoided as assiduously as skinny hips. It didn't appeal to bridegrooms.

Dena felt much more drawn to the world of her boy cousins, who were up to more adventurous things. They stole their fathers' cars and went on joy rides through the city. They sailed small boats on the Blue Nile. They spent evenings in shisha cafés that were full of the cozy noise of water bubbles and the smell of apple-scented tobacco. They were sent on exciting errands into the giant markets of Khartoum—to locate a hard-to-find car part or a filter for a broken air conditioner. They went horse riding. They went on overnight camping trips to the pyramids in Meroe, packing up sandwiches and blankets and firewood. Theirs was a world of freedom and adventure. It was the world to which she wanted to belong on her summer holidays, and the boys let her tag along, indulging their American cousin. She paid no heed to the comments of her girl cousins and aunts, who worried about her darkening skin and messy hair.

At the end of each summer, she returned with her parents to the gray and the chill of Seattle. Her mother spent all day watching crime shows. The America she saw on television convinced her that the country she had escaped to was no better than the one she had fled: dictators and militiamen in Sudan, serial killers and psychopaths in America.

And so her mother retreated deeper into the house. Curtains shuttered, doors double- and triple-locked. There were all kinds of rules for Dena: no hanging out after school, and certainly no sleepovers with friends. Arabic lessons every Saturday. No talking to boys on the phone. No movies with explicit sex or violence. Her parents vacillated between fearing the enemy without—the predator who might snatch their daughter from the street— and the enemy within, that Dena might herself turn alien, that she might fall prey to influences beyond their control, boys and drugs and sex.

When it came time to let her go to university, they were wary. Hoping to safeguard her from the myriad hazards and corruptions of their new country, they sent her to Mount Holyoke, a women's college in western Massachusetts.

Her parents had no clue that a women's college was, in fact, the one environment in which she was most liable to be corrupted. At Mount Holyoke she found girls who broke every convention of womanhood drilled into her by her family. Girls who walked about holding hands, who fondled each other openly, who didn't shave their legs, who wore no makeup, who behaved as though the world put no limits on their ambitions.

Dena knew from a young age that she had no romantic interest in boys. Never had crushes on them. Never sought to be pursued by them. She knew this about herself, though did not know what to make of the knowledge. Growing up, it was yet another thing that set her apart from her schoolmates in Seattle and her girl cousins in Sudan.

That first year at college she watched the girls, flabbergasted. She got to know her neighbors, becoming privy to the unbridled passions that roiled the dorms. Kaitlin, who was in love with Jessica, who had dumped her for Elizabeth. The orgy that had taken place in Lily's room.

Still, she didn't forget herself. A link to the world of her parents she maintained through her studies. She toiled over Arabic, the language she spoke at home, but which she didn't command.

She fasted the whole month of Ramadan, gathering with the Pakistani and Bangladeshi and Egyptian girls to break fast. But the pull of this newfound liberty, three thousand miles away from her mother and father in Seattle, was irresistible.

In the spring of her second year she became entangled with a thin, tousle-haired Bangladeshi called Rifah, whom she met at one of the Ramadan iftars. Encouraged by Rifah, she shaved her hair. She went shopping in thrift stores and acquired a new wardrobe. Lumberjack shirts, cargo pants, Dr. Marten's.

And then it was summer and she had to go home. It had been a year since she'd last seen her parents, having skipped winter break with them after making up an excuse about studying for exams.

At the airport, her mother and father waited in the arrivals hall. When the doors glided open Dena walked out in her boys' clothes with her suitcase to a crowd behind the metal barricades, some with flowers and balloons and signs, feeling, as she always did after a flight, like she was stepping onto a stage—never more so than at that moment.

She spotted her parents almost immediately. They were both craning their necks—her mother on tiptoe trying to get a glimpse of those emerging through the doors behind Dena. Evidently they didn't recognize her. She walked up to them. Her mother, closer to eye level, caught sight of her first. Her smile faded and her eyes grew wide and she fell back as though she'd seen a ghost. A confused, frightened look overtook her father's face.

"Dena!" Her mother put a hand to her chest. "What's happened to you?"

She didn't answer, reaching instead to hug them awkwardly over the barricade.

That night she told them that she had a girlfriend. That she would live with a woman and maybe never have children. Her mother pulled at the lapels of her lumberjack shirt and threatened to kill herself. Her father looked as though he was about to weep. The plan to travel back to Khartoum that summer was hastily canceled. Her mother couldn't bear the thought of what her sisters and brothers would say when they saw their niece turned into a boy.

None of this had she disclosed to anyone in Saraaya. Not to Alex, and not, of course, to William and Layla, who, startled out of their intimacy just now, were still standing against the kitchen counter as she went to the table to pour herself tea.

"Sorry to disturb," she said, "Alex has invaded the gazebo."

"Stay with us then," said Layla. William seemed to wilt a little as she moved away from him. "Here, have these, they're fresh," she said, setting down a bowl of sugared dough balls on the table.

"Thanks."

Dena picked up a piece. William came over to the table and put an entire dough ball in his mouth. Layla touched her face to indicate the powdered sugar that had gotten all over his. He took out a handkerchief from a pocket and wiped his lips.

"Where're you off to today?"

"To shoot south of town. Along the road the refugees are taking."

He stopped chewing, swallowed. "Dena. I've warned you."

"I can look after myself."

"Listen, the authorities are arming nomads. Last week Mustafa and I came across militias on the highway. A cattle raid. They had guns, they had Nilot herdsmen tied up. These men are dangerous."

"But you and Alex go out all the time."

"That's different. I know my way around. You're a woman, and you're not from here." Then, half in exasperation, he said, "We should marry you off. At least then you'd have a husband to follow you around and keep you safe."

"I can keep myself safe." Did she want to shock them? Or

was it that she was tired of always having to hide herself? "And besides, I don't like men."

William agreed wholeheartedly that men were generally useless. Women were infinitely more intelligent, more beautiful, more refined, were better cooks, and—he winked at Dena—better filmmakers—

"No, I mean I don't *like* men."

His mouth was still open with his unfinished sentence. Then, as her meaning slowly dawned on him, his eyes, always so limpid, reflected a commotion of confusion. Disbelief followed by shock followed by embarrassment. He frowned and smiled and shook his head all at once, standing tall as a tree with its top tousled by a gale of astonishment. Layla, half turned from the stove toward them, was perfectly still, her hand on the ladle as she stared at Dena. The smell of burning tomato sauce filled the room.

Dena averted her eyes by sipping on her tea. The kitchen was silent for what felt like minutes. In the quiet, Alex and Mustafa's voices came to her distinctly from the yard.

She looked up.

"Now you know." Somehow she was more afraid to look at Layla, and so she addressed William. "Is it a problem?" Suddenly she was ready to battle them.

Layla moved abruptly to turn off the fire. William bestirred himself, struggling to compose his expression into something like mild—albeit still perturbed—equanimity. His gaze rested on the surface of the table.

Finally he looked at her. "No. It's not a problem."

She waited for him to say more.

"It's not?"

Layla occupied herself with the pots, though her head was tilted, listening.

William thought for a moment.

"Yes." All traces of turbulence had passed from his face now, and he looked at her steadily with clear, candid eyes.

Of course, he said, he was surprised, because he'd never met anyone who'd acknowledged this openly about themselves before. But it was her business. "Besides, my grandmother told me."

"Your grandmother told you what?"

When she was still alive, he said, his grandmother told him stories about Nilot women who, back in the old times, before the arrival of the English, would marry each other.

"Really?" It was the first she was hearing of this.

Seeing the doubt on her face, he grew animated. As she listened to him, speaking quickly now, about the old times, about how it was all done officially, with one woman giving a bride-wealth for another, in a proper ceremony attended by kinsmen, about how it wasn't frowned upon back then, she felt suddenly inarticulate with gratitude. He had no inkling, she knew, of the gift he was giving her.

ſ

LAYLA ONLY VAGUELY GRASPED what Dena had confessed and was too embarrassed to ask directly. By the time she got up the courage, the conversation had moved on, and soon after Dena left to gather her film equipment.

Now she turned to William.

"What does she mean, William?"

He looked at her. "She likes women. She falls in love with women."

"A woman? liking other women?"

She asked him to elaborate. He did. It was what she'd guessed: Dena wasn't interested in marriage with a man. But how could a woman be in love with another woman the way she was in love with William?

"It's impossible," she said. "It's wrong."

"Many people," William said, "would say that you and I together are wrong. You're a nomad, and a Muslim, I'm a Nilot, and a Catholic."

It was true—her own family would disapprove of William. And yet she'd chosen him. She liked Dena. She was strong-willed, with a quiet, watchful quality about her that allowed you to be yourself. She'd never met a woman like her before—disdainful of marriage and entirely consumed by other things. Dena often interrupted a conversation to dash out to the yard to shade the camera, fretting that she'd left it under the sun for too long. She was anxious when it wasn't near her, or in her lap. It often struck Layla that she treated the camera as though it were a child.

But this new information confirmed that Dena was more rebellious than Layla had imagined. And yet, as had often happened to her since she'd started working at the compound, she had one of those moments when she felt her view of the world alter. If Dena made her own choices, who was she to judge? She could fall in love with a Nilot. Dena could fall in love with a woman.

"Poor Alex," said William.

"You think she told him?"

"No. She probably didn't plan to tell us either."

They had noticed the animosity—even more than usual—between the two of them, though neither she, Mustafa, nor William knew exactly what had passed between them. Beneath her veneer of self-possession, Dena was prickly as well as stubborn. She was reserved, didn't share more than she needed to. Even William was wary of her. But Alex was talkative. And yet all he'd told William was that Dena was angry with him.

It made Layla wonder. In befriending Dena, she realized that there were other things a woman could want, besides marriage and children. But in the end, she knew what she wanted. She wanted William. She lowered the fire and went to sit with him, reaching for his hand across the table. Since the driving lesson, when he'd touched her, they held each other's hands often.

"You're right."

She took in his face, the eyes in which she could always find warmth and affection, the lips always on the brink of a smile. How wonderful to be with such a person, who was so open, who accepted others on their own terms, and who made her see that she, too, could and should be open to others.

IV

MUSTAFA WENT TO SEE DENG A FEW DAYS AFTER THE driving lesson. He took his friend Ibrahim along. Ibrahim was a year younger than Mustafa and looked up to him. He was usually happy to follow wherever Mustafa led, but on this occasion he came along reluctantly. Guns were something else entirely. What if his mother found out, he asked. What if they got caught? What if they ended up in jail?

Mustafa told him that they didn't have to commit, wouldn't commit, until they learned more. But hadn't Ibrahim told him that his mother was struggling to look after him and his siblings and was threatening to take Ibrahim out of school to work? This might be a quick way to earn some cash. And so Ibrahim had relented.

It was the first Monday of March. On their way to the garage, Mustafa eyed soldiers and security men on the streets. A contingent of five hundred men had been sent as reinforcement from Khartoum. Checkpoints had popped up everywhere. Along the main road, army trucks extended from the football field on the edge of town all the way to the crossroads near the gas station. Weapons were as common a sight as jewelry displayed in market stalls.

Either people were hoarding supplies or supply routes from Khartoum were disrupted—these were the only explanations for half-empty shop shelves. Prices, too, were rising, he realized, as he heard peddlers hawking wares at double what they had been a month ago.

Everyone seemed to be waiting—for what, no one was entirely sure, but for some kind of trouble. Soldiers dozing in the shade of their army trucks waited. The townspeople waited, in the meantime walking hurriedly past the keen eyes of the security men. The militiamen waited, though their fellows were already at work sacking villages on the edges of the district, which was why straggly groups of shell-shocked refugees had descended on Saraaya.

This was the other big change: shanty settlements had sprung up in empty spaces—near a rubbish dump not far from the butcher's, in the unfinished skeleton of a health clinic that was supposed to have been built years ago but whose money had mysteriously vanished, thus leaving two floors of exposed cement and brick and jutting metal beams and stairwells leading up into blue, empty sky.

This, a favorite play site of Mustafa and his friends, was now crammed with displaced Nilot villagers, who'd unfurled mattresses and cardboard and set up coal stoves and strung up laundry lines. The villagers wandered the streets like ghosts, cowering before the soldiers, who harassed them, and begging food from market women, who more often than not refused them. He could tell them apart not only by their frightened demeanor but by the fact that they were even worse off than the townspeople—in clothes that were not so much ill-fitting as shreds of fabric, walking barefoot, and often lugging mountains of belongings on their heads and backs.

And he was beginning to see other things. The week before, as he was walking by the police station on his way back from an errand, he saw soldiers surround an old woman. A displaced villager newly arrived in town. Her eyes were gray and her skin stuck to the bone. Her legs were as thin as twigs. Her dress was a rough square sack with holes. She was half-starved. On her knees she followed one person after another, begging for food.

Soldiers saw her, told her to get lost, and when she didn't, one of them found a rope and tied it around her neck. Mustafa stopped in his tracks. A crowd gathered. The soldier pulled her behind him. She crawled on all fours, making small, strangled noises. No one dared intervene. Seeing the crowd, one of the soldiers took off his beret and went around thrusting the hat at spectators. Contributions for the entertainment. People drew back. The one holding the woman jerked on the rope. It tightened around her neck. She squealed and kicked her legs and fell forward. A few people, wishing to put an end to the scene, dropped notes into the beret and begged the soldier to stop. But seeing the crowd respond, the soldier tightened the rope. The woman was soon on her back, scarecrow legs kicking in the air, hairless genitals exposed.

Only when they were satisfied that everyone had emptied their pockets did they stop torturing her. The crowd evaporated. Mustafa remained, unable to take his eyes off the woman as she crawled off into an alleyway.

∫

NOW, ON THE OTHER SIDE of town, he and Ibrahim stepped into a dim garage that smelled of benzene, a layer of black grease coating floors and walls, with rows of rough wooden shelves cluttered with rear axles, riveters, cable cutters, nut pliers, soldering irons, pipes, plastic canisters. Beyond the square of light illuminating the space in front, the garage was dark, except for white gleams reflected in pools of oil.

Mustafa called out. Deng materialized out of the darkness in stained mechanic's overalls, goggles strapped to his forehead. He greeted them, flipped on a light switch, and led them to the back, where he pointed them to stools. Nearby, a car hulk sat on bricks, its doors stripped, its windshields missing. It reminded Mustafa of the burnt corpse.

"So, you've come at last. It took you a while." Deng handed them cold Pepsis from a cooler. "Your friend here trustworthy?" he lifted his chin at Ibrahim.

"He's my best friend. Won't say a word to anyone. I made him promise."

Ibrahim, wide-eyed, buckteeth edging over his lower lip, looked from one to the other.

"I won't say anything."

"You'd better not." He looked at them. "Now, to business." The arms supply route from the south, from Uganda, was cut off, he said, what with the authorities worried about an attack from that direction. Most soldiers were piled up along the district's southern border. So weapons were now coming from the west, from Chad. Making their way through Darfur and the Nuba Mountains into Saraaya, where Deng had a small side business delivering to the rebels—the authorities hadn't yet worked out that arms were being smuggled right under their noses.

Still, with more security men on the streets, it was risky. That's why he needed help. Mustafa was a nomad, an Arabic-speaker. He looked like the authorities. He sounded like them. It was an advantage that he was so small—"How old are you?" he asked. "Twelve," said Mustafa, and pointed a thumb at Ibrahim, "Eleven."—Good, they looked even younger than their years. Not being Nilotes the authorities wouldn't suspect them. But, he said, this was about business, not about which side they were on.

"You want to earn some good money?"

Mustafa nodded, hypnotized by the lull of Deng's voice. Even Ibrahim had stopped fidgeting and listened attentively.

"So," Deng continued, "five deliveries. I get you a mule cart, watermelons, and the guns will be packed beneath them. You pass by one or two villages on the way to sell melons, as a cover. You head to a meeting point ten kilometers south of here, in the gum-tree forest. I'll give you twenty, maybe thirty rifles at a time. You show up and someone will pick up the guns. You get the payment from them—I'll tell you how much—and bring it back to me. Once you've done all that, I pay you. First delivery would be next month, in April. Then May. And so on. One drop-off per month."

"And how do you know we won't report you?"

"If you do, you're dead." He paused. "Besides, the authorities stole from you, didn't they? They stole your money, they beat you up." Mustafa didn't contradict him. "It's a chance to make up your losses."

"How much? Do you pay us?"

"I pay enough to make it worth your while. But you have to follow my instructions exactly."

"OK. So how much?"

"A hundred thousand, for each trip."

Mustafa's jaw dropped. He looked at Ibrahim, whose mouth was also agape. One hundred thousand pounds for a few hours' work, even shared with Ibrahim, was a sum such as he had not imagined. But a short life's worth of experience had taught him that there was always more to be got. He turned to Deng.

"There's two of us."

"Who told you to bring a friend?"

"Two's better, in case something goes wrong. Make it a hundred each."

"I'll think about it."

"One hundred," he insisted, "each."

When Deng continued to eye him, he thought he had a chance. "We'll do the job," he said. "You won't have to worry about a thing."

"Tell you what: Seventy-five each. And if you do well, there may be more."

Ibrahim came to life. The sums frightened him. So much

money could only mean trouble, he protested. This was too dangerous, and the town was crawling with soldiers, and he didn't even know how to drive a mule cart, and—

Mustafa pinched him so hard he yelped.

"We're in," Mustafa said.

ſ

WILLIAM WAITED at the checkpoint leading into the market area. Layla stood beside him. Mustafa was out on some errand of his own. It was eleven a.m. and it was getting hot. They'd been standing in line for an hour, taking refuge in the shade of a homestead fence. Ahead of them fifty or sixty people sat on the ground or leaned against the fence, fanning themselves with newspaper or screening their eyes with their hands. Truck tires barricaded the road beyond. To one side, soldiers played cards on an upturned crate, a howitzer-equipped truck parked beside them. Shards of broken glass winked in the late-morning light. Vegetables and fruit littered the road. Black patches stained the mud walls of homesteads, where people had lit fires to cook while waiting.

They were short on fuel for the generator, which was why he was going into town; Layla wanted to pick up groceries from the market. The errands should have taken less than an hour, but every day there were more barricades put up. New regulations. People crossing into the market had to be searched. No unauthorized vehicles allowed near the police station. North and south ends of the town patrolled by soldiers. Checkpoints along the narrower roads that led east and west.

Over the previous weeks he'd felt a change. Some of the nomads he knew passed their eyes over him as if he were invisible. When he went to their shops, they refused to serve him. Security men he'd known for years, whom he regularly chatted with, who asked after his health and whose health he asked after, stared at him dead-eyed. The privilege of his job with the organization, wrapped around him like a protective cloak, was evaporating. His good English, his relationship to the white man, his neat clothes, the organization's truck that he drove, were suddenly offensive, made him a target. He was a Nilot who did not know his place, had forgotten that this town belonged not to his people but to the other side.

What worried him most was the arrival of more militias. They were dusting off their AK-47s, lacing up their army boots, mounting horses and military trucks to loot undefended Nilot villages. There was the cattle raid he and Mustafa had stumbled upon six weeks ago. And three days ago, he'd been walking with Alex when they saw a group raining blows on a Nilot teenager. It was early morning; the streets were cool and empty. The boy was huddled on the ground, right arm twisted out of its socket. William went up to them.

"Hey."

The militiamen turned. Three of them, three shades of brown, hair dusty, beards overgrown. Telltale army boots beneath their jellabiyas.

"You've beaten this boy enough."

One of them moved. He had no time to flinch before the rifle butt landed in his stomach.

"Stop!" Alex's shadow over him.

The men cursed and spat in the dirt and left, doubtless because of the white man.

Every day more clashes between groups of herdsmen. Rumors of arms being smuggled into the bush. News of nine people dead in a confrontation in a far-flung village the week before. Soldiers patrolling streets and villages and oil fields. Young Nilot men arrested.

He kept warning Dena, who was going out alone to film

along the desolate routes through which villagers escaped. But she refused to listen. She left the compound before sunrise and returned only with the curfew that had been imposed. This morning he'd caught her before she left, had begged her to wait for him so that he could accompany her, but she'd brushed him off.

He worried. Not only about Dena, but about all of them, and about his own capacity to protect them. It didn't help that wherever he turned he ran into walls. The security men had stopped talking. Men with links to the rebels in the bush sat with him, drank tea with him, but when he asked questions, their faces grew stony. They shifted in their seats and changed the topic of conversation.

Since his return from Khartoum three years ago, things had been calm in the district. He'd almost begun to believe that he could live a normal life here. He'd felt protected by his job working for the organization, protected by the contacts that came with the job, contacts among the police, the army, and the security men. He got on with the young men with links to the rebels. They forgave him his relationship with the authorities only because they knew his work made it unavoidable. He'd stopped caring who controlled the town as long as he was left to live in peace. But it wasn't peace, it was merely quiet.

ſ

THE LINE MOVED. A murmur rose. He and Layla looked over the heads of the crowd. Guards separated people. A new group formed to the right, only nomads. There were shouts, pushing, and pulling. Nilotes disgruntled upon realizing that they had to wait while nomads were let through.

A guard came down to them.

"Other line," he said to Layla. "You, wait here," to William.

Layla was reluctant to leave him.

"Everyone's been waiting together," she said. "We should be let through together."

"He stays. Or you can wait in this line but you'll be here for a while."

"Go," said William. "I'll catch up with you in the market."

She hesitated, but he insisted. She crossed to the other line and looked back at him in farewell. He felt a pang in his chest. He always did whenever he was separated from her, even for brief periods.

He turned back to the crowd ahead. Only Nilotes now. A man stepped out of place, was shoved back by a guard. Suddenly the two were in a headlock; soldiers rose from their card game and came running. People jostled to escape the knot of uniforms converging in the street.

Things were bad, were getting worse, he thought as he watched soldiers haul the man away. He'd never gotten involved in the insurgency, though his father had died in the first civil war, after going off to join rebels in the bush, leaving his mother pregnant with the youngest, William. His mother looked on his father's death as an abandonment. He had been young and stupid and strongheaded, she told William, had insisted on joining the insurgency even though he had three children to feed and a fourth on the way. She had pleaded with him not to go. Went to the healer, who'd made up a charm to keep her husband from leaving Saraaya. But it hadn't worked. He left, and within a year he was killed in a skirmish between government forces and rebels near Malakal.

The only token William had of his father was a black-and-white photograph sent to his mother shortly after his death. In the photograph his father posed in uniform with a group of fellows. His right hand on a rifle planted in the ground. A tall, lean man, wearing a mustache, a corner of his lip lifted in a smile. William had inherited his father's eyes and frame. Though his father was handsomer, stronger, in his uniform and cap. Now whenever William looked at the photograph, he was struck by how young his father was. He had been twenty-six when he was killed, seven years younger than William was now.

William was born into the war. His earliest memories were of airdrops. Back in those days there were no paved roads in Saraaya—the district was entirely cut off during the wet season. He still remembered the first time he saw a plane—he must have been three or four. A loud rumble made him scurry into his mother's skirts. She picked him up and pointed. There was the plane flying low: it was bigger than a house and made the trees go wild and cattle scatter, and the children come running. He remembered the terror and excitement of the noise as dust flew into his eyes and he hid his head in his mother's shoulder and then looked to see the plane tilting its nose up and a door opening, and bright-orange bundles tumbling out into the sky. When the packets thumped to the ground a cheer went up, and people waved goodbye as the plane became a speck above the horizon. Women's bright dresses bobbed in the grass as they ran out and opened bundles and pulled out sacks of flour and rice and sugar. He followed his mother into the field and back again to town, a sack balanced on her head.

And then an afternoon playing outside with his sisters. That same rumble that he recognized. Thinking it was the other plane, bringing the bright-orange parcels. He dropped his stick and ran out and saw the plane flying low, so low that its shadow was huge, its noise deafening. He skipped and hopped and waved, waiting for the bright-orange packets. People screamed. Sounds of terror that he mistook for joy and he laughed, dashing into the field. People were running away—mothers wailing and men shifting their cattle toward the trees.

And then above the screams he heard his mother's voice. There was a whistle, which made him look up. The plane was so low now that grass flew into his face and pebbles struck his chest. Oblong shapes dropped out—they were not orange. They wavered in the air, and he stood there gaping until someone lifted him and threw him to the ground. His mother was on top of him. The earth shook. Clods of dirt landed on his arms and his mother squashed him, and he cried, terrified, for the earth was swallowing him up and his mother wanted to kill him, her sweat mingling with the dark, wet soil.

And then the sky went quiet, and from the direction of the houses he heard screams and crying. He couldn't tell whether he was up or down. His mother's heart thudded against his ear as he choked on his own snot and tears. He saw a glimmer of sun on dirt through the smoky air. A patch of grass near him stirred. A woman got up. She clutched firewood to her chest and walked. A triangle of jagged metal stuck out from her head. Her face streamed blood, and she kept wiping it and stumbling, careful not to drop the firewood. His mother covered his eyes. But through her fingers he saw the woman suddenly fall to the ground like a felled tree, and then all he could see was the metal glinting from her head.

He couldn't remember much after that. How he and his mother got back to town, what they saw there. His memories were mainly stories that he'd heard—that six bombs had fallen, splaying open the insides of people and houses and animals. Destroying the grain storage and a cattle byre. That his three sisters had miraculously escaped, hiding with a neighbor. They had all made it out alive, though half the town had lost people or animals.

His mother decided then to flee Saraaya. They headed to the safest place—to Juba, the biggest city in the south, where thousands of other people were taking refuge. He had vague memories of the road, of being carried on his mother's back. The steady rhythm of her march, his cheek against her warm spine. Envious of his three older sisters who walked beside them—he wanted to do that, too, but when he walked, he grew tired and whined for his mother to carry him again.

All of his sisters married young. His mother needed the bride wealth—it was the thing that saved them from destitution. And the Catholic Church. His mother was so grateful for the church hand-outs that saw them through the first difficult years in Juba that she became a devout Catholic. They were at Mass every Sunday. She sent William to Catholic school, where he acquired his good English.

He had fond memories of the smell of incense during the Sunday services, the crisp robes that the priests wore, the candle-light and the whispers and the darkness, and that image of a suffering Christ on the cross, hovering above William and the other schoolchildren like a bird—or at least that's how William liked to think of him; the idea of the nails driven through his hands and feet was terrible to him as a child, so that, day-dreaming during the services, he imagined him as a bird in midflight, wing-arms floating in the air.

The one lesson William had learned from his father's death was that he was not to think of going into the bush, ever. He was to take care of his mother. She'd lost a husband and couldn't bear to lose her only son. And so instead of joining the insurgency, as many of his age-mates did, he went north to eke out a living in Khartoum, sending whatever little he could to his family in Juba.

f

FINALLY THEY WERE being let through. People picked up children and bags and pressed forward. At the front of the line a guard looked at him.

"You're the one who works for the white man?"

"For the organization. Yes."

"This way."

It was becoming a pattern. Every time he was out alone, he was delayed by extra searches and questions.

He had to bend his head as he was led into a dark tent. Three men sat on the ground.

The guard ordered him to stand in place and lift his arms. He was turned and searched roughly along his torso and shoulders and legs. Then the guard felt for the wallet in his breast pocket. He took out notes and casually tucked them away.

"That's money for fuel," said William. "I need it. You have no right to take people's money."

A sharp, throbbing pain between his eyes made him double over. He touched his knuckles to his nostrils, breathed through his mouth, and waited for the pain to recede, stepping back from the guard's fist.

"Next time," the guard said. "Shut up and move on." He opened the tent flap. "You can go."

William straightened, outrage mingling with the warm pain suffusing his face. He touched his nose again. The men on the ground watched him. He looked at the guard, who was daring him, waiting for him to react. He bit his jaw and walked out into the sunlight.

He was on the other side of the barricade now, but there was no point in going for fuel without cash. He stood there, not knowing what to do. If he went back to the compound to get more money, he'd have to stand in line once more only to be robbed and assaulted again.

A sense of helplessness and shame came over him. He glanced back at the long line of Nilotes still waiting to pass, the guards shouting orders, corralling them against the wall. He decided to return to the compound. They would have to do without light tonight.

ſ

AN OLD MAN STOOPED under giant bundles. On his head plastic canisters strung together with rope atop a mattress rolled tightly. On his right shoulder a straw bag out of which peeked two startled chickens. On the other metal kettles that clanked against a pink tricycle missing a wheel. A blue sheet of plastic tarp and a bundle of firewood on his back. His feet were caked white with road dust. His hands, a study of twisted veins and tendons, clutched a stick that he dug into the ground. He walked on the edge of the great river of people moving faster than he could keep up. Nilot refugees fleeing their villages, taking with them all they could load on their shoulders and backs and heads, dragging behind them thumb-sucking infants, propping up bowlegged grandmothers and fathers.

For three days Dena had hauled the camera up and down the dirt road that cut its way through the semi-desert just beyond Saraaya, through the greener plains farther south, around the swamps of the Sudd and into the lush stronghold of the rebels three hundred kilometers south. Here, five kilometers beyond the town, the promise of green was still distant. It was mid-April, late in the dry season. The sun bore down on the road and on the people and on the parched grass standing stiff in the windless air.

She'd turned dark in her days of filming. Her clothes were grimy and her lips were chapped and her ears and mouth were full of dust. Her feet baked in her sneakers. The camera was so hot it scalded her fingers. She had to scrape away at particles lodged in the crevices of the lens, inside the eyecup, along the grooves of the tape compartment. She'd never felt more affection for her EC-325, which emerged day after day from its cushioned backpack with its luminescent eye whirring to life without protest or hindrance.

She'd spotted the old man a few minutes before, struck by his loneliness. There were no children or grandchildren turning to check on his progress. Everyone else marched in groups. Mothers passed babies they were tired of carrying to their husbands, men with bandaged arms helped one another, small children carried smaller children. Teenage boys heaved an arched zinc roof over their heads. A gang picked apart a destroyed truck in the middle of the road, stripping the steering wheel, the bumper, the backseat.

Some behaved as though they were on an outing. Boys chased one another through the crowd. She filmed two drunkards veering left and right, passing a bottle of sorghum beer between them. She filmed mothers sharing their food with the children of other mothers. Three people carrying a hammock with a hugely pregnant woman asleep in it. She filmed boys moving up and down the procession with mules pulling giant barrels, selling water to those who could afford to buy.

No one stopped to help the old man. Herdsmen caught up with him, and for a moment he disappeared in a thundercloud of hooves and horns. They moved on, leaving him coated in dust. He managed twenty steps before he had to stop, the mattress on his head swaying precariously, the chickens squawking, the kettles clanking faintly. Then he began to move along the flat road again as slowly as though it were the face of a mountain.

William kept telling her it was too dangerous to go out filming, especially with news of escalating clashes in the villages. But William assumed that being a woman made her vulnerable, when often it worked to her advantage. The soldiers and militiamen sought her out to film them with their bullet belts and rifles, happy to strut and pose for the camera like peacocks. A few days of mingling with them, of delighting them with their own images beamed back at them on the viewfinder screen, had done wonders. The checkpoint guards raised the barricades for her willingly. The militiamen smiled at her. There was nowhere in town or on the plains to which she didn't have access. She was a Northerner, and so they trusted her instinctively.

Only once did she have an unpleasant encounter. Two days ago, she was stopped on her way to the river. The soldiers were friendly—they asked questions about the camera and bustled to have a look, passing the device around.

Except for one. He stood apart from the others, leaning back against a truck, arms crossed over his chest, watching. She felt his gaze on her. He interrupted the conversation to ask who her guardian was.

Guardian?

Yes, her husband or father.

She told him she didn't have one.

"You're here alone?"

"Yes."

"Where are you staying?"

"At the NGO compound."

"You live with the white man and the Nilot?"

"Yes."

A mean lascivious gleam came into his eye then. His gaze descended to her chest. The other men stared, looking at her anew, their eyes traveling over her body. She flushed, lifted the camera to hide herself.

The soldier reached for her face. "Some lipstick, some long hair, then you'd be a treat."

She batted his hand away and hurried off, the soldiers' laughter trailing her.

The encounter shook her. Had she been too friendly? The soldier with the lewd gaze—it was as though his thoughts had infected the others—she saw their looks and their intentions change too. For the first time, she had felt unsafe. But she'd brushed it off. Things were bound to happen sometimes. And so far she'd been able to move freely, even as a woman, even with the camera.

And what sort of a filmmaker would she be if she let images like this of the old man pass? She followed him as he fell farther behind. Children skipped around his legs and mules trotted by. A group carrying a backseat from the destroyed truck stumbled around him.

He steadied the mattress on his head, oblivious to Dena as she stepped across the trench that marked the edge of the road. His shoulders drooped under the firewood strapped to them. The blue tarp came loose from its rope and dragged behind him like a broken wing.

Dena walked beside him, lens angled in his direction, as he fell back among the women held up by small infants carried two a time. She stuck with him even as those moved on and he fell in with the wounded hobbling on sticks. She stuck with him as he fell behind those, as the crowd became a speck in the distance, until finally he was a lone figure on the parched tongue of the road, the featureless sky above and a broad sweep of nothingness ahead.

Those weeks she'd spent struggling with her images were only practice. Now her muscles knew instinctively what to do: the smooth flow of her pan shot taking in the sweep of the desolate road, her knack for catching a faltering step, or his old man's mouth slack with exhaustion, or a sliver of thin, wrinkled thigh revealed through the torn trousers. A sixth sense for what was going on outside the frame, and when to turn to it—as she did now, the lens ascending to the cloudy eyes gazing up the empty road. The camera traveling down again to the chickens that flapped their wings as he let them drop to the ground. The camera watching, too, as the old man climbed down his stick, the mattress tumbling backward from his head, the blue tarp swelling and wafting down again as he settled amongst his heap of things.

She crouched a meter away and still he didn't look at her. The camera lingered on the haggard face, the gray eyes lost beneath their hooded lids. For two minutes she filmed, waiting for him to move again.

Suddenly she came to herself. She switched off the camera and rose. He looked up, startled, registering her presence for the first time as she reached out a hand to help him up.

∫

THROUGH WILLIAM, Alex followed news of the fighting, the torched villages on the edges of the district, refugees fleeing to Saraaya. For two months the security situation had been deteriorating. Men in jellabiyas with rifles slung over their shoulders, nomad militiamen armed by the authorities, had appeared in town. They were destroying sorghum and maize and millet farms. They were looting cattle and land. Oil companies were dismantling their encampments in the desert. There were fewer supplies in the shops, because deliveries were disrupted. One day, William arrived at the compound with a swollen nose. He'd been robbed at a checkpoint.

Alex was terribly anxious. Things were getting out of hand. But instead of arranging for his evacuation to Khartoum, his boss, Greg, was pressuring him to stay put. The upheaval, Greg reasoned, represented an opportunity. The violence was making international news. They were the only international NGO on the ground in the district. More villages destroyed, more refugees, more chaos, more money for the organization. He wanted Alex to report back to headquarters on the clashes, promising that when it was all over he'd send him to one of the more pleasant duty stations—Kinshasa, Cape Town, Addis.

And so, in mid-May, on news that there was a lull in the fighting, Alex ventured out with William to the Nilot villages.

In the first village they found homesteads reduced to charred ashes, black circles where mud walls once stood. A scent of incineration in his nostrils, footsteps muffled by ash as he walked past flattened byres and twisted tin roofs pointing jagged in the air. He saw a tree scorched from root to stem, a black shadow of its own black shadow. He stepped over the red-stained pages of a child's schoolbook. Walked on quickly before he could ascertain whether the stains were blood or not.

Beside him William stooped every now and again to examine an object. A doll or shards of a clay jug or a torn magazine photo of a lush tropical waterfall that had hung on someone's wall. A singed tulle dress standing stiff in the middle of a deserted road. He kept muttering to himself in Nilotic, shaking his head and sighing.

A terrible smell reached them as they walked deeper into the village. They swatted away at green-twinkling flies that landed on their eyes and lips and noses.

"The well," said William.

William trotted forward. Alex stopped. Something rotting. Someone dead, in the well. His knees went weak; bile rose in his throat.

William looked over the edge and then turned, waving away foul air.

"Dogs," he called.

Alex joined him and held his breath as he leaned over the lip of the well. In the half-light he made out blood-matted fur, fangs glinting, bloated limbs. Carcasses that had been thrown down the well to poison it.

They drove back in silence, brooding.

Upon their return to the compound, they found the yard transformed into a refugee camp. Villagers in various states of disarray, decay, illness, exhaustion. Old people sprawled on cardboard by the kitchen wall. One man emerging from the bathroom with a crutch fashioned out of a forked branch. Mothers breastfeeding babies under shawls. Women stringing laundry along a clothesline. Other women standing over coal fires outside the kitchen.

Sacks of possessions cluttered the entrance. Discarded newspaper, rotten bread, watermelon rinds piled in a pyramid of trash in one corner. Shacks and rooms hastily constructed out of dry grass and tarp in the empty space behind the gazebo.

Alex stared. "What the hell is going on?"

William shook his head, at a loss.

Layla and Dena were handing out water by the kitchen, tugged at by children and mothers and old men impatient for the cup to be passed to them.

Alex called out to Dena. She gave the cup to a child and came over. A wild air to her in her dusty clothes and her rolled-up shirtsleeves and the sweaty bandanna around her forehead.

"What are these people doing here?"

"They've left their villages," she said. "They need a place to stay."

"They can't all stay here."

"This is a humanitarian organization, is it not?"

"We can't house fifty people. There's only one bathroom for God's sake!"

Dena turned to William. "What do you say?"

William took in the yard. "I don't know. We can manage for a few days, maybe."

Mustafa appeared with his clothes, playing cards, shoes collected from various corners. He chattered angrily at Dena and William in Arabic.

"Mustafa doesn't like it," Alex said.

"You two are outvoted," said Dena. "Layla's fine with people staying. Oh, and some women are using your room, Alex. Hope you don't mind."

"Office is off limits," he said.

But when he went to the office he found the door ajar. Children on the floor, on the desk, in the chair, on the windowsill. They had found his maps. They had found his box of pens and markers and pencils. Two sat on the desk scribbling on maps pinned by the window. Another group hunched naked over unfurled maps on the floor, coloring. A plump baby sat in the lowest drawer of the filing cabinet, in a nest of crumpled maps, gleefully destroying one of his most important—the blueprint on which he'd made all his markings. She was taking bites with her two teeth, spitting out bits of map on the floor.

He went for the baby. Startled betrayal in her eyes as he prized remnants from her hands. She threw her head back and wailed, revealing pink gums wedged with bits of paper. She pushed small angry fists into his cheek as he lifted her out of the drawer and deposited her outside.

He snatched pens from children on the floor. Two girls fled shrieking before he reached them. The baby, still wailing, crawled back inside and he picked her up again. A boy slid down the side of the desk, bringing a heap of maps down with him, which he trampled as he ran out.

He picked through the ruins. What was not torn or shredded was covered in scribbles, doodles, colors. Child's drawings of warscapes and dead cows. The map of grazing routes was disfigured by red ink squiggles and loops. A black marker had blighted the cadastral map that he'd spent days gathering information for. The ink had leaked; the paper was soppy with black blots. In the scuffle with the baby his master map had been destroyed, shreds of it lay wet with saliva on the floor.

"What's going on here?" William stood on the threshold with Dena and Layla. People had gathered at the door.

"Your maps," Dena said, looking at him. "You should've locked up."

"Locked up?" he said. "Did I know you were going to turn the compound into a refugee camp?" He waved a torn map. "Look at this. This is months of work!"

The next days were as chaotic as he'd feared. When he went to the kitchen for a glass of water he tripped over babies. The bathroom was so dirty it was practically unusable. There were so many mouths to feed that there was never enough food. He was left to scavenge for remnants of the brown beans and lentil soup that Layla and the village women cooked up daily.

Only a day or two, Dena and William said. But each day there was a new reason why the refugees couldn't leave. Militias were targeting the road taken by Nilotes fleeing south, it wasn't safe for them to go. The old people needed more time to rest. A pregnant mother was feeling unwell. Already two weeks since their arrival, and no signs of them moving on. And so he guarded the little peace he could find behind the locked door of his office.

∫

AFTER THE EVENING MEAL, Dena and William gathered with villagers in the yard. There was no fuel for the generator, and so they sat in the fading twilight. The compound was shadowed with makeshift brush fences, screens constructed out of cardboard and tarp. Someone had splashed water over the ground, and a coolness rose from the wet dust. Alex was in the office. Sounds of dishes came from the kitchen, where Layla and Mustafa were clearing up after the meal.

Over the past few days Dena had been filming and gathering stories. Many of the refugees didn't say much or told only the basic facts. The few who did speak at length told of terrible scenes. Parents killed in front of children, women dragged into trucks or backyards, militiamen lining up to do with them as they pleased. Families separated in the chaos of escape—brothers disappeared, infants missing, a lifetime's worth of land and cattle lost in a moment.

They spoke of the dread of landmines blowing their limbs to bits or the fear of a slow death from starvation on the road. They spoke of illnesses picked up from filthy water, infections festering through their insides. They spoke of walking until they couldn't walk anymore, heads heavy with fever, stomachs light with hunger, eyes seeing double and hardly any strength left to pull up breath.

They didn't say it all—many were still in shock. Having barely escaped death, they carried its atmosphere around with them. But what they didn't say the camera caught glimpses of in lifeless gazes, in the silence between words, in the way that a child clung to their mother's neck, in the sounds of nightmares that broke from sleeping lips. The camera caught glimpses of it in the women who held themselves as though broken, in listless limbs that had lost the will to move.

It was often in the evening, as darkness fell, that something unknotted and one or another of the villagers ventured to share their story. Now Dena and William and the crowd hushed as an old woman began speaking. The camera, set on its tripod, recorded the cadence of her voice. It recorded the postures and shapes of the gathered listeners: women lulling infants to sleep; two men with bandaged heads; a teenage girl with her arm around a friend; children piled together in a chair. They all sat around the woman, her feet up on a bed, her head propped up with a hand.

She had arrived the week before from a village that had been attacked, carrying her grandchild. His cheeks drooped onto his shoulders and his eyes were huge and black above a tiny, wet-lipped mouth in which two small white teeth gleamed whenever he smiled. A down of hair covered a head round and smooth as a pebble. He hardly spoke but used his hands and face, constantly

pointing and gesturing. He had recently learned to walk and teetered during lunchtime with his mouth open, demanding bites of
soup or beans in addition to the ones already fed to him by his
grandmother. It was hard to say no to him—everyone gave him a
bite just to watch his cheeks bulge and his tiny teeth show as he
ate and smiled at the same time.

His grandmother spent her days feeding him, putting him to
sleep, comforting him when he scraped a knee or an arm. He was
always in a playful mood, but his grandmother was grief-stricken.
Even when she smiled at him, she looked on the brink of weeping.
Now the baby sat huddled in the crook of her arm, playing with a
toy bull carved out of wood as she began speaking. Occasionally,
she paused so that William could translate.

"We come from Yarol, four days' walk from here," she said.
"I was born in the village. My three children and their children
were born there. It's a village like any other. There's a road that
winds down between the homesteads, and fields to the east, and
a river to the south where we water the cattle. At the end of the
village there's a big tree, where we gather for special occasions. I
remember playing under that tree when I was a child. I watched
my children and grandchildren play under it. I know my neighbors and they know me, and we know the nomads who come
through every year. It's my home. I'm like that tree with its roots
planted there. It's the place that nourished me.

"But the last time I remember peace was when I was a child.
Even then, my mother told us stories. About slave raids—men
who came from the North on horseback and snatched up villagers
and took them away. This was back during the Turks' time. But
even after the white man came to the country, the slave raids didn't
stop. Sometimes years went by without one. And then sometimes,
two or three raids in one moon cycle. Half the village tied up
and marched north across the desert. My own grandmother was
taken that way.

"And then we heard that the white man ruling us was going back to his own country. We had a new government, made up of our people, in Khartoum. We'd get schools and water wells and hospitals. And for a while, things were good. The government dug a well. A teacher came from Juba. I spent two years learning to read and write with the children in the village. But the hospital was never built, nor were the roads, and the teacher stopped coming. Still, we went on with our lives. We grew our crops and herded our cattle and helped one another.

"Before we saw the war, we heard about it. People passing through told us about a fight between our men and the government in the North. They said that our men weren't happy with the new government in Khartoum. We were being ruled again. Not by the white man but by the Northerners this time. And so our men were fighting to get what was promised to us in the South. We heard about guns and raids and airplanes that dropped fire from the sky, and about abandoned towns and villages and crops left to die.

"But it was all stories. It wasn't until I became a mother that the war really arrived in our village. The rebels were supposed to be on our side. But they snuck in at night and forced us to hand over all our grain, leaving us with nothing. Soldiers came in the morning and said we were helping rebels. They torched our houses and fields and took our cattle. We ran away, but we always came back. We didn't have anywhere else to go. Many left the village for good, but I stayed with my three children. My husband was taken young with an illness. And so it was just me looking after them, through all those years of running and coming back."

Someone brought a kerosene lamp, and the light fell on the woman's eyes, which were wet and old. The light played on the baby who lay against her. He'd dropped the toy, had put a thumb in his mouth, staring up at his grandmother, absorbed by her voice as everyone else was. She wiped her eyes as she began speaking again.

"These last weeks, we kept hearing that rebels were close by. We stayed. If it were rebels, then at least they were fighting for us, even if they stole from us and abused us too. And we were waiting for the rains—we wanted to plant. Some others said it was the army coming.

"This time, when we heard the rumors, I told my children to go without me—let rebels or army or militiamen do with me what they willed. I was too old to run again. But my children refused to leave me. They stayed with me, and the grandchildren too."

She stroked the baby's shoulder. Her voice dipped, the kerosene lamp flaming and flickering against her eyes.

"They arrived in the early morning. Militias first, in army trucks. I was sleeping outside and heard engines. My daughter called to me to come inside. My other daughter and son arrived with their families. We wanted to run to the trees, but this one"—she touched the child's head—"was missing. We searched. I ran out to the garden behind the house and found him playing and picked him up. When I turned, I saw militiamen coming down the road. They shot at people running away. So I ran into the field and dropped down in the grass with my grandson.

"I watched them go into my daughter's yard. They rounded up everyone—my two daughters, their husbands and children, my son and his wife and children—and forced them into a hut. Twelve of them, all in one hut. They barricaded the door with beds. They splashed gasoline along the walls and the roof."

She lifted her hand from the baby and wiped her face again. When she spoke her voice wavered. "They set the house on fire. I watched flames eat up the thatch, black smoke rise from the windows. I heard my children's and grandchildren's screams. I wanted to run to them. But the militiamen were there. And I had this little one with me." She touched his shoulder. "If it weren't for him, I would have thrown myself into the flames with them. But I just lay in the grass and pressed him to me and covered his ears, so he wouldn't hear his mother burning."

She wept. Seeing his grandmother's distress, the baby cried, too, and she reached to comfort him. The camera filmed on. It framed the woman and the child surrounded by the somber listeners. Beyond the light cast by the lantern, shapes dissolved into darkness. No one spoke. They listened to the boy's whimpered breath as he finally fell asleep.

⌡

SITTING ON A MULE CART, feet swinging as he leaned forward to peer along the dirt path along which the cart was parked, Mustafa thought about his payment later—a whole seventy-five thousand pounds—which he would stash along with his first payment in a can he'd buried in the compound, near the kitchen. And still three payments to look forward to.

He'd never made so much money. He could quit his job and go to school and even buy a bicycle to transport him to school. Maybe, he thought, as he glanced down the path, his attention caught by a bearded goat rearing on its hind legs to get at foliage, he'd leave Saraaya altogether. It was enough money to set him on his way.

"Where are they?" asked Ibrahim, sitting beside him. They were parked in the grove of gum trees ten kilometers south of town. Apart from goats, they were alone. It was a few minutes past five p.m. Splashes of light fell on them through the leaves.

The mule's bottom twitched, its tail flicking. The cart on which they sat was stacked with watermelons, beneath which were two wooden crates lined with guns.

"They'll show up," said Mustafa.

On their first delivery the month before, they had arrived fifteen minutes late, having been delayed by the mule, which went right instead of left, left instead of right, suddenly diverged off the road to munch on a patch of grass. At one point it simply stopped while they were five kilometers from their meeting spot. Mustafa whipped, yelled, jumped down, and pulled at the bit. In the end they made their way by luring it forward with slices of watermelon.

Mustafa thought they might have missed who they were meant to meet. He thought maybe he had taken the wrong way. There were any number of dirt roads and dirt paths leading to the villages that could have been confused with that one. But he had followed Deng's directions exactly, and they had arrived at the end of the third dirt path that led away from the wadi and into the gum-tree forest.

Eventually, a four-wheel-drive appeared around the bend. Two Nilot men stepped out, one in a mesh vest and long shorts, the other in khaki pants and a T-shirt. They carried rifles. Mustafa had never come face-to-face with rebels before. Many young Nilot men were sympathetic to them, and some even worked for them. But in town, where the authorities were in control, no one openly acknowledged links to the men in the bush. These two could have been any ordinary Nilot herdsmen. Except for the rifles.

"Who's Mustafa?" one of them asked.

"I am."

"And who's he?"

"My friend. We work together for Deng."

"You have the delivery?"

Mustafa hopped down from the cart. He and Ibrahim removed watermelons, sackcloth, straw, landed the crates with a metallic thud on the dirt. He lifted the cover. In the shallow crate was a stash of AK-47s, burnished snouts gleaming, curved magazines ridged, wooden battery packs scuffed.

One of the men picked up a gun and examined it, ejecting

the magazine and then reloading. The other one opened the second crate.

"They're Russian," said Mustafa. "The real thing."

The men laughed. "Of course they're Russian. Kalashnikovs, aren't they? How many?"

"A dozen in each crate."

"How much does Deng want?"

"Three million."

"We paid two last time."

"Deng says it's not easy getting weapons in these days. Security's on the alert. He's had to pay more to get this in."

The taller of the two considered him.

"Tell me, which side are you on?"

"Not the government's."

"Why?"

"Because they're thieves."

"But they're your people."

"They're still thieves."

He smiled. "That's right."

The men counted out the weapons. One went to the car and returned with rubber-banded notes, which he handed to Mustafa. The notes bulged in Mustafa's fingers, and he had to start over a couple of times as he counted.

They lifted the crates into the car trunk.

"Next week," the one in the vest said. "Same time, same place."

ſ

NOW THEY WERE HERE, on their second delivery, having arrived at the appointed time: five p.m., on the last Thursday of May. It was six, and still nothing. Again Mustafa looked up the dirt path that wound its way through the bush. No sign of a car. No sound of a car. Just the chatter of birds, and trees, and wind. The goats had moved on. He hopped down from the cart and walked up the bend.

"Nothing?" Ibrahim called.

He shook his head. He thought. It was getting close to curfew. "Let's go back. We'll tell Deng they didn't show."

"Are you sure?"

"Yes."

He climbed up, turned the mule around. They wound their way through the forest and along the wadi. Guns clattered faintly in their boxes. They reached the plains around town. Dry yellow grass stretched out around them. Above them, gauzy clouds hung in the dull light of the day's end. The rainy season was coming. Bird flocks heaved and twisted in the sky. The low line of homesteads came into view. They rode on, the mule obedient, flicking its tail as it trudged forward, cart wheels creaking, guns clinking.

"Hey, look." Ibrahim pointed.

A strange illumination, a faint glow above the town, which could have been sunlight, except that the sun had already set. Distant noises, shouts. Clusters of people, some walking, some running, moved in their direction. Some herded cattle along, which should have been in byres this time of day.

"What's happening?" Mustafa called out to a Nilot woman hurrying past with a child on her back.

"A fire."

"Where?"

"At the police station."

When they turned into Saraaya they could hear the uproar coming from the market. Flakes of ash wafted in the air. Crowds of people were running toward the plains. The mule grew skittish. Watermelons tumbled off the cart. They were at the north end of town; to get to Deng's they would have to cross the market.

"What do we do?" asked Ibrahim, clutching the edge of the

cart. Mustafa forced the mule into a loop, heading into a quieter alleyway.

"The guns, we have to hide them. We can't go to Deng's now."

He circled along the town's outskirts, steering the mule through alleyways until he reached the compound. He parked the cart by a side wall.

"Wait here."

It was dark now; they could hear noises coming from afar, honking and shouts and the fire, but the chaos had not yet reached this part of town.

Not possible to move the weapons in through the front gate—the compound was full of villagers, and Dena and Alex and William were there. There was a way in only he knew about, through a broken storage-room shutter that had never been fixed. Now he went to the storage-room window, surveyed the alleyway again. Quietly, he pushed the shutters open, praying that he hadn't blocked the window with boxes or brooms. With a creak they gave way. He crept along the wall back to Ibrahim, who was huddled on the cart, a small shape in the darkness, and though Mustafa couldn't see him clearly he could see his head move.

"Come on. We'll move the crates in through the window."

They hauled down the first crate, which, in the darkness, and with the fear that they might be set upon at any moment, suddenly seemed impossibly heavy. They stumbled with it to the storage room. Mustafa shouldered the crate up to the frame while Ibrahim squealed with effort as he lifted. It seesawed on the windowsill as Mustafa climbed through to balance it on the other side. Ibrahim followed him, and slowly, carefully, they slid the crate down, the two of them tripping over buckets and bags and brooms and newspapers, going perfectly still when they heard someone in the yard on the other side of the door.

They moved the second crate in, and Mustafa covered both boxes with newspaper and old sheets. Out in the street again, they tied the donkey to a post and went around to the compound gate—Ibrahim was eager to get back to his mother's and whispered a good-bye to Mustafa over his shoulder before running as quick as a furtive animal into the darkness.

Through the compound gate Mustafa heard voices and thought he should shelter inside, with William and Alex and Dena. But instead he turned toward the fire, which, though he couldn't see, he could hear and feel; it was hotter than usual for this time of night, and the air crackled. He left the gate and went in its direction. Figures flitted in and out of doorways and men called to one another. Someone ran with a flaming torch down the street.

He heard questions and answers hurled into the night—a rebel attack, an ambush by army soldiers, a bomb. A few neighbors ventured out to their doorsteps, trying to see farther down the road. A rooster crowed, confused by the light in the sky. Shrieks and yells and noises drifted from courtyards, as though people were hurriedly collecting their things.

Dogs barked. Up the street, people came running with piles of clothes and food. A group of boys smashed the windows of a parked car. Farther along, he saw men up in the acacia tree on which he'd displayed his underwear. They were looking out toward the fire. The night was full of the sounds of revving engines—army trucks coming from the military garrison.

He reached the stalls and small shops that marked the busiest part of the market. Soldiers chased people into alleyways. Gangs were tearing down canopies and kicking at locked grilles. Someone's byre had broken open and cattle were rampaging in the streets. A shimmering light hung over zinc roofs and brick walls. In the middle of the street, men piled on top of one another, kicking and punching.

He stepped over tumbled sewing machines and tripped over a sheep's carcass splayed outside the butcher's. A cracked television set, plugged in somewhere, cast a haze of static in a doorway. He saw mothers hauling their children up by their arms and torsos.

In the brightness cast by the fire, he caught a glimpse of a face contorted in a scream, shoes flying off someone's feet, a man writhing like a worm as soldiers hauled him into the back of a truck. The fire rumbled, and the street churned with light and shadow. Gunfire pierced through the noise of burning wood and paper and straw.

Black smoke swirled and stung his eyes. Still he went on, ducking into a doorway whenever mobs charged past or a rock flew by his head. He inched his way deeper until he reached the police station, where a crowd was held back by soldiers and policemen. Here the street was as bright as day. Flames rose from the station's windows, whipping up into the night air. The veranda's pillars collapsed, and the roof followed, caving; papers set alight billowed up into the darkness and were extinguished, cascading down in a haze of embers over onlookers.

Soldiers and policemen were helpless; with covered faces they passed along buckets of water, splashing uselessly at the raging flames. They couldn't get close enough—it was too hot. Mustafa's head was scorched, and his eyes streamed tears.

The building adjoining the station—an ammunition depot—caught fire. Weapons exploded. A curtain of flame flared twenty meters high and he was knocked to the ground as people screamed and heaved back. He got up, coughing, his chest hurting and his eyes burning, the fire a deafening roar in his ears. Beyond the blaze he saw more army trucks speeding down the main road. He ducked into the shadow of a wall, then turned and ran, as fast as his legs would take him, back to the compound.

ALEX STARED AT THE CLOCK, BLEAKLY CONTEMPLATING the fact that at this very moment—one p.m.—he should have been touching down in Khartoum. But he'd missed his flight. Or rather, his flight had missed him because of unforeseen bad weather. It was June and the wet season had officially commenced a month ago—but there had been no rain. It was his sheer bad luck that a deluge arrived just in time to ruin his evacuation.

And he was desperate to evacuate. Two weeks before, rebels had fire-bombed the police station; the market, too, went up in flames. On the evening of the attack, he'd been in the compound. They'd heard screams and gunfire. He and William and Dena and the refugees had poured out into the street. They saw smoke billowing above the market. They gathered from neighbors' reports that rebels had slipped into town and set the station aflame.

William had herded everyone back inside. To their relief, Mustafa, who had been missing, showed up. He'd been to the market, he had seen the fire. He gave an account of the chaos—looting and patrolling soldiers and shops set alight. Not only the police station fire-bombed but an explosion at the ammunition depot.

They huddled in the yard, listening to the rat-a-tat of gunfire and the boom of exploding shells. No one slept. The villagers held on to one another, recalling terrors they'd lived through in the homes they'd fled. William paced up and down. He was frantic over Layla, worrying that the fighting had spread to the as. Alex and Dena and Mustafa sat at a table, between them. Dena was stiller than usual, her eyes huge, dark pupils. Mustafa jumped every fire, asking, "Did you hear that?"

The next morning, Alex got through to the office. He threatened Greg that he'd make his own way to Khartoum if the organization didn't evacuate him. Greg acquiesced, and Alex was booked on the UN flight scheduled to arrive today.

He'd been waiting for it ever since the fire-bombing. Throughout these last nights he was often jolted awake, falling through himself. He had lost his appetite. Everything startled him. He took up doing push-ups and pull-ups off the beam that ran across the gazebo in the hope that wearing himself out might help him sleep. Children gaped at him, mimicking his exercises. He tried to read the Africa-themed novels he'd brought with him. *Things Fall Apart. Season of Migration to the North. Waiting for the Barbarians. Heart of Darkness.* All turned out to be about men losing their minds. They didn't help.

What had kept him sane through that week was the thought of that flight. At night, when he tossed and turned on his mattress, he'd imagine himself high up in the air, the town receding into haze, clumps of trees growing tinier and tinier, wispy clouds casting shadows on his face. The steady whir of the engine calming him as he breathed with relief at his ascent into the atmosphere.

For days he kept that vision before his mind. He turned to it as army trucks trundled up and down the roads, as soldiers hauled people off the streets. He turned to it when news reached them that more militias were being armed.

He had no faith in William's ability to protect them. The day after the fire, Alex found him kneeling on a newspaper beside the truck, sleeves rolled up as he dipped a brush into a can of green paint.

"What're you doing?"

"I'm repainting the emblem."

Alex glanced at the truck door. The paint had faded and the globe floating above two hands, which had almost completely vanished, was reemerging under William's green varnish.

"It protects us," William said. "This way the authorities know when we're in the car that we're with the NGO."

"A logo? That's your idea of protection?"

William placed the brush in the can.

"And what do you want me to do, Alex?"

"Find out what's going on. When is this going to stop?"

"I've sent out Mustafa."

"Mustafa's your source of information? A twelve-year-old? You're paid to be a fixer. So fix things!"

William glared. "I'm not paid to be a fixer. Nor am I paid to be your security guard. My official title is translator. The authorities are arresting any and every Nilot man under the age of forty. Maybe you forget that I'm a Nilot. I can't go knocking on the door of the security men or chatting to the militias about what they're planning next. That's why I'm sending out Mustafa. He's a nomad. He looks like them. He knows how to get around. If you prefer to talk to the authorities yourself, go ahead."

Helpless, he occupied himself with preparing for his departure. He packed up his things—stuffing his clothes into his rucksack and suitcase, collecting whatever equipment he could take with him—while William, Dena, Layla, and Mustafa watched.

"You're leaving?" Dena asked. "Just like that?"

He could see that she was casting his departure as a cowardly abandonment. He didn't care.

"Yes, I'm leaving. If you want to stay here until this compound crumbles over your head, that's your choice."

"What about Mustafa and Layla and William? You and I can just go but they can't."

"Why can't they?"

"Where would they go?"

"Anywhere safe. As far as I'm concerned, you're all crazy for staying."

Today, the day of his departure, he'd woken up before sunrise. Picked his way through the sleeping refugees to brush his teeth. Stacked his luggage by the office door and waited for ten o'clock.

But he was beginning to believe that something about his presence here, at this latitude and longitude of the world, had released the vindictive powers of the universe. What else could explain a storm on the morning of his flight, of all mornings?

It had started just after breakfast as he was saying goodbye to Dena, Layla, and Mustafa. The three of them had assembled by the compound gate to bid him farewell.

He'd thought that he would feel sad saying goodbye, but he found that he was only impatient to catch his flight.

"Bye, Mustafa." He ruffled Mustafa's hair and hugged him.

He said goodbye to Layla in Arabic, doing the modest salute that the men and women did here—something between a hug and a handshake.

He was hesitating over how to say goodbye to Dena—whether to hug her or to do the same half-hug, half-handshake—when he was distracted by a coolness. The others felt it too because they all looked up. Leaden clouds tinged with white loomed over the compound walls. Fat splotches of water exploded against his face. A flutter of activity as the refugees collected their things and dashed for cover.

William, who had been waiting in the car, darted in and told him to hurry. Dena waved, and then she, Layla, and Mustafa scurried to the gazebo, only their outlines visible through the fog of water.

On the way the storm intensified. Rain thudded against the roof and the hood of the truck and crashed against the windshield. They could barely see three meters ahead. The engine strained as they dipped into depressions. By the time they arrived at the airstrip, the atmosphere was a moldy brown-orange substance, weighing down his clothes and fogging his vision. Mud spattered against his trousers as he splashed up and down the dirt runway, uselessly searching the sky for the plane. By the time the rain stopped the airstrip was a shallow lake, orange islands of mud peaking up here and there. The truck tires were half-sunk in water.

In the end they drove back to the compound. They found Layla, Dena, and Mustafa along with others scooping out water from the flooded courtyard.

A call to Khartoum confirmed his worst fears: the plane had skipped Saraaya because of the bad weather. The next flight wasn't due to come this way for another three weeks.

∫

HE LIFTED HIS HEAD. Rain-washed light fell on the poster of the green globe floating above two open palms. His luggage—bags, a box of equipment, two cardboard tubes containing what was left of his maps—was back by the desk. Drops plopped against the windowsill. Outside, the din of refugees—the racket of children and the hum of conversation and the clatter of pots cooking up the same bland soups he had looked forward to leaving behind—were like the sounds of a purgatory.

He got up. His wet sneakers squeaked as he crossed past children splashing in puddles. William stepped out of the bathroom patting his neck with a towel.

Alex marched up to him. "We need to drive to El-Obeid."

There was an airport in El-Obeid. If he could get to an airport, he could get to Khartoum.

William shook his head sadly. "With this much rain the roads will be blocked. We can't get there."

"There are highways."

"We'd have to drive through a hundred kilometers of dirt road to get to the highways. Those roads are mud. Soon as we start we'll get stuck."

"Truck keys." He put out a hand.

"What for?"

"I'll drive myself."

"It's three hundred kilometers from here to El-Obeid. You don't know the way. You'll get lost, you'll get stuck, you'll kill yourself."

Alex lunged for the keys in his pocket. William shoved him. Alex crouched low and attacked. William's great height worked against him—he grasped desperately at the air for balance as he tipped backward, his arms flailing and a leg flying up, and crashed into the soaked earth. Villagers left off their washing and children collected around them. Mustafa appeared and stood gaping.

William raised himself on his elbows, shaking away mud. Eyes blazed as he sprang at Alex, who found himself whirling in the air. The cold smack of mud against his forehead, mud in his mouth and nostrils. He wiped away at his face uselessly. His arms made sucking noises as he lifted himself. Fear for himself, the canceled flight, his helplessness—all melded into a knot of diabolical, destructive fury. He hurled himself at William.

Mustafa jumped up and down.

"Dena! Layla! They're fighting!"

Dena and Layla rushed out of separate corners of the compound. Dena stopped and stood, staring; Layla ran toward them.

Fingers in Alex's mouth, digging into his cheeks. A long arm grabbed hold of his shorts and hauled him to the ground. Alex clung on and pulled William down with him. They rolled through the yard, Alex half-blinded by dirt, William's hot, angry breath on his face mixed with the smell of cologne, slimy squishy sounds of struggle, curses hissed into each other's ears. He scratched at William's eyes. William cried out and rolled away. Alex rose quickly. His clothes weighed on him. He'd lost a sneaker and kicked off the other one. William rose, too, barefoot, his shirt gaping open and his chest streaked with dirt. He lurched free of Layla as she reached for him and hurtled at Alex.

Villagers sprang out of the way as the two of them crashed on the table. They rose; they fell into the hammock. Alex was tangled up in fabric. The hammock twisted and dumped them onto the ground. They rolled back into the middle of the yard, William's elbows like daggers in Alex's ribs. Alex bit William's shoulder. William's nostrils distended to the size of a dragon's, eyes so huge they seemed ready to burst, teeth as hungry as a crocodile's. But Alex's rage gave him strength. He couldn't tell his own limbs apart from William's. They had become one color— mud-smeared, earth-tinted arms and legs and torsos piled in a seething, slippery mass in which he was sunk sometimes downward and sometimes upward.

Astonished women and children and old men followed them as they flung each other around. They ended up on one of the bare bedframes, William pressed Alex's face into the coils. Alex threw one of the tires used to keep rainwater out of the compound at William. William got hold of the tire and pinned Alex beneath it and landed slaps and punches through its hollow circle. Alex twisted aside. He heard Layla and Dena shouting, and then finally, men heaved William away. The tire lifted off Alex. Dena and Mustafa helped him up. He blew his nose free of mud as he was led, dazed, toward the gazebo.

∫

LAYLA PULLED WILLIAM to the gate and stood him there. Bloodshot eyes and mud-spattered clothes gave him the look of some crazed creature that had just crawled up from underground.

Carried away by his own rage, he ground his teeth and thrashed his arms, gesturing so vigorously that she stepped aside to avoid an accidental swipe of his limbs. He glared over her head at the gazebo, where Alex was out of reach, and hurled abuse at that pampered, useless, thankless—

"Shut up."

His eyes dropped to her face. She pointed to the boys and girls staring at him.

"These children are better behaved than you."

"*He* attacked me."

"William, we have forty, fifty people who need help. We have enough on our hands. And you decide to fight with Alex now, of all times?"

It was difficult to keep her temper in check. They were all on edge. A month of looking after so many people was taking its toll. William was constantly on the move, shuttling the sick to the health clinic and securing whatever supplies he could—blankets, medicines, firewood—for those continuing on their way south. Mustafa was often in town on errands. Alex had been getting ready to evacuate. Only Dena seemed untouched. She spent her days filming villagers and, when she had time, helping Layla in the kitchen.

Layla herself was needed every second of the day—to care for sick children, to attend to the sleeping arrangements of a family, or to resolve a squabble over blankets. Because it was so busy, she hadn't gone home for days, sending Mustafa with a message to her father that she was helping at the compound. She was overwhelmed with having to cook for so many people. Especially with stocks of beans, lentils, and rice running low. Because the market was still shuttered, people hoarded food, locking up supplies in cupboards or hiding them under their beds.

She and William hardly had time together. Only sometimes, at the end of the day, they managed to steal a few moments. She

saw the lines around his mouth then, brow prominent above
eyes sunken with exhaustion. Otherwise, they encountered each
other while rushing around the compound. He might zip into the
kitchen to carry out a tray of food, and they would exchange a
few words. Or she might remind him to see if he could find bread
at the neighbor's.

The patience with which he helped the villagers, his energy,
his tirelessness in braving the road to the health clinic made her
adore him all the more. But this William possessed with rage
standing before her was something new entirely.

Still, her words had struck a chord. He grew shamefaced.

"If Alex attacks you, then just walk away."

He averted his eyes, but a slight movement of his head indicated that he understood.

A boy tugged at her thoub and asked when lunch
would be ready.

"Soon," she said, touching his shoulder. The morning's
upheaval had set everything back—she hadn't even started on
lunch yet, and children were getting hungry. She turned to William. "I have to go. Stay away from Alex."

She left him and walked past old women resting on tarp
spread over the wet ground. A young man with a bandaged
shoulder sat by the potted plants. The children were full of
energy, shrieking and chasing one another around the ridgepole
of the gazebo.

Because her family had been on the move, she'd always been
one step ahead of the war, or one step behind it. They'd leave
one village only to hear weeks later that it had been torched. Or
arrived at a small town to find houses reduced to rubble, shops
riddled with bullets, buildings bombed.

Only now that she had settled in Saraaya was she beginning
to feel the fear of being in one place, a sitting target. They were
all feeling it. The morning after the rebel attack, she'd walked the

ten kilometers from her homestead to the compound, past the smoldering police station and the looted market and ash-covered alleyways, past checkpoints staffed by security men and soldiers.

Streets empty of neighbors, friends, market vendors. More and more compounds and farms abandoned. In town, they measured the violence by the waves of refugee villagers who arrived daily. Still, she was luckier than most. She was a nomad, her family were nomads, and soldiers and militias were only going after Nilotes.

In the kitchen, she found some of the village women had already started on lunch—two of them sat sifting through rice. Another woman chopped onions. She smiled at them gratefully. She couldn't have managed all the cooking without the help of these women.

Now she was surprised to find them laughing. Mustafa stood in the middle of the kitchen reenacting the fight. He pummeled the air mimicking Alex's clumsy blows, then, impersonating William, tangled up his legs and fell about, crashing into tables and chairs. The women laughed so hard they had to wipe their eyes with the edges of their dresses. Layla, too, laughed. It felt good to find a reason to be merry after the morning's upheaval.

The women asked her about William.

"He's fine." She turned to Mustafa. "And Alex? Where is he?"

Mustafa righted a chair. "He's locked himself in the office. Don't think he'll come out for a while."

The women wanted to know who had started the fight, why the white man was angry. All expressed amazement at two grown men rolling around in the mud. Mustafa made them giggle again by sprawling on the ground in a star shape, recalling Alex trapped under the tire.

But a sharp, terrified scream made laughter vanish from their faces. Mustafa sat up. They all turned to see people hurrying past the doorway. Layla and Mustafa exchanged glances, then Layla followed him out into the yard.

The sun had come out and reflected off the rain puddles. She saw William at the gate surrounded by men in fatigues. A dozen soldiers already inside, some around William, another group walking deeper into the compound, scattering people who crowded toward the back, hiding behind one another. Alarmed villagers picked up their things and rushed into the shadows of the walls, under the gazebo, into the rooms, muttering prayers and exclamations.

Soldiers fanned out. Though some were taller and some shorter, some wore beards and some were clean-shaven, in their green uniforms she could hardly tell them apart—as they laid claim to the space, they moved with the same threatening energy. They surveyed the rooms, went behind the kitchen and the bathroom, the tent by the gazebo. The compound was full of the noise of trudging boots and villagers' breathless whispers and the whimpers of children.

Trying not to draw attention to herself, she inched closer to the entrance, Mustafa beside her. William stood with one hand on the gate, answering the officer in charge—a large man with slow, precise gestures. The whites of his eyes were stained. His air of boredom, as he glanced around the compound and took in William, seemed calculated.

"Occupation?" he asked.

"I'm the translator." William was trying to hold his ground by standing taller. But his uncertain hand on the knob gave away his powerlessness. The soldiers were already inside. It was too late to shut the door on them. Still, he tried to meet the officer's regard on equal terms. "I help look after the compound."

The officer nodded at the villagers, then leveled his gaze at William.

"How long have these people been here?"

"About a month, since mid-May."

"And you let them stay all this time without permission?"

William hesitated. "They're old people and sick people and mothers." She could tell that he was weighing every word. "They've left their homes and came here for help. We let them stay. We're a humanitarian organization."

"The town's under emergency. Gatherings are prohibited."

"It's not a gathering."

"That's not for you to decide."

A child wailed, despite his mother's frantic hushing. William's eyes followed the sound and his gaze fell on her and Mustafa. He made a motion for them to stay back.

She glanced toward the gazebo. Dena stood with villagers, watching. Alex stepped out of the office. When he saw the soldiers, his face—still smudged from the fight earlier—blanched.

The officer gestured to him. "His permit."

William called to Alex to bring the work authorization. Alex went to the office, followed by a soldier. They came out again and the soldier handed over papers.

The officer looked over the documents. Then he gave an order to search. Soldiers standing still as statues moved with a violence that took everyone by surprise. Two men dragged old people off their mats. Another three kicked over makeshift rain canopies and coal stoves, ripped open bags, dumped Alex's satellite devices in the mud. Pairs of men opened doors, and through the doorframes Layla caught glimpses of them breaking glass and slicing open mattresses. The string of flags hanging along the compound walls came down as women scuttled along the perimeter; plastic chairs flew as soldiers tried to get at people barricading themselves behind furniture. Shouted orders mingled with the screams of villagers, things breaking and crashing, water splashing as people scampered through puddles.

Mothers clung to their children, hiding them behind their backs or dragging them anywhere they could hide them. Those trying to escape through the gate were butted with rifles. An old woman lay on her side, moaning, her walking stick out of reach. One man bled on the ground; another wept against a wall.

Layla lost sight of William and Alex. She held on to Mustafa. They were pushed and pulled. Two soldiers came toward them and they rushed into the kitchen with other women and old people. The soldiers followed inside. They toppled the fridge and tipped over pots. Dishes smashed against walls, windows, counters. Barefoot children yelped as they stepped on glass. Men blocked the doorway, and people crowded into the pantry. Three women cowered behind the fallen fridge; another group hid behind the table.

Pressed against the counter, Layla kept her grip on Mustafa. A soldier reached for her. She tripped over her thoub. Mustafa clung to her as they were marched outside. They were ordered to sit against the kitchen wall, and huddled with a group of villagers, the sun bearing down on them, flashing up at them from puddles, their clothes soggy, clots of mud splattering their faces as soldiers trooped about rounding people up.

On the other side of the compound, soldiers congregated around the storage room. One yanked at the locked door.

"Where's the key?" he called to William, standing under guard by the office.

"In there." He pointed to the kitchen.

The soldier led him there. As he neared the doorway, he caught sight of Layla and Mustafa again. A question in his eyes. Layla nodded that they were all right. A minute later he reemerged, the key in the soldier's hand.

Mustafa gripped Layla's arm. He half rose, following William and the soldier with his gaze as they crossed to the storage room.

"No," he said. "They can't go in there."

He squirmed, squeezing her arm so hard it hurt. Suddenly he let go of her and made to stand.

She reached for him. "Sit down, Mustafa!" But he twisted out of her grasp and bolted after William.

ſ

MUSTAFA STOPPED a short distance from the storage room. William stood opposite him, flanked by two soldiers. Three men entered the room; he heard them rummage through boxes and furniture, their voices drifting out muffled over the din. Shelves crashed and things tumbled—what sounded like his buckets and mops and brooms. Dust wafted out of the doorway. He prayed that they might search sloppily, that the noise might stop soon.

He looked at William, whose attention was fixed on the storage room, though he seemed calmer—the fear that Mustafa had glimpsed on his face when the soldiers first arrived was gone. He stood between the two men, arms slack, waiting for them to finish their search and move on.

Layla was trying to get his attention from across the yard. She was still seated by the kitchen among women pressing children to their chests, some weeping and others staring at the ground. She was asking him something—what was happening, was everything all right. He shook his head. He didn't know, not yet.

Mustafa swallowed as he turned back to the storage room. The soldiers were taking their time, searching in earnest. His throat was dry and his ears hummed. He'd had no chance to move the guns. He'd gone to Deng's the day after the fire to find the garage destroyed. Deng had limped out of the darkness, arm in a brace, cheek bruised and one eye swollen shut. The authorities were turning the town upside down looking for weapons, he told Mustafa. They had come to the garage and left it a mess; they had roughed him up. If they moved the guns now they'd get caught.

He ordered Mustafa to keep the weapons out of sight and his mouth shut. The authorities wouldn't suspect the compound, he said. A white man lived there; they would leave it alone. He paid Mustafa one hundred thousand pounds to do as he was told.

Mustafa had returned to the compound with the money hidden in a milk can. No one ever stepped into the storage room except him—it was his domain, where he kept his cleaning rags, his soap and mops. When things quieted down he'd move the guns to another hiding place. He'd get Ibrahim to help. They'd bury the weapons by a tree or hide them in one of the abandoned villages. In the meantime, he could only sit tight and wait. With so many people it was impossible to move, and it was risky to sneak the guns out the same way he'd brought them in, through the window. Soldiers and militias were patrolling back streets. And so the guns had stayed put.

Until now. For, just as he was beginning to feel that anything was better than the suspense in which he stood, eyes flitting between William and the storage-room door, so tense that he could hardly breathe, someone called from inside. And then soldiers streamed out carrying two crates, which they set down with a crash outside the door.

He watched, transfixed. He should have run, but instead he just stood there as a man alerted the officer in charge. The officer came over. William and now Alex were surrounded by soldiers. Someone lifted a cover. There they were—a dozen rifles, snouts gleaming in the sun. The officer knelt and picked up a weapon and examined it, handling the pistol grip, weighing the buttstock, checking the magazine as though evaluating it for purchase. In the background, children whined and women stifled their sobs.

The officer held up a gun.

"Where'd these come from?" he asked William.

William's eyes moved from the guns to the officer and back

again, a confused expression on his face, as though he couldn't make sense of the weapons, or of the officer's question, and most especially the officer's question directed at him.

Alarm came over his face as consequences sank in. He started to say something, then stopped. His arms moved. He shook his head, staring at the guns.

"I have no idea."

The officer threw the rifle into the crate; Mustafa jumped at the noise.

"You're responsible for this compound."

Mustafa stood half-hidden between the soldiers. All activity had ceased around them.

"Who else has access to this room?"

"I—" William's eyes roamed beyond the soldiers to the refugee villagers. For an instant, a brief millisecond, they passed over Mustafa. Mustafa's face or posture must have communicated something to him, because his eyes veered back. William stared at him, mouth slightly agape, the epiphany so clear on his face that the officer turned to follow his gaze, but Mustafa scuttled back.

Dread and terror mingled in Mustafa's chest. He peered from behind a uniform at William. His eyes were white, something like hurt passing over them, the muscles of his face tensing with the effort of composure, then his mouth went slack, as though he were winded. Mustafa's heart thumped so wildly, he could feel it in his throat. He watched as William's gaze hardened, eyes narrowing to points and lips coming together as though there were a bad taste in his mouth.

"Well?"

William turned to the officer. Mustafa wanted to plead with him not to give him away, but William didn't look at him.

William said, "The key's in the kitchen."

The officer rose. "And?"

"The key's hanging in the kitchen, behind the door. Your men saw. Anyone could have hidden the guns in the storage room."

The officer waited. But William went quiet. Relief washed over Mustafa and he made a movement; he wanted to catch William's eye. But William looked right through him, and he realized with shock that he was willfully refusing to see him.

"You're saying that even though you're responsible for this compound, that someone brought in dozens of weapons under your nose and you, and this white man there, had no idea?"

William's jaw throbbed. "That's what I'm saying."

"You hid the weapons here thinking we wouldn't search. A good cover, this being a humanitarian organization."

"I've told you what I know."

A ripple of movement amongst the soldiers. William glanced around him. Alex sensed that they were in danger. He kept asking William what was happening, but William, caught up with the officer, ignored him.

There was a moment of stillness. Then the officer gave a barely perceptible nod, and one of his men stepped out of the sea of uniforms and struck a blow to William's shoulder. William collapsed. The soldiers closed in. Mustafa couldn't see any more, a wall of uniforms blocked his view. Children screamed. Villagers made a dash for the gate. Old men tumbled over as they tried to use their walking sticks to beat off soldiers, women cowered with their children and grandchildren. By the kitchen, he saw Layla shoved so hard she landed on her hands and knees in the mud. He looked to the gazebo but couldn't see Dena—she had been there a minute ago. He turned to the knot of men around William. More trucks arrived. Soldiers herded villagers out through the gate.

Mustafa inched his way along the wall, beyond fallen planters, and bounded to the office, knowing only that he needed to hide, that if he didn't, he might be dragged out and taken somewhere terrible.

ſ

UNDER THE GAZEBO, Dena watched men surround William. Mustafa stood on the edge of the circle of soldiers and across the yard she saw Layla half rise to her knees, trying to see what was happening to William. By the gate, villagers wept beneath the soldiers' guns—they were trapped, not only by the soldiers but by the compound walls penning them in.

She smelled people's fear. Injured men shrank away and old people too weak to move propped themselves up, trying to keep soldiers in sight. Beside her a woman made a low, keening sound; every now and again a wail or a prayer broke out from someone, and this, along with the sounds of children crying, amplified the panic beneath the gazebo.

Soldiers broke off from the group around William and came toward them. She held the camera but didn't dare raise it, dangling it low in her hand, so that it was invisible. The crowd pressed away as the men approached, but then soldiers pointed guns and ordered everyone to sit. A man tripped and trampled a child; an old woman rushing too quickly to sit ended up sprawled beside Dena. The villagers settled down, still and unmoving as they could manage to make themselves.

She was afraid to film. But another part of her resisted the fear. The war that had been so distant, looming over them but always, somehow, eluding her, was now in front of her—right here in the compound, and she knew that if she didn't have the courage to raise her camera now, she might never forgive herself.

She glanced to her right. A soldier was looking away toward the storage room. To the left, by the kitchen, two men stood guarding women amongst whom Layla sat. She twisted around and surveyed the space behind the gazebo. No men there. She adjusted herself on her knees and lifted the camera, her eye on a soldier questioning a man at the front of the crowd.

The soldier was asking for the man's name and village. When the man answered in Nilotic, the soldier demanded that he speak in Arabic. The man answered again in his own language; he didn't speak Arabic. The soldier pulled him up by his shirt. Already threadbare, it ripped as a seam unraveled. The man fell limply, and for a few brief seconds was still, as though passed out. Suddenly, he raised his head and spat in the soldier's face. The soldier recoiled, letting go and wiping his mouth. Then he knocked the man so hard he fell backward onto women and children.

Noticing the commotion, two soldiers left the group around William and came toward the gazebo. Now the soldier who'd been spat at pressed the villager's cheek into the ground with the muzzle of his rifle. He pressed so hard that the man began to whimper. The image blurred in the frame as she focused. She zoomed in on the man's face, his eyes tearing, his lips moving against the rifle.

A shove from behind and she dropped the camera, bumping her head against someone. Her forehead pulsed. A woman turned around to scold her, then quieted. Dena followed her gaze to a soldier standing over them. He was tall, eyes set wide apart, cap askew, a sparse mustache over his mouth. His eyes flickered over her with interest. He bent for the camera and hauled her up by the arm. The soldiers at the front looked up.

"She's filming," he said, holding up the device. She wriggled but he tightened his grip and pushed her through the crowd, and she stumbled as she tried to avoid someone's fingers, tripped over a knee. The soldier holding his gun against the villager's head relaxed it; the villager had gone quiet. He told his companion to stay and fell in beside Dena as the other man marched her through the yard. Wedged in between them, she felt the scratch of their uniforms against her arms, heard rifle metal clinking against bullet belts.

"Where are you taking me?"

She looked around for help. Layla and the women by the

kitchen were being led to the gate. Alex was trying to get to William, who was surrounded by men. Mustafa was gone. She called out but no one heard her, and the soldier yanked her so violently she caught her breath.

The other man opened several doors to find soldiers searching, and so they went on until they got to her bedroom. It was empty—the search party hadn't gotten to it yet. They pushed her inside and closed the door behind them.

She stared at them, wary. She could dash for the window behind her, but outside she heard men laughing. Her gaze flitted over the room—the bed she'd made up that morning, camera brace on the floor, dated and stacked tapes on a table by the wardrobe.

The soldiers' eyes fell on the tapes. The one by the door went to the table, opened a cassette case, and unspooled tape ribbon on the floor. She wanted to snatch the cassettes from him, but when she made a movement, his look made her stop. He picked up another cassette, and another, the noise of rippling ribbon filling the room.

"I've been seeing you around town," said the one with the camera. The other one stepped on the cassettes, ribbon dragging on his boots, and came to stand beside him. This one was a little smaller, his uniform baggy on his thin frame, his hair shaved, a narrow face marked by dark, reckless eyes and a wide, full-lipped mouth.

"What are you? A boy or a girl?" the first one asked. He turned to his friend. "What do you think?"

"Looks like a boy. Then again, moves like a girl."

The first one pressed buttons on the camera and looked through the eyecup. He hadn't unscrewed the cap on the lens.

She jumped when he moved. "Turn it on."

She uncapped the lens and pressed the Power button and

handed the camera back to him. He squinted at her, twisted the focus dial. "Is it recording?"

"Yes," she lied. She hadn't pressed the Record button.

The other one jostled to get a look.

"Show us," he said, taking the camera from his friend.

"It's recording."

"So show us."

He put the camera in her hands.

"You have to take out the tape and replay."

"She's lying," said the other one. "She filmed us at the checkpoint the other day. She showed us on the camera."

She stared at him, suddenly placing the narrow face. The same one who had looked at her with lewd eyes, touched her face all those weeks ago, when she'd been stopped by soldiers on her way to the plains.

The tall one grabbed her.

"OK," she said. "Press this. If the red light's flashing, it's recording."

"Think we're fools or what?"

He stepped back and looked through the lens.

"Take off her clothes."

The other swung her to face him and pulled open her shirt. She collapsed against the wall, whimpering, and tried to hide herself. He pulled her up and yanked the shirt from around her shoulders.

"Good," said the one with the camera. He adjusted the lens. "Take off that thing she's wearing."

He scratched at her bra. She screamed and fought him, and when she couldn't free herself writhed again against the wall, feeling the soldier's heat against her back and bare breasts.

"She's a stick." The one behind the camera laughed. "No meat on her at all."

The one holding her breathed into her ear. He reached up a

hand and caressed her. The one filming came closer now, and she saw the camera traveling from her face to her shoulders to her exposed breasts. Again she tried to lift her hands to cover herself.

"Make her show us more," the one behind the camera said.

The other one's fingers slid along her waist and fumbled at the zipper of her pants. He lifted her with one arm and pulled the jeans until her shoes came off. She almost fell when he placed her back down. The jeans were tangled at her ankles.

"Take them off properly. Otherwise, I'll get angry."

Her legs had turned to water and she felt light-headed. She kicked off the jeans, stood in her boy shorts, barefoot.

"Even her underwear is like a boy's," laughed the one with the camera. "You want to be a boy or what?"

The one holding her yanked at her underwear, but now she scratched him. He slapped her hard. She bit his hand. He twisted his fingers into her short hair and pulled her head back until she screamed.

He looked at the bite mark on his hand. She thought he'd hit her, but instead he pulled her to him and cupped her breast and ran his tongue along her cheek.

"That's good," the other one said. The lens traveled over her face, her neck, her chest.

The door opened and Alex tumbled in, almost falling. His face was flushed, his clothes and arms mud-spattered. He looked about him, disoriented, and made to rush deeper into the room, but when he saw the soldier nearest the door, he shrank back, fright blanching his face. He glanced around the room anxiously and saw the other man. He saw Dena but didn't seem to recognize her until she squirmed and made a sound. Something like terror passed over his face as he spoke her name in a gasp.

Sweat broke out on his forehead. He hesitated, swallowing, one arm held out to forestall a blow. He stared at her again. She wept, twisting against the soldier, fighting him uselessly as he barred her against the wall with his arm. Through the open door the noise of the search, of terrified villagers and shouts and abuse reached her.

Alex scoured the room helplessly. His feet got tangled in tape and he looked down. He looked up and saw the camera in the soldier's grip. He took a step in, tape rustling under him.

"Get out," he said.

The soldiers observed him curiously. He walked deeper into the room, edging toward them. He looked at Dena, who was heaving with small, breathless sobs now, the only thing holding her up the soldier's arm.

The one barring her spoke in Arabic. "You don't give us orders, white man." He reached up his other hand. For a moment the hand wavered by her face. Then a hard smack across her cheek, the force of it dashing her forehead into the wall.

Alex lunged at him. They fell against the wall and she slipped down. The other soldier dropped the camera and bounded forward, treading on her as he went for Alex. She crawled under the bed. Alex fell over with the soldier, who found his footing again while his companion restrained Alex on the ground. He fought as they kicked at his head and chest and spine. They brought their rifle butts down on him until his movements grew weak, his arms flailing, his legs limp. He curled up and covered his face. She dragged herself from under the bed and raised herself, but her limbs were too weak and she collapsed again and slid back, trembling.

Alex hadn't moved for minutes, but she now saw him reach for the camera pitched on the ground and shove it under a chair.

"Still awake?" one of the soldiers asked.

"Go to hell," said Alex. He spat out blood. He was looking up at them, his chin angled and his eyes dazed. She could see what was coming but Alex, blind or delirious, kept saying, "Go to hell."

The soldier raised his boot.

"Go to—"

She closed her eyes and heard a crack like wood splintering and felt blood spatter her.

ſ

A BREEZE RUSTLED THE thatch of the destroyed gazebo roof. Scattered straw against the kitchen wall, floated papers and maps up into the air. The canvas of the tent billowed and sagged. The kitchen door had been pulled off its hinges; drawers were dumped in the middle of the yard. Tape from Dena's cassettes streamed out, spider-webbing onto toppled chairs and plants. The ground was trashed with wet clothes and upturned shoes, hairbrushes and canisters of cooking oil and firewood.

William leaned against the office wall. His ribs throbbed and the back of his neck was sticky with blood. His lip was swollen. The compound gate was open, and he wanted to shut it. Still, he sat, his head bent, breeze brushing against his face.

The soldiers had left as suddenly as they'd appeared. An order from the garrison—an ambush, men were needed. They'd herded villagers into trucks and hauled out gun crates. William was left behind—why, he wasn't sure. Lying on the ground, he'd watched refugees shoved out, old people kicked and slapped, young children pulled from their mothers, men marched into the street. Soldiers stepped over and around him. He'd closed his eyes, and when he opened them again, they were gone.

He hauled himself onto his knees, but something dug into his side and he doubled over. Steadying himself against the wall, he stared at footprints, waiting for the pain to recede, then pushed himself off and limped through the mess, sidestepping papers and belongings. No sign of Layla, Alex, or Dena. Nor of Mustafa. The thought of the boy made him curse out loud; he tensed with rage and halted again as a spasm constricted his abdomen.

At the kitchen door he stopped, eyes adjusting to the semi-darkness. The fridge lay on its side in a pool of water. Soup streaked and dripped down the stove. The table was upside down. Knives and spoons tossed on the ground, amidst shattered glass and ceramic.

He thought he heard sobs. Someone was breathing, or crying. Layla. His heart jumped. He stepped carefully to avoid glass and followed the sound to the small pantry.

It was darker here than in the kitchen, light barely entering through two small windows above the shelves. Layla was hunched over on the ground, rocking. She looked up at him and put a finger to her lips. Her other arm was draped over Dena, who was curled up in a ball, her head in Layla's lap.

He went to her and bent down. "Are you all right?"

"I'm fine."

He surveyed her features. Her eyes were clear and her face was unscathed, though her dress was torn and covered in mud. Her thoub was bundled on the ground beside her. She nodded down at Dena and looked at him.

Dena lay motionless. Her knees were drawn up and she'd buried her face in her arm.

"They didn't . . . ?" he trailed off, staring at Layla.

"I'm not sure," she whispered.

He stared at Dena again. "Does she need a doctor?"

"She says no. But something . . . ." Layla dropped her voice. "They took her into the room. She won't tell me."

"Let's take her to lie down."

"She doesn't want to go to her room. We'll stay here for a bit." She touched his arm. "Are you all right?" her eyes moved over his face. "I saw them hit you." Her voice shook. "I was so scared."

"I'm fine," he said, and drew her to him. "Layla, listen."

Her face was grave, mirroring his own, her eyes huge and hollow in the dim light of the pantry. "Listen. Will you marry me?"

He couldn't read her expression, and as he spoke he became afraid that he'd blundered, that it was the wrong moment, it was callous of him, with Dena lying hurt between them, to ask. But when he'd found her in the kitchen, relief had flooded over him, along with the certainty that he had to ask. He'd been thinking of asking for weeks, as he'd watched things unravel, as he thought of what would happen to them should they all have to leave. The only way they could leave together was if they were married.

"I love you. I want to be with you, I want us to be together if things get worse, and they are getting worse. We can be together if we're married and—"

"Yes," she said. "Yes."

She pulled him forward and kissed him on his bruised lips, and he yelped with pain, and happiness.

∫

MUSTAFA CROUCHED UNDER the desk in the office, hiding. The clock, which he could see from his place, hung shattered on the wall, both its hands stopped just before eleven. He didn't know how long he had been waiting here. He'd dashed into the office and crawled under the desk, listening to the trudge of boots and chairs tumbling and glass breaking. There were yells from the road, and then it went quiet.

He sat with his chin on his knees staring at the closed door. The low wood above his head, and the metal sides of the desk pressing in around him made him feel safe, cocooned. He imagined that he was in a box, floating down a river, lulled by the gentle sway of the current, the ripple of water. He closed his eyes and pictured it until the room began to sway softly, and the sound of the current was in his ears. Thoughts of water recalled him back to his own throat. He was thirsty. Also, hungry.

He opened his eyes and studied the door, considering whether to risk stepping out. Soldiers might still be in the yard. But the quiet suggested otherwise. He needed water. And he needed to find William.

William, he thought fearfully, was either dead or enraged.

Or arrested. Or hurt. He hoped William wasn't dead, but just a little hurt, hurt enough not to bother with being angry, so that Mustafa might have time to explain himself, to apologize, to swear to never, ever, do such a thing again. Still, dreadful options weighed on him. William's death or William's rage. It was safer to stay here, under the desk, from where he could just stare at the door, forever. But what if William needed him? What if he were bleeding to death while Mustafa sat here, staring at the door?

He crawled out. One of the chairs sat on top of the desk. The poster of the green globe had been ripped from its place, leaving a dustless square patch on the wall above the filing cabinet. He went to the door and opened it a crack. The immediate surroundings were quiet, and he stepped out. As if a storm had passed through the compound—plants knocked over, wet ground heaped with clothes and pots and glass, mattresses, bags dropped as people fled or were marched out.

No trace of William. Nor of the others. The compound was deserted and forlorn, as if it had been abandoned. He crossed the yard and went into the rooms. They'd been turned upside down, empty of people.

By the time he reached the kitchen, he was beginning to fear that he'd been left behind. They had all gone, escaped. They'd left him. Just as the panic was rising in his chest, he heard voices coming from the pantry. He hurried past the upturned fridge and stopped in the entryway.

The floor was cluttered with tomato tins, onions, and spilled rice. William and Layla on the ground whispering over a person who, by the clothes, Mustafa took to be Dena—he couldn't see her face, which was buried in Layla's lap.

William and Layla were smiling at each other. Kissing. He moved and glass cracked beneath his flip-flops. Layla looked up first. Her hair was messy and her dress was ripped and soiled. In her lap, Dena didn't move.

"Mustafa."

William turned. His lip was swollen and the collar of his shirt was bloody. A gash cut across his brow. For a moment all was still, Layla and William staring at him. Then William's brows knitted. Glass skidded as he rose and bounded toward Mustafa. Layla moved Dena's head from her lap and got up. Mustafa ducked behind her and held on to her waist. There was a struggle, a flutter of fabric, bodies pulled and pushed, Layla lost her balance as William reached around her.

"Has everyone gone crazy?" Layla pushed William away. "Stop! Mustafa, let go!"

William got a hold of Mustafa's ear and twisted. Fire leapt up Mustafa's brain. He wriggled and screamed as William pulled him through the kitchen so quickly that he bumped a knee against the table and half-limped into the yard, his nose running and his head aching and his knee throbbing.

Behind him, Layla yelled at William. William stopped abruptly and turned. Mustafa sobbed, dangling from William's grip, feet dragging in the mud.

"Tell her why I'm throwing you out." When Mustafa continued to sob, William shook him. "*Tell her.*"

"William, let him speak." She looked at Mustafa. "Mustafa, tell me."

He was sobbing so hard now that he couldn't catch his breath. He focused on Layla, trying to ignore William looming over him. Layla, maybe, would understand.

"I put the guns in the storage room."

She stared at him, then at William.

"He was running guns," said William. "Out of this compound." He jerked Mustafa. "I should have handed you over to them, see what they'd do to you."

"Wait." Layla held William back. "Why, Mustafa?"

His gaze faltered, reverting to William's face, then back to Layla's. "I was hiding them."

"For whom?"

"A guy in the market. He was paying me to deliver them to the rebels."

William erupted. "I could beat you right now. I could kill you." He hauled Mustafa through the yard.

"The night of the fire-bombing," he wailed. "I got stuck with them and had to hide them somewhere."

William stopped. "So you hid them here," he said. "To save your own skin, you put us all in danger. They could have killed me right now. They could have killed us all."

Mustafa heaved with sobs. He raised his eyes to Layla, appealing to her. But he could see that something had changed. She was no longer on his side. Now she only halfheartedly held William back.

"Out." William towed Mustafa to the gate. "Don't show your face here again."

Mustafa spluttered and coughed as William swept him into the street. Through the blur of his tears, he tried to push his way in again, but William shoved him so hard he fell, and the gate slammed shut. He got up and banged, put his ear to the metal, but inside there was only silence.

ſ

"ARE YOU SURE?" asked Layla when William shut the door. She stood back from the gate, looking at him. "He could be hurt out there."

"Serves him right."

"He's sorry."

"I don't care."

Rage bubbled in his chest. He'd spoiled the boy. Mustafa thought he could get away with anything. High time he learned a lesson. He limped past her, then stopped, his anger receding as he remembered that she'd said yes. He went to her and reached for her shoulder.

She drew back. "It's not right, William. He'll get hurt."

"Layla. I'm not letting him back." He waited for her to relent. "Don't be angry. Please."

She looked away, unconvinced. Suddenly her face changed. He turned and saw Dena in the kitchen doorway. She looked haggard, frail, her eyes red and puffy from crying. She held her elbows as though cold.

"Where's Alex?" she asked.

Layla turned to him. "Where's Alex?"

He glanced from one to the other. "I was about to look. I haven't seen him."

Dena slid down the doorframe. Unnerved, Layla went and crouched beside her and held her. Dena began to say something. William went to her, trying to make sense of her words.

The more she tried to speak the more upset she became. Something about her room. Two men. He gathered that Alex had been assaulted by soldiers there, that Dena had witnessed it, that the men had dragged him away. Layla pulled her close and exchanged troubled looks with William.

"Layla, take Dena inside, I'll find Alex."

Layla nodded. She spoke softly to Dena, coaxed her to her feet and led her into the kitchen.

Right as the soldiers were closing in, he'd seen Alex trying to get to him. But then men had surrounded him, and he saw nothing beyond uniforms and rifles.

He surveyed the yard again, walking to the space behind the

gazebo. It was empty. The tent had been pulled down and canvas hung over boxes of equipment. He limped back to the office. No trace of Alex there, nor in his room.

In the storage room he found a mess of newspaper and toppled brooms. Alex's rucksack and suitcase gaped open by the door, clothes and equipment flung about.

In Dena's room the camera tripod leaned out of a shattered window, and the shutters hung halfway off their hinges. Closet doors were open and clothes and a camera brace spilled out. He lingered, taking in the smashed window, the table pitched forward. What had they done to Dena? She was always in control, so sure of herself. To see her in this state unsettled him. It brought home to him how vulnerable they all were. They had to leave town. All of them, and soon.

Back in the yard, he called to Layla. She stepped out of the kitchen.

"I can't find him."

She walked over to him.

"What do you mean you can't find him?"

He looked around helplessly.

"I can't find him. He's not here."

"Did they take him?"

A feeling of foreboding gathered in his chest. He went to the gate and opened it. Mustafa was gone. Other than cars parked in the distance, the street was empty, quiet.

He shut the gate and stood, at a loss. Layla went to the office.

"I've checked there," he called to her. "I've looked everywhere."

She crossed to the bathroom—he'd overlooked it. The door was closed and when she turned the knob, he saw that she had trouble opening it. She leaned against it, pushing more forcefully. Something blocked the door from within. She pushed harder and squeezed in through an opening and then he heard her gasp.

He half limped, half ran, and made his way inside. Alex was

slumped on his back, on the ground. His feet had been block-ing the door. His face and T-shirt were bloody. His right eye was swollen, turning purple. A dark patch of blood on his forehead, coagulating along his temple and cheek. The tap was running. Water sprayed from the hose over the low basin, mingling with blood on the floor.

"Is he dead?" Layla whispered. "William, is he dead?"

Her words jolted him. He leapt to the ground and put his ear to Alex's mouth. Breathing. He checked his pulse. Weak.

"Let's get him outside."

Layla opened the door wider and he cradled Alex under the arms, his head lolling as William stumbled out, shouldering his weight into the yard. He laid him down on a wet mattress.

"I'll get some things," Layla said, and hurried to the storage room.

William picked up a shirt on the ground and pressed it against Alex's head. Gently, he propped his head up. Layla came back with a first-aid box and took out sterilizing alcohol.

"We need to get the doctor," he said. There was one doctor in town, not really a doctor, but a nurse who had worked in Juba during the war.

"How? We can't go anywhere."

As he was thinking of what to do someone banged at the gate.

"Dammit. Mustafa."

"William, let him in. We can send him for help."

He stared at her, undecided. But she was right. They needed to get help for Alex as soon as possible. He got up and went to the gate, already giving Mustafa instructions as he swung it open.

"Run to the doc—"

Three soldiers in the doorway. He recognized them from the raid earlier. The shock of it made him freeze, giving one of them time to step inside. The other two followed. Outside, another group stood.

"William Luol," said the soldier facing him. "By order of the military commander, you're under arrest for weapons smuggling."

William's mind worked in slow motion; he heard Layla yelling, and, as he was turned around, he found himself facing her across the wreckage of the compound. She had gotten up, leaving Alex on the mattress. Her eyes were wide, her mouth working. Her expression reflected the fear that was beginning to turn his spine cold. Rope bit into his wrists as a soldier tied his hands behind his back. Layla was running toward him. One of the men stepped in her way. Instinctively, he moved to help her, to protect her from the soldier forcing her back, but the other men twisted him around and forced him through the gate.

VI

HE FELT RATHER THAN SAW THE DOOR OPEN—A HEAT ON his face, brightness behind his eyelids. He opened his eyes to a blur of movement, sun framed by the doorway, through which he could make out a strip of courtyard. He was lying on a mattress in the office. The window above the desk was shuttered, and he was in that part of the room in darkness. Dena and Layla crouched over him, whispering in Arabic. It felt as though he hadn't seen them in a long time. Dena's face seemed different—the bones more prominent. Her shirt collar exposed the tendons of her neck. Layla's moon-shaped face looming over him also seemed tired. Dark circles ringed her eyes and there were faint lines around her mouth. A scent of cooking spices wafted from her thoub.

They grew quiet, studying him as he looked at them. Finally Dena spoke. How was he feeling. The words traveled to him as though through water, blurry and indistinct. A tight metal helmet, a torture instrument, was clamped invisibly around his skull. He could hear his pulse thudding in his ear. He could feel, too, heat everywhere on his body, but in his head it burned steadily, like a gas flame. He had a premonition that he shouldn't move. Terrible pain might spring on him if he did. He felt it lurking in his joints, in the thrum of bruises on his skin. With each breath, something like a splinter needled his lungs, and he breathed shallowly. His tongue was a wedge in his throat. He was terribly thirsty. He twisted his head. Layla followed his gaze to a water bottle by the mattress. She reached for it and tilted it to his lips. The water was cool, fresh. The heat lifted.

Layla spoke, Dena translated. Was he hungry.

He nodded.

Layla rose and went out, shutting the door behind her. The room darkened. Dena perched on the edge of the mattress, her arms around her knees, looking at him. He let his gaze wander away from her. How long had he been lying here, hours or days? He'd been dimly aware of people coming and going, hands on him, things put into his mouth—a thermometer, water, pills. But mostly he was elsewhere, amongst landscapes splashed with green and pink. Streaks of black. A sandstorm—the grains of sand were sparkling atoms of water. The storm was blinding; he couldn't see beyond the rush of whirling droplets. Floating, being lifted up into the air, that sudden emptiness in his stomach that took his breath away, and then drowning. The sandstorm turned into an ocean. Thick purple liquid, in which he could see fish swimming hazily toward him. Among these scenes were glimpses of others he'd witnessed with William on mapping expeditions. A field of water lilies swaying softly with the current of the swamp. The desert bounded by the tripwire of the horizon. He had voyaged amongst these strange and familiar scenes sometimes with wonder, sometimes with terror—the journeys felt real, the effort exhausting—fighting the ocean to breathe, fighting the desert to walk—to where?

And then there was the corpse. In his dreams it came back to him—the twisted intestines and the exposed teeth and eye sockets. Sometimes the corpse raised itself from the ground, its ligaments bending stiffly as it walked around the courtyard. It dragged its entrails behind it, tugging on them as though on a leash. In other dreams it sat under the gazebo, drumming its burnt, nailless fingers against the table. Often it turned its eyeless gaze on him.

A strange, terrible sound—like the whir of a chainsaw—issued from its jaws. And then he woke up, sweating.

He focused his gaze on the wall, anchoring himself in the room again. Above the filing cabinet, a blank space where the poster of the organization's logo once hung. Boxes, books, papers by the door. Clothes flooded down a chair onto the ground. Dena sat, attentive, but silent. Again he became conscious of the heat on him like a second skin. He kicked off the sheet to reveal pale, wasted legs that he hardly recognized. White thread projected into his field of vision—he was wearing a bandage.

He had trouble reaching beyond the throbbing in his head. There were other things, before the dreams, that he needed to grasp. His mind worked. Slowly, the fog lifted. He remembered the canceled flight and the fight with William. The raid. Dena in the room with two soldiers. Pain—excruciating pain—its memory deep in his body.

Light flooded in. Layla entered. She handed a bowl to Dena and murmured some words. She looked at him and smiled faintly, then left again.

Seeing that he was frowning in the light of the open door, Dena got up in one swift movement and went to shut it. He could do that once. Now, just moving his head sent currents of pain rippling through his body.

She sat down and picked up the bowl.

"Some soup for you."

He hauled himself up. The room wavered and he shut his eyes, waiting for the spinning to stop. He opened his eyes and tightened his grip on the spoon—even his fingers were weak. Dena held the bowl as he dipped into it and sucked one mouthful after another. He lay back, breathing as though he'd just lifted a weight, and steadied his eyes on her.

"How long? Have I been like this?"

She put down the soup.

"A week." In the darkened room her face was all shadows. "Since . . . the soldiers. We wanted to take you to the clinic, but there's been more rain, the roads are blocked."

It was quiet—eerily so. He could hear sparrows.

"The villagers?"

"Soldiers swept them out. And"—she hesitated—"William's been arrested."

He stared at her. "When?"

"Same day. They came back for him. Layla's trying to find out where they're holding him."

He remembered William repainting the organization's logo on the truck door, saying it might protect them. How exasperated Alex had been at that pathetic attempt at protection. Alex had been worried for himself. But now it was William in trouble. Whatever the danger to him, it had always been greater to William. He flushed at the thought that their last encounter had been a fight, started by him.

"I'll call the Khartoum office." He tried to lift himself, but the room began spinning again and he fell back on the mattress.

"Later," Dena said. "I wasn't sure I should tell you."

He looked at her.

"What?"

"You're worrying over me."

She half smiled. His impression that her face was more gaunt was confirmed now. She'd lost weight. Her jawbones were more pronounced, the hollows of her cheeks deeper. Even her eyes seemed sunken. His mind cast back to the soldiers. He saw her naked, the soldier holding her up, the other behind the camera. He shuddered. He wanted to ask about it, but thought better of it.

"How's Layla?"

"Not good. But she's hanging in there. She goes to the security office every day to ask about William. I should help her more, but . . ." She trailed off.

She didn't feel safe leaving the compound. Although how safe was the compound? Its walls with their shards of glass, the metal gate, had been useless in protecting them. He remembered his fear after the corpse, his doubts about whether the compound was secure enough. But over the months, even through the clashes, he'd lulled himself into the belief that it was safe inside. Or safer, at least. The refugees' arrival had changed things. It became impossible to draw a line between inside and out.

"Mustafa?" he asked. Surely if Dena couldn't go out, Mustafa could.

"William threw him out."

She explained that Mustafa had been gun-running for the rebels, had hidden weapons in the storage room. William realized it the moment the guns were found. Still, he didn't give Mustafa away. But then suspicion fell on William.

Alex listened. To think that Mustafa, bold as he was, was capable of this. And now William in prison.

"Where's Mustafa now?"

"We don't know. Maybe with his mother. Anyway, he hasn't come back. And Layla won't let him. She's furious with him, now that William's been arrested."

He let his gaze drift to the pale square on the wall. So much had happened since the soldiers.

"But there's some good news."

He looked at her. What could possibly be good, with William in prison and Mustafa gone?

"There's a cease-fire." The government and rebels were meeting in Kenya to negotiate, she told him. "There might even be a peace agreement, eventually. The news is all over town."

"Really?"

"Yes, really. No one's holding their breath, but the fighting has stopped. For now."

A cease-fire. Maybe even a peace agreement. It seemed almost unbelievable. Why now, he wondered. In the end, the pieces were simply falling into place. The rebels had been chipping away for decades. They were weaker, seemed to be losing, but the scales had finally tipped. To think that the war might end in a room in Kenya, around a table laid out with teacups and cake.

Dena's brow creased. It wasn't just her face that had changed; her posture had too. She seemed to shrink into herself. Different from the quality she had when she was filming, when the sureness of her movement allowed her to disappear into her surroundings.

Through the shutters above the desk sunlight fell across her forehead. She leveled her gaze at him. Her lips parted, came together. She unclasped her arms from around her knees. He watched all of this with interest, aware that she was about to say something. He wondered what had happened to the camera.

She said, "I wanted to say thank you for helping me. With the soldiers."

They looked at each other. She read the question in his mind. "No, they didn't. But if you hadn't come . . ."

He thought about this. Did he deserve the credit? In fact, he'd gone to her room to escape soldiers outside. They'd turned violent, had closed in on William. When he tried to help him, one of them pointed a gun at him. He'd stumbled back and ran through the nearest door, which was Dena's.

That was when he saw her—naked against the wall, the soldiers filming her. He simply had to put an end to that scene. And so he'd spoken up. They had turned on him. Had he willed them to? Maybe, maybe not. He'd been terrified, but in that moment it felt as though there was no choice.

He had come to within an inch of his life. Was that why he felt relieved, in spite of the pain ravaging his muscles, his bones?

As though he'd plunged deep into a body of water—one of the liquid landscapes of his dreams—almost lost his breath there, and came up just in time for air. He was battered, but he'd survived.

"Truth is," he said, "I was looking to hide. So I went into the nearest door—yours."

"But you stayed."

He looked at her. It occurred to him that this was a chance.

"I'll take your thanks," he said, "on one condition."

"Which is?"

"I want us to be friends."

She smiled faintly, nodded, and drew her knees up. She leaned her chin on them and looked beyond him. Her expression darkened.

"I keep thinking about William. What's happening to him." She paused. "And those two soldiers."

She avoided his gaze. He realized that she was ashamed that he'd seen her. She'd been exposed to him as well as the soldiers. He wanted to reassure her but didn't know what to say.

Instead, he shifted to make space for her on the mattress. She looked at him, a little dubious. But then she kicked off her sneakers and stretched out beside him. They lay side by side in the dim room, staring at the ceiling.

_ʃ_

THE WAITING AREA of the security office was packed with supplicants. They sat propping their heads on their hands, rising whenever a guard appeared, trying to catch the eye of the stone-faced men who moved between back offices and the reception. They were mostly Nilot women. Grandmothers in search of disappeared grandsons, mothers in search of sons, young brides looking for husbands snatched in the night, daughters fearing for fathers who'd been picked up on their way to pasture. There were men, too, but only a handful—it was as though all the adult men in Saraaya had been detained in the sweep of arrests overtaking the district. Those who hadn't yet been detained were afraid to show themselves. And so only a few boys and very old men ventured out to ask about disappeared relatives.

Almost two weeks of coming every day made Layla a familiar face here. When she'd arrived earlier that morning, a guard registered her name in a logbook. No one understood the point of this logbook. At first, Layla thought it was to record the order people arrived in. But there was no sequence. Sometimes someone who arrived last was called in immediately, while someone who'd been coming for weeks was left waiting. Some days there was no registration; the visitors were allowed to flood into the waiting room chaotically.

Today, as every day, she was told to wait. She'd been waiting five hours. Hunger crept up on her, bladder pressed in on her; her back ached from her cramped position on the floor. Though the windows were open, the heat was stifling. Sweat trickled down somber faces, and mothers fanned fussy children with newspaper.

By the entrance, a young woman argued with a guard. She held a screaming baby, her hand protecting his head. The guard was pulling her toward the exit. He was rough, ignoring her pleas to mind the baby, whose arms made small, helpless swipes at the man hurting his mother. The woman fought but was hindered by the child. She'd gone up to ask how long she had to wait. It was a mistake that every new arrival made—asking for help or information from the remorseless sentries. A mother might ask a guard if he could deliver a message. A very old man might venture forward, pressing his palms together—he was too old to look after himself and needed to find out what had become of his sons.

Each day someone learned the lesson the hard way. They were entitled only to wait, never to ask questions. The guards insulted people's sons and husbands and brothers, until women and old men and children were reduced to tears. They could bear insults to themselves, but not to their disappeared loved ones.

Now, the guard hauled the woman to the door. He was throwing her out. She resisted him uselessly, weeping along with her baby. Some ventured timid words of reproach. But the guard clamped his hand around her shoulder, his voice booming with insults as he pushed her into the street.

People mumbled, shook their heads, looked down at their hands or at the door through which the baby's cries could still be heard. Sighs and prayers rippled through the room. But there was nothing they could do—it was a drama that repeated itself daily.

The supplicants retreated into themselves, finding solace in one another's company. She was overcome by a feeling of kinship with these women who kept her company through her days of waiting, made her burden lighter because they bore it with her. They passed the hours in stories of losses, in inquiries, in despairing and hopeful speculations. Whenever someone was finally called in, the others squeezed her shoulder and blessed her and wished her good luck. They waited with bated breath until she came out again—as though it were their son or husband she'd gone in to ask about. Often the women came out crying—either having learned nothing new or having learned the worst—that their husband was dead, their son was lost for good. More rarely they stepped out with a hopeful smile on their lips. Their brother was alive, their father was being held at this or that facility.

They wondered at Layla. She was one of few nomads in the room. Why was she here? The authorities weren't arresting nomad men, only Nilotes. In answer to their questions, Layla told the basic facts—she was a cook at the NGO compound, she worked with William Luol, the translator, a Nilot. He was arrested in mid-June. He was needed at the compound. She'd come to find out what had happened to him.

In those first days after William's arrest, she'd been torn between tending to Alex and Dena and fearing for William. On the third day her brothers arrived. She hadn't been home, and her father was asking after her. Since the refugees, she'd taken to sleeping over at the compound. Now, in the aftermath of the raid, she told her brothers that there was no going home for her. With William disappeared, who else would look after things?

Four days after William's arrest, she left Dena and the neighbor in charge and ventured out to the security office.

But more than the men in uniforms, she feared her own weakness. She was overwhelmed by pressures and responsibilities. She didn't trust that she was strong enough to keep herself together. Her link to William stripped her of her privilege—that she was protected from harm because she was a nomad. But any injury done to him struck at her own heart.

When she doubted her own strength, she tried to keep faith in his. She told herself that he'd keep himself safe. She pushed aside thoughts of his proposal, their marriage, because thinking of such things seemed brazen. It was hoping for too much, and the superstitious part of her didn't want to tempt fate. Only a few weeks before she would have thought of a thousand obstacles to their marriage—beginning with her family's disapproval. Now she would fly in the face of her family if need be.

In the meantime, she pinned all her hopes on his release. Each morning, she felt panic at the prospect of the security office, the crowd of women, the cruel guards, the hopelessness of another day of waiting. But she couldn't bear the thought of William suffering. And so even though it felt like a hopeless ritual, she rose each morning at sunrise, dressed, drank her tea, and, after check-

ing on Alex and Dena, went out to face yet another day of waiting, taking her place at the end of the line of women who had
come from faraway villages and, having nowhere to sleep, camped
out in the street.

Someone called her name. She roused herself, so flustered that
she tripped over her neighbor, and hands reached up to steady her.
The women whispered their blessings as she stepped over slum-
bering children and hurried to the guard who was frowning impatiently in the doorway.

As she followed him into a hallway, it crossed her mind that
she might emerge, like some of the women she'd seen, in tears
at some terrible news—that William was dead. The thought rose
and bubbled, and with effort she pushed it away. She focused
instead on the guard's back. She focused on the hallway through
which she moved—it was lined with dark-green doors. She noted
these details as though they were of great importance. Already
her legs were unsteady and her chest felt tight.

Finally they stopped at an office. The guard spoke to someone
inside, then stepped out of her way and she walked in, mustering
her courage. At the back was a desk behind which sat a security
officer in plain clothes, elbows on the table. Layla had little experience in such offices and was intimidated—the national flag that
leaned from a penholder on the desk, the nameplate with silver
calligraphy that she couldn't read—she could only pick out one
or two letters.

She was relieved that the man didn't look at her as she
approached. Surely he would see her terror. She stopped between
the chairs and waited. Finally the officer looked up at her, a little
weary. But his eyes weren't cruel. She had become so accustomed
to the rough treatment of the guards, that she expected worse
from their superiors.

"Yes?"

She cleared her throat. She needed to get the tone right—supplicating but determined.

"I'm here to ask about someone . . . someone I work with. He was arrested during a raid."

"Name?"

"William Luol."

The officer looked at her intently. She could almost read his thoughts. He was registering that she was a nomad. Inquiring about a Nilot.

"Where do you work?"

"At the humanitarian compound."

"When was he arrested?"

"Two weeks ago, during a search—we had refugees staying at the time." She stopped, confused, worried that she was digressing. "I was sent by the American in charge. Wanted me to ask when William might be released."

"What work do you do at the compound?"

"I cook. William—William Luol—he's the translator. And he looks after things at the compound. The American needs him. That's why I was sent to ask."

The security man looked at her for a while. Though trying to keep calm, she could feel that he sensed her agitation. She didn't mention the assault on Alex.

"You say soldiers arrested him?"

"Yes."

"In that case, he's not under our jurisdiction. Likely we don't have information."

"But you haven't checked. Can you check?" She was desperate for news, at least confirmation that he was alive. "Please, sir. I've been run ragged coming here and waiting every day. I'll get in trouble at work if I come back with no news. Please, just look, or ask. At least tell me where he is. Please."

She watched him decide whether to be helpful. Her tone seemed to have an effect, because he called to someone, and an assistant came in.

"See if you can find anything on William . . ."

"Luol," she supplied.

"William Luol."

The man disappeared again and Layla stood, nervously looking at the nameplate she couldn't read. The officer invited her to sit. She sat tentatively on the edge of a chair while he turned to his papers.

A few minutes later the man came in and placed a file on the desk.

The officer ran his finger down a page. "What date was he arrested?"

"Fourteenth June." She held her breath.

"Here."

Her heart jumped, and she got up and came forward, looking down at the file though she couldn't read anything, couldn't understand anything.

"Search of the compound. Illegal sheltering of refugees. It says here he was arrested for weapons smuggling."

"It's just a misunderstanding."

She could feel her face working. She tried to collect herself. She had to remain cool, pretend that William was nothing to her. She was simply here to inquire about someone she worked with.

"He's been moved," said the officer.

"Where to?"

"Military prison."

"When will they let him go?"

"I don't know."

"Is there someone to ask? Who do I ask?"

The officer closed the file, his face emptying.

"Ask at the garrison," he said. "That's all I have. If he's been taken to the military prison he may be held for a while—why are you crying?"

She didn't know whether it was from relief that William was alive or whether from helplessness, her inability to do more, to get him out.

She said thank you. She turned into the hallway, walls swimming around her, and stepped out into the waiting room dashing tears from her eyes. She was greeted by a cacophony of questions from the women, who, seeing her distress, took her in their arms and soothed and comforted her against their shoulders.

*

AN HOUR BEFORE CURFEW, Mustafa stood charting his ascent into the canopy of the acacia on which he'd displayed his underwear all those months ago. The trick was to scrabble up to the middle of the trunk, where a knob stuck out on which he could rest his weight—from there he could reach the lowest branch, and climb deeper into the leaves.

He scanned the street. This part of the market was almost completely deserted now. Abandoned stalls and shops lined the road. Some of them had been destroyed in the May fire-bombing. Only one of three garages was open. Plastic bags spun and somersaulted outside shop grilles. Military trucks were parked by the gas station. Farther down the road, soldiers were busy searching a car stopped at a checkpoint. The hood of the car was lifted, and men poked their heads into its open doors. Now was his moment—while the soldiers were busy with their search.

He took off his flip-flops, tied them together with rope, and slung them around his neck. Then he stepped back and threw himself at the tree, bark crumbling beneath his feet as he clambered up and hugged the trunk like a lizard, steadying himself.

He stretched an arm to the lowest branch, swung himself, and grabbed hold with his other arm, his stomach tightening with effort as he lifted his legs to the branch, then climbed up onto two sturdy boughs shadowed by leaves.

From his perch he took in the view—shuttered shops and checkpoints and army trucks stationed at intervals. The destroyed police station, the minaret of the mosque rising above thatched roofs, the church, and, on the very edge of town, army barracks, beyond which he could make out refugees moving through the plains. Above him, clouds like faint white thumbprints flecked the sky.

Here, in the tree canopy, he was invisible to the soldiers and militiamen who patrolled beneath, the drunkards and herdsmen, safe from rabid dogs that roamed howling in the night. He was lucky to have a hiding place. For days after his dismissal from the compound, he'd been lost, bouncing from friend to friend. At first, Ibrahim took him in. But Ibrahim's mother began grumbling soon after his arrival. Four children to feed and she couldn't feed another. No space in the house. Why didn't Mustafa go to his family?

Omar at the juice stall let him sleep in his shop for a while, but then he'd dismantled his shack and left town, like others were doing. Jane, the tea lady, put him up for a few days, until her husband objected. People were hardly able to look after themselves, let alone strangers. So Mustafa went to Deng's, only to find the garage broken open, shelves ransacked, tables overturned. A neighbor told him that Deng had been arrested.

And so Mustafa went home to his mother. Walked three days to the village—a hunk of cheese he'd filched and stale bread in a plastic bag and a water bottle under his arm, which he filled up from wells along the way. He walked barefoot to save his flip-flops, except during the warmest part of the day, when the dirt beneath his feet was as hot as smoldering coal.

Sometimes he came across nomad encampments swarming with sheep and oxen, men tending to animals, women cooking over open fires. But all the Nilot villages were abandoned or destroyed. He came across refugees fleeing toward Saraaya. From them he heard about militia raids and rebel counterattacks on the district's outskirts.

On the road his feet blistered. He coated them with a layer of dirt sprinkled with water, mud bandages to cover sores. He was careful with his water and bread and cheese. Whenever he felt himself flag, he stopped and rested on his haunches or took a nap. He whistled tunes he knew from the radio as he walked, thinking of his mother. He wasn't sure how she'd react to his arrival—anger that he was coming empty-handed, or relief that he was safe.

But he arrived to find the village deserted. The last time he had gone home was four months ago, in the truck with William. Then the village had been full of life; children chasing one another and old men laughing in the twilight. Now most houses were rubble and ash. The few that stood looked like they'd been left in a hurry. Doors creaked and curtains fluttered through windows. His mother's house was still standing, but empty. He climbed in through a low window and found mattresses rolled up on the floor. A bare table in a corner of the room. The wardrobe had been cleared out and the one suitcase stored on top of it gone. He looked around, the enormity of the silence sinking in.

He had thought about his mother on the way to the village, but now it was his little sister and brother he missed. How long before he saw them again? His little sister with her thumb always in her mouth, his brother with his big ears. Were they safe? Would they remember him?

He spent the night in the abandoned house and started back to Saraaya the next morning. There, days of sleeping on the streets, of having to slither belly pressed to the ground into a hollow beneath a market stall, scrunching himself up into the shadow of a doorway, or cutting himself climbing into an abandoned truck through a broken window, only to lie on springs that poked his ribs.

All to escape the threats of the night. Thieves and militias prowling after curfew. Worst of all, the hand combing through his hair as he slept in the doorway of a shop, the touch soft, like the touch of his mother. Only it wasn't his mother. It was a soldier, an ogre who'd wanted to touch him. Mustafa had yelled and fought him off. But after that he slept with ears pricked for footsteps, a rock by his head for a weapon. One afternoon, as he was passing by the tree, his gaze fell on it and it occurred to him that it was the perfect hiding place—he could sleep up there, safe from the streets below.

∫

HIS BOTTOM GREW NUMB, and he adjusted himself on the branch, watching the horizon darken. Rooftops and trees blurred against the sky. A crisp breeze wafting in from the northern desert chilled him, and he pulled his arms in through his sleeves and hugged himself beneath his T-shirt. If he'd had money he would have left Saraaya, but he didn't even have bus fare's worth to get to El Obeid. All his gun-running money was still buried in the compound. Every day he wavered over going to William and falling on his knees in apology. To get it back—a safe bed, friends, a salary. But whenever he thought of going back, he remembered William's rage, and was afraid.

He was sorry for the guns, but it wasn't right to cast him out. William might be angry with him, he might scold him. But to cut him off from the compound, which had become his home?

He comforted himself with the thought that they needed him. Who else would clean and sweep and go into town, if not him? He pictured himself running into the compound, into William's arms, everyone beaming at him and telling him how they missed him. For things to be as they were, before the raids and the militias and the fire-bombing—his bed with its mosquito net, lunch under the gazebo with everyone, riding with William and Layla in the truck and going into the market on errands.

Just then, as if in answer to his thoughts, he spotted Layla crossing the checkpoint. He narrowed his eyes and crawled through the foliage to get a better look—yes, it was her, the same gait, the bent head. He scrambled down the tree and fell at her feet, then jumped up and wrapped his arms around her, awash in her scent of cooking spices, the compound, its smells and tastes and sights that he missed so much flooding back.

"Layla!"

William had forgiven him. He'd sent her to bring him back. She grabbed him so tightly that suddenly a sharp pain pierced his collarbone.

"You!" She pushed him and he staggered.

She fixed him in her glare, her teeth bared, her eyes burning. Why was she looking at him like that? He'd never seen her so angry. He was so sure she'd come to bring him back to the compound.

"William's been arrested," she said. "They're blaming him for the guns. They're holding him in the garrison prison and I don't know if I can get him out."

The words knocked about in his head. The guns. William arrested because of the guns. His guns. His body suddenly went numb. It was a big mistake. He shook his head, opened his mouth, but no words came out.

She said, "He was right about you. You're a selfish, worthless, ungrateful little boy."

He took a step toward her. "I didn't mean to. I didn't."

"You didn't mean to?" She stared at him. "It's all your fault. He might get hurt . . ."

"I'm sorry. Let me come back. Please."

"No." She shook her head. "He was right to throw you out. You stay away."

She stepped back, still staring at him, then walked around him and down the road in the direction of the compound. He stood in the stillness of the empty street, surrounded by closed-up shacks, and watched until her thoub vanished into the gray light.

It was almost dark. At the checkpoint, lanterns flickered. Voices reached him from a distance. He was terribly tired. He looked up. The tree was suddenly very tall, and it seemed impossible to muster up the strength to climb up once again to his hiding place.

∫

ALEX SAT ON a chair, facing the open office door behind Dena. She stood behind the camera framing a close-up of his forehead. A bruise radiated up from his brow and disappeared into the tousled hair. The bruise was bright red in the center, faint pink at the edges, blending into white, translucent wrinkles. The lens picked up obscure scratches and inflammations. She moved the camera down to his left eye. His lashes were stuck together, strangely lush and feminine. In the close-up of his pupil she could see her own reflection, a black speck in the orb of his eye.

She asked him to turn his face. Another long wound ran down his left temple. Unlike the forehead bruise, this one was sharp and defined. The gash had scabbed over and a ridge of rough skin rose along the cheek, cutting across stubble. This close, the face had the aspect of an undulating landscape, with slopes and valleys and soft patterns. As she moved inward, the skin of his cheek turned blue, then raw purple near the jaw. She moved down along the wound to his jawline.

Filming him had become a pastime. One afternoon, as they sat together in the office, he'd asked her to bring her camera.

"Why?" she asked.

"Just because."

She hadn't touched the camera since the day of the raid. She went to get it. When she held it in her hands, it felt alien, cold. The dark glass eye was ominous. She studied the metallic angles of the body, looked at the lens, and felt as though she was holding a weapon.

When she returned to the office, Alex took off his T-shirt and lay down on the mattress. He looked even worse than a few days before. Bruises were coming to the surface in purple and blue and yellow blotches all over his chest. Cuts were hardening into scabs. He had lost so much weight that the arcs of his ribs showed clearly and his arms lay beside him like spindles.

"Shoot," he said.

"You're just going to lie there?"

"Sure."

She stared at him for a moment. Then she took off her shoes and positioned her feet on either side of his torso and, standing above him, pointed the lens at him.

"How do I look?"

"Like crap."

They giggled.

She started with the ribs. She liked the outline of the bones above the hollow of his stomach. She focused in so closely that the image became abstract. The camera roamed along a ridge in his chest. Black and white slopes alternated, moving ever so slightly with his breath. She could see goose bumps and fine hairs. Sometimes, translucent skin was disrupted by the green and purple and red of a bruise.

Over the next days she traced his arms and shoulders, filming broken skin. She lingered over scars along his stomach. She experimented with illumination. Sometimes she shut out almost all the light in the room, so that his limbs were indistinguishable blocks of shadow in the frame. Other times she had him stand outside in the noon sunlight and filmed him there exposed, shadowless.

Alex enjoyed being her model. He gave himself up entirely to her. She, in turn, liked this new, gentle, cooperative Alex. He'd become softer, more interesting since waking up from his injuries. There was a new shade of affliction in his eyes—it gave his face depth. All of his intrusive, knowing boldness was gone. Instead a shy, uncertain smile broke out unexpectedly from time to time.

Every day he insisted that she film the same spots on his body. When she asked why, he said he liked to see how his bruises were healing. Under the camera's eye, they watched cuts close up, scabs harden, skin gain back its luster.

She found relief in dwelling on his bruises. She could forget about her own wounds, and her shame. Her mistake was thinking she could stand outside of things and observe. Hiding behind the camera—distant, in control of the picture but not in it. But of course she was always in it. And now all that was left of her months of filming was the footage of her own assault.

It was her link to the others that kept her afloat. Alex who had helped her, and Layla who looked after both of them, and William, whom she was scared for. And Mustafa, whom she worried over.

When she wasn't filming Alex, she spent her time cleaning up. This, too, had become a routine. Two weeks after the raid, the compound was still in disarray—clothes and papers strewn in the yard, smashed glass in the rooms, Alex's mapping equipment damp by the gazebo. Layla was out most of the day and so Dena worked alone. She gathered up gear, swept up dishes and spilt food in the kitchen. She often thought of Mustafa as she went about these chores. She couldn't bring herself to be angry with him, though she understood the danger he'd put them in—William especially. When Layla told her she'd run into him in town, Dena was secretly relieved to know that he was safe.

Each day she waited for Layla, who often returned hollow-eyed and listless from searching for William. The only concrete information she'd managed to gather was that William was being held at the garrison prison. But when Layla visited there, the guards neither confirmed nor denied his detention. The fear at the back of all their minds, though none of them spoke it out loud, was that if they didn't get William out soon, he might disappear. It happened all the time to Nilotes suspected of ties to the rebels. Dena wanted to help Layla, but she was afraid of stepping out. She dreaded running into the men who had her in the room. And so she helped indoors, leaving Layla to venture out on her own.

Everything was uncertain—not only William's fate but the fate of the whole town, the whole war. She and Layla and Alex waited expectantly, putting their hopes in the cease-fire. While cleaning up, she often listened to the radio, following news reports of peace negotiations in Kenya, which were full of vague talk of progress. But if an agreement was struck, a prisoner exchange was likely, and William and others might be released. Alex called the Khartoum office every day to follow up on his case. From town, Layla brought news. People were looking forward to a deal, in the hope that their men might be released.

Amidst all this waiting, there was nothing to do but put the compound in order. And film Alex. She was aware of the office darkening, the messy bedding behind him as he shifted in his seat, the pile of papers on the desk. The ache at the back of her neck, which always came when she bent over the tripod for too long. She'd filmed all the bruises on his face and now tilted the pan-handle, descending to his neck and moving along his right shoul-der. There, a pattern of marks, like hieroglyphics. The sole of a boot imprinted into the muscle. The bruise was paler than the day before, healing. She could already see the marks fading, their edges softening. She liked this bruise especially and lingered on it.

Alex touched his shoulder.

"Does it still hurt?"

"It's better."

She considered him.

"Can you stand?"

He rose and stepped on his uninjured leg. His appetite had returned and she saw for the first time the weight on him. He seemed more solid, wider and taller.

She asked him to turn. He limped around, revealing the width of his shoulders against his narrow torso. She focused on the point on his nape where his uncut hair faded. The lens moved slowly down his neck, tracking vertebrae.

*

LATER, THEY SAT on the mattress, leaning back against the wall. Dena held the camera in her lap and replayed footage on the viewfinder screen. It was the part they both looked forward to—going over the day's images together. They compared marks from today and yesterday. They noted improvements, deteriorations, color developments. Alex joked that Dena was making a map of his bruises.

As she watched she felt him lean against her, ostensibly to get a better look at the display. Each day he came a little closer. It had happened enough times that she'd stopped wondering whether it was accidental.

Now when she tried to lean away, he shifted nearer, his shoulder pressing against hers, though he continued to gaze at the viewfinder as though engrossed.

She stopped the video and turned to him.

"Alex, I'm gay."

His eyes swiveled to her face.

"You are?"

"Yes. So, stop trying to kiss me."

He sat up. His eyes flickered over her eyes and mouth and hair.

"How come you never said?" He looked at her. "When I told you I liked you. That day you almost broke the camera over my head."

"It was none of your business."

"You should've told me."

"I just did."

He continued to stare at her. He opened his mouth to protest, but then closed it.

"OK." He looked sheepish. "Sorry."

He settled down beside her. She pressed Play on the viewfinder, and soon they were absorbed by a purple bruise blooming on the screen.

ſ

EARLY ONE MORNING, Mustafa trekked twelve kilometers to the fortresslike garrison rising out of the flatlands beyond town. Two guards perched high up in a tower, keeping watch over the plain. Outside the gates, soldiers in green uniforms jogged, huffing and sweating, past military SUVs and canvas-covered trucks. Farther away, another group stood in rows, lifting their rifles in answer to the barked commands of an officer. Near the road, a handful of hawkers and merchants sat beneath umbrellas and canopies, displaying cigarettes, snacks, water bottles.

No one paid him attention as he looped around and approached the main gate. A barricade blocked cars from entering into an open area beyond. Three guards clustered near a booth, telling jokes. He paused, surveying the entry. He could try to slip in behind the booth without being noticed. But once inside he might get caught. And besides, he didn't know where to go, or whom to look for.

He went up to the guards. One of them stood with a boot propped on a chair, telling a story. Mustafa tugged on his arm and announced that he had a message to deliver to the military commander.

The guard looked him up and down, then waved him off.

"If you don't let me in, you'll regret it." He walked into the middle of the circle. "All of you. The military commander will want to know. I have information about arms smuggling."

The guards glanced at each other and, calculating that it was risky dismissing him if he did have information, decided to let him in.

The one sitting rose with a sigh. Mustafa followed him into the yard. On one side were barracks spread over two floors—a balcony ran along the length of the top floor. Soldiers lounged in undershirts. Some played cards, others dozed on camper beds, still others polished boots or rifles.

Beyond the barracks, at the back of the complex, was another inner courtyard, sealed off with a fence and a locked gate. This inner yard was darker, filthy. Smeared paper and plastic bags littered the ground. Stained walls covered in scratches, blurred charcoal marks, and childlike drawings. He saw Nilot men chained to blocks of concrete. They wore rags and their faces and limbs were covered in dirt. One slept with the chain reaching from his neck, like a dog. Another rocked back and forth and made strange sounds, the metal clanking as he moved. The yard was crowded with others who shuffled around shoeless, limping or wincing as they walked in circles. They wore stained clothes, their beards and mustaches and hair full of muck. The faint disgusting whiff of unwashed bodies and human waste reached him.

The prison. He strained to get a better look, searching for

William. He tried to see into the dark corners of the prison yard. His gaze fell on three locked doors at the back. Cells. William was in there somewhere. He trotted to catch up to the guard, who had turned right and entered through a doorway into an office.

The guard pushed Mustafa forward, informing a soldier that the boy had information. Mustafa was directed to a bench. He sat, his legs dangling. Men came and went through another door, some in uniform, some in civilian clothes, giving instructions and orders.

Finally, after an hour, he was led into a a windowless room in which sat a heavyset man in uniform, arms like logs on the desk piled with folders, eyes hooded beneath his beret. He held a gold pen in one stubby hand. At a table to the left officers gathered over papers.

When the commander's eyes fell on Mustafa, a crease of displeasure appeared on his brow, and he turned to the soldier who had brought him in. "What's this?"

"Sir, he says he has information about weapons smuggling."

The commander looked at Mustafa, the crease deepening. He motioned for him to come closer.

"Talk, quickly."

"Three weeks ago, those guns found at the NGO compound," said Mustafa.

"Yes."

"You arrested William Luol, the translator." If he gave himself up, admitted his guilt, William and Layla might forgive him. He would have to suffer for his betrayal; it was the only way to make it up. He swallowed. "William Luol isn't responsible. I am. I hid the guns. I was delivering weapons to the rebels."

The commander's eyes narrowed, chair squeaking as he swiveled. "Come here." Mustafa went to stand in front of him.

"How old are you?"

"Twelve."

"You look younger."

Mustafa stood taller. Why did no one believe him? "I'm twelve."

"Well, listen, little man, the cells are full. We don't have space for a nomad boy playing pranks. Go home, OK?"

"I'm telling you, you arrested the wrong person. Let William go. Arrest me. I hid the guns."

"Nilot boys work for the rebels. Why would a nomad boy like you get involved with them?"

"Because you, and the government you work for, are thieves and thugs."

"Watch it."

"You're all sons of dogs." He continued with a stream of filthy epithets directed at the commander, his private parts, his mother's private parts, his daughter's private parts—every dirty word he'd picked up in the market. The room went entirely still with shock. An involuntary snigger burst from one of the men. The commander heaved forward to smack Mustafa, but Mustafa sank his teeth into his wrist, tasting ashy flesh.

Soldiers were on him. A blow across his head made him see double. He was lifted up and dropped onto the tiles. He looked up from the ground. The commander's beret had been knocked off, revealing hair pressed sweatily against his ears. He scowled, holding his right hand.

"Lock up this little shit."

Mustafa smiled, feeling something come loose in his mouth. A tooth fell out, clinking faintly against the tile. A string of bloody drool trailed from his lip as he was lifted from the ground and hauled to prison.

*

WILLIAM LAY SUFFOCATING in the dank, musty smell of the man pressed up against him. The odor mingled with the reek of his own soiled body. He smelled his sweat mingling with the other man's and his sickly breath, he could hear him breathing in his ear.

On the other side of him, a second prisoner snored, his mouth open, his teeth black. His elbow kept falling against William's temple. William turned his head. There was no getting away from others. Beyond the two men next to him prisoners lay in sweat-soaked shirts and undershirts, amidst shoes and flip-flops and stained cardboard, crowded so tightly that their limbs tangled. Desolation and shock and exhaustion on their faces. A man leaned against the barred gate at the front, sweat flowing off him so quickly it was as though his entire body were weeping. Another slept with his head on his neighbor's shoulder. In one corner someone had been beaten so badly he lay moaning, bleeding from his ear. A teenager with knees pulled up and face hidden sat still as a statue in the middle of the room.

The floor was slick with substances. To one side stood a bucket full of piss and shit. Stains mushroomed along the walls. Etched drawings of stick men and guns and phalluses and cattle. Senseless, misspelled declarations. In places nails protruded from bricks. Plastic bags hung from them, containing prisoners' meager belongings—clothes in shreds, one or two cigarettes bribed from a guard, plastic bottles with trickles of water saved from the day before. The only light filtered in through the one small window above William and the barred gate at the front, which looked out onto the prison yard.

He spent twenty-three hours of each day in this cell, his muscles wasting away with hunger. Always having to gather his body against a shoulder digging into his spine, a foot in his cheek, or a torso taking up the little space he managed to press himself into. Twice a day, a guard pushed buckets of beans into the cell. They scrambled to the food and slurped up what they could with their fingers. Water was handed out only morning and night, at a different time from the meals, so that he had to wait to quench his parched throat.

Sometimes hours went by with little movement, the room as still as a mass grave. Then suddenly two men might pounce on each other—a fight for space. There was no escaping the blows then. Inmates fell on top of one another and the latrine toppled and guards came running.

At other times the prisoners shared their tragedies. The young man who'd joined the rebels to raise a bride wealth, only to be caught up in an ambush. The old man arrested for refusing to disclose his sons' whereabouts. The Nilot boys rounded up from the streets. They cared for the injured and sick among them, doing what little they could with rags and drops of water. They made space for one another or offered their shoulders and laps as cushioning from the soiled floor.

For an hour each morning they were allowed to walk around the prison yard bordered on the far side by a fence, beyond which were the barracks. Sometimes soldiers threw bread morsels through the bars, watching prisoners scramble for them like animals. They laughed and pointed, cheered when a fight broke out.

In the prison yard concrete blocks stood at intervals. Prisoners were shackled to them for hours, sometimes days. Some were chained because they were violent or disorderly. Some were deranged—men who talked to themselves or cackled at invisible presences. Others who smeared their faces with dirt. One who dug his nails into his cheeks, opening up wounds again and again, so that his face was covered in red, festering welts.

William didn't know if these men had arrived mad, or whether prison had unhinged them or war had. They terrified him more than the prison bars, more than the guards who beat their charges or the threat of hunger and thirst. They were an image of the collapse he needed to keep at bay. By the end of his first week he felt unbalanced. He counted days, afraid to lose track of time. He'd been inside for three weeks. He didn't know how long he'd be held for, whether he'd ever be released. He couldn't predict what the soldiers might do to him. He feared that Layla, Dena, and Alex might never find him. He found himself crying. He wept into his arm, trying to hide his sobs. His neighbors were too sunk in their own miseries to notice or care. He mourned for himself, for his dead father and his mother and sisters whom he might never see again. He wept for Layla. He missed the compound—he missed Mustafa and Alex and Dena.

At other times he lay motionless, his limbs numb, his mind empty, his heart dead and heavy as stone. Nothing mattered. He didn't care if the next meal came or not, if the soldiers took him out and shot him. What did it matter? He had no energy to think forward or backward. Those he loved came to him distantly—they would carry on with their lives, things would go on without him.

More and more, during the long days in the cell, he thought of the corpse. He found himself brooding over it in the small hours of the night, when he was woken by fitful sleepers, and in the middle of the day, when the heat was so unbearable he became delirious. Again he saw the rigid limbs, the burnt lips drawn back in a mute scream, the hollow sockets of the nose, the sac of intestines spilling out beneath the rib cage, and the horror came back to him.

At times he wondered whether he hadn't dreamt up the corpse. No one had ever come forward with information. The authorities never revealed what they knew. The body was forgotten, as if it had never existed. There had been more bodies in the villages and in the plains since. His only confirmation that the corpse was not a dream was that Alex, Dena, and Mustafa had witnessed it too.

Had he missed the signs? Why hadn't they packed up and left as soon as news reached them of the village raids? Even as soon as the corpse appeared? Had he been careless in looking after the others?

But Alex had been the only one anxious to go. Dena was too

stubborn. As for himself, he couldn't have left Layla or Mustafa behind. His thoughts circled until smells and sights intruded on him. A man's open wound, the unwelcome intimacy of a neighbor's knee in his groin. The sounds alone were enough to drive him mad. At night, moans of injured and sick men. Each afternoon and evening, someone begging for mercy during a beating.

And he was in pain. For three days now, just as the sun slanted through the one window, soldiers came to take him out. "For a walk," they said. A short march to the prison yard. There they struck his face, dug their boots into his torso, stepped on his arms as he tried to cover his head. They called him scum, slave, heathen.

And then there was the interrogation room. Here they wore him down with questions. Hour upon hour, one soldier after another. From whom did he pick up the weapons? Who did he deliver them to? How long for. Who was his contact among the rebels? Who was his contact in Saraaya? He told them he didn't know. They didn't believe him, and so they kept him in the room through mealtimes and refused to give him water.

He turned on his side and stared beyond his neighbor to the wall. There was no escaping the war if you were a Nilot. He was surrounded by men who'd risked themselves for the rebels. Like any Nilot he supported their cause. But he'd also taken his mother's lesson to heart. War only destroyed—it took his father's life. The thing to do was to survive it. And so he'd provided for his family as best he could, made as much of the scant opportunities that came his way.

Had it been selfish to think only of himself, of his own survival? He wondered what his father would make of him, his father who had given everything, not only for his children but also for his people.

He held on to the thought of Layla, still there on the other side. She'd said yes. They'd be married—if only he managed to get out. Looking back, he regretted his shyness. How often had he stopped himself from touching her, or held his tongue when he'd wanted to tell her that she was beautiful? Why did he wait so long to ask her to marry him?

He'd wanted to give her space to make up her own mind, but at last the war had forced things. It was the memory of their kiss in the kitchen that kept him going. Nothing had prepared him for her lips, the warmth of her cheek against his, her fingers on his face.

He closed his eyes, wanting to escape the sounds, the men, the suffocation, and thought of Mustafa. He was like a son, the person closest to him, after Layla. William relied on him more than anyone. It was why Mustafa's deceit was a shock. Sometimes, thinking of it, William was so angry he regretted not handing him over to the soldiers. But when the rage passed, he saw that he could never give him up. The habit of protecting him was too strong.

He opened his eyes. The injured prisoner was now sleeping. An old man leaned against the cell bars, dazed. He wanted to stretch his legs, but someone had already spread themselves out in the space by his feet.

It was the getting out that was the thing. It was what gave him hope—the thought that he and Layla would be married, would leave Saraaya and start again somewhere new together. They might try Khartoum again. Alex had promised to help him get a job there with the organization. They would live in a house with a mango tree in the yard. They would have two boys and two girls, who would be tall like him and beautiful like her. They would speak Nilotic and Arabic and English, would go to university and do things neither he nor Layla dreamed of.

He came to himself when he heard voices. A guard stood in the frame, holding someone by the arm. There was a stir as men moved or woke up or lifted themselves to see. A new prisoner. A ripple of curiosity went through the cell.

Someone said, "It's a boy."

Through the throng of bodies, he saw someone small squirming in the guard's grip. He recognized the slithery movement, discerned the willful limbs. Mustafa, barefoot, his mouth bloody, his face covered in dirt, his features wrinkling at the foul smell in the cell.

William blinked, unable to believe his eyes. He rose. The movement caught Mustafa's attention. When he saw William, his features opened up—his mouth a red circle and his eyes huge. He jerked free and tumbled over prisoners' legs and arms and collapsed in front of William, who was up on his knees now. Mustafa panted, a bloody grin on his face.

"What on earth are you doing here?" William asked in amazement, staring at the agitated face, which, after so much time, or because of its bruises, seemed different, with its eyes aglow and cuts along his cheek, and a missing tooth.

"I confeshed," Mustafa lisped. "I told them I was the one who smuggled the guns."

An upheaval in William's chest. He didn't know whether to embrace or hit Mustafa.

"Are you out of your mind?" He felt feverish with hunger and thirst and emotion.

"I told them to let you go," said Mustafa. "But they won't." He buried his head in William's shoulder. "I'm sorry." He was crying, and William held him, the boy's small bones quivering in his own big arms.

∫

LAYLA, DENA, AND ALEX sat around the kitchen table, the satellite phone between them.

"Will they call soon?" Layla asked.

Dena translated the question to Alex.

"They said around two maybe," he said.

He'd just hung up with the secretary in Khartoum. They had spent the morning waiting for a call from the office there. Layla was at her wits' end. For three weeks now she'd been going to the garrison. She was refused admission—the guards wouldn't even confirm whether William was being held there. She argued with them, but two days ago, one of them had threatened to hit her.

She still went every day, taking refuge with the hawkers who sold snacks and water near the road. The thought that she was close to William, that only a few hundred meters separated them, comforted her.

Today she didn't go only because they were waiting for news from Khartoum. Alex had informed the office that the compound had been raided, that weapons had been discovered, and William arrested. The organization was in contact with the Ministry of Interior, trying to exert pressure to have William released. The rebels and the government were signing an agreement in Kenya—it was expected any day. But the agreement wasn't official yet. Rumors and counter-rumors flew. In Saraaya, people ran down the street hollering that a deal had been signed, only to be contradicted five minutes later by others who declared the negotiations had fallen apart.

But today there was something to look forward to. Alex's boss had managed to get a meeting at the ministry. He'd promised to call afterward, and so they were waiting.

Dena scraped her chair back. "Tea?"

Layla shook her head. Alex nodded.

Dena was almost back to normal—except that she was still afraid to leave the compound. Alex, too, was recovering well. The color had returned to his face. He'd removed the head dressing and was walking, though with a limp. She and Dena were surprised to learn that he planned to finish his map report. Hadn't all his maps, his documents, been damaged?

"Yes and no," he said mysteriously.

He was even well enough now to help Dena with putting the compound back in order. It was good to find a bit more of the yard cleared up when she came home after a long day of searching for William. Once, returning late from the barracks, she walked in on the two of them sitting on the hammock, shoulders touching, the camera in Dena's lap. They were looking at footage together. Light from the viewfinder cast a glow on their faces. That picture of companionship made her pity herself. She missed William terribly.

⸘

AN HOUR SINCE Alex's last call. They waited. The teapot sat empty on the table.

"Call again," said Dena. "Before the office closes."

Alex dialed. "Hi, Alex McClure again. Yeah. Greg back yet?" Silence. "OK. We're waiting. Thanks." He hung up and shook his head.

A few moments of silence passed.

"Any news from Mustafa?" asked Alex.

Layla knew that Alex was concerned, had been asking after Mustafa. She shook her head no—she hadn't seen him since the day he'd surprised her on the road.

"Don't you think we should try to find him? He's learned his lesson. Keeping him out isn't doing anyone any good."

"Drop it, Alex," Dena said. "William threw him out and Layla doesn't want him back. So let's leave it at that, OK?"

Layla caught the gist of their words, though Dena didn't translate. Mindful of Layla's feelings, Dena was careful not to express strong opinions when it came to Mustafa. But Layla sensed that Dena, like Alex, wanted him back. It made Layla wonder whether she was being too harsh. Maybe they were right. Maybe Mustafa had been punished enough and there was no point in keeping him out—it wouldn't change anything for William. But she didn't trust herself. If Mustafa were in her presence, she might box his ears. She'd barely been able to restrain herself when he'd fallen out of the tree that day, running to hug her, as though what he'd done could be forgiven so easily.

"I don't want him here," said Layla.

Dena turned to Alex. "Did you understand?"

Alex sighed, staring at the two of them with a look that said they were making a mistake.

⸏

THEY WAITED. Shadows grew long on the kitchen floor. Alex went to the office to work. Dena and Layla sat with the phone between them. Layla leaned back, hands folded in her lap, eyes on the satellite phone.

Dena glanced at her watch.

"Four." She sighed. They'd been waiting for the call since ten in the morning.

Dena rose, went to the stove, came back, and poured herself a cup of tea.

They both jumped when the phone rang, its screen flickering green. Tea spilled onto Dena's hand. Layla snatched up the phone. She didn't know which button to press and shoved it at Dena, who pressed something and then Layla put the device to her ear.

"Hello? What news? Is William being let go?"

Only when she found herself unable to understand the words on the other end did she remember that this was Alex's boss, who didn't speak Arabic. Still gripping the phone, she ran into the yard, followed by Dena. Alex stepped out of the office and reached for the phone.

"Alex speaking."

She could make out the sound of the voice on the other end. Dena was now beside her. They both crowded in, listening. She tried to read Alex's face. He kept saying "umm-hmm." Every once in a while he asked a one-word question—"When?" "Where?"—which she understood, and other, longer words which she didn't, and then she looked to Dena, but Dena was engrossed in listening and didn't translate.

When he hung up she grabbed his arm and Dena pulled at his T-shirt.

"So?"

His eyes crinkled and his lips parted, and his teeth showed in a grin.

"The agreement's been signed in Kenya." Dena translated as he spoke. "They're exchanging prisoners. The ministry's spoken to the authorities here. They're letting William go. We can pick him up in a couple of hours."

Layla shouted and Dena laughed and Alex bounced up and down, and then the three of them were embroiled in a hug.

Then over their own shouts they heard shouts from the road. They went to the gate and saw people opening their doors. The news was out. The rebels and government had signed an agreement. The word "Machakos" was on everyone's lips. Only a first step, but it meant hope. The cease-fire would hold, maybe permanently.

They decided to drive to the garrison immediately, before the streets got crowded, to wait for William. But when Dena told Alex to get the truck keys he stopped.

"I can't drive. My leg."

They'd forgotten about his injury. And Dena didn't know how to drive.

They stared at one another.

"I can drive," said Layla.

"You can?" said Dena.

"Yes, I can. William taught me. Where's the key? Alex?"

Alex and Dena were dubious, but there was no stopping her, and so Alex went to get the keys.

The truck was parked where it always was—by the gate. Dena sat beside her, and Alex took the backseat. It had been weeks and weeks since she'd last practiced with William. They'd stopped the lessons with the start of the fighting.

She did all she'd learned to do—adjusted her seat, the side-view and rearview mirrors, and turned on the ignition. She was so focused on clutch and gear that she forgot to put the gear stick in reverse. When the car moved, it lurched forward almost into the compound wall. Dena buckled her seat belt and Alex looked at her anxiously.

Another mistake and they might bolt from the car. This time she was careful—she asked Alex to check behind her before revers-ing. She managed to maneuver the car onto the road. It bumped forward, going too far to the right. Alex and Dena watched in tense silence. Her palms were already sweaty, the muscles of her calves tight.

After being cooped up in their compounds for weeks, people were flooding out onto the streets. The town, which had seemed so empty except for soldiers and militiamen, was suddenly full of dancing women and laughing men and children and honking cars and cattle and dogs and goats noising their approval. She tried to focus on the road. Behind her, someone honked in exasperation. In front of her, a donkey cart came to a halt and she screeched to a stop just in time.

But even as she concentrated on the road, the festive atmos-phere flooded in. Music blasted from cars. Displaced villagers came out from their tents to celebrate with the rest. Men with guns let people stream through barricades. Three girls led a beautiful, long-lashed bull with carved horns through an alleyway. People banged on the hood of the car and reached their arms in through the windows. Boys leapt up onto the bed of the truck and made a stage of it, dancing and jumping. Layla nearly crashed more than once, while Alex and Dena panicked and laughed by turns.

The destroyed stalls and burnt shops seemed like the aftermath of a lively town party. Only the militiamen watched sulkily. The agreement meant an end to their looting—and they couldn't be happy about that. But even they were powerless in the face of the decree that had come from Khartoum.

They made it out of town and entered the highway that crossed the plains. Now that she'd driven through the crowds, this stretch of the road felt easy. She pressed on the gas. Only when she found William safe, only when she had him back beside her, only then would she dance and sing and join in the jubilant scenes around her.

VII

IT WAS JUST AFTER THE ASR PRAYER. LATE-AFTERNOON light washed over the brick walls of the mosque, reflecting against its arched windows, sweeping over its green dome and the finger of the minaret gesturing to the sky. By the gate, William followed the comings and goings around him. Worshippers walked out of the archway; a little boy scampered by; a mother ushering her children along sang with them; young women coming from the market laughed together. Others stood in groups, exchanging pleasantries and farewells.

Under the cease-fire, and with news of the agreement, there was a special pleasure in greeting one another, in gathering, in ambling through the streets. He felt it too. After prison, it was a gift to linger or move as he pleased, to soak up these daily scenes.

Sixteen days ago, when a guard unlocked the cell door and announced that he was being released, he'd thought a trick was being played. The guard called his name twice, and still he didn't move. Only when the other inmates congratulated him and ushered him to rise did it sink in. In his happiness, he got up and rushed to the door, and then suddenly remembered. He stopped and looked back to see Mustafa resting against the wall, staring at him. For two weeks Mustafa had slept beside him, shared his water with him, kept him company in the prison yard.

William told the guard he wasn't leaving without the boy. The guard answered that the order was only for his release. But William refused, and so the guard left and locked the gate behind him.

When he went back to his seat, Mustafa curled up against his side.

"We'll get out," William said.

It happened sooner than expected. Three hours later the guard came back and told them both to follow him. The prisoners shouted blessings and congratulations, told them to hurry up before they squandered their chance again.

They collected their things—a plastic bottle, some rags that Mustafa used for a pillow—things for which they had no use but which they took along anyway. He held Mustafa's hand as they crossed the prison yard, his eyes passing over the men in chains. He didn't trust the soldiers. A fear gripped him that they might be walking into a trap—a place worse than this one. He was tense even as the guard unlocked the fence and led them past the barracks. Mustafa clutched his hand. The closer they got to the main gate, the more fearful William grew—at any moment their hope might be dashed.

But they arrived at the gate without incident and the guard pointed them out. He and Mustafa took a few tentative steps, looking over their shoulders, then passed through to the other side, where they saw soldiers drilling in the plain.

He stood blinking in the clearing. After five weeks in prison it was strange to be surrounded by so much space. The sky was a vast blue slate, and the earth was endless. He didn't know which direction to walk in. And then he saw Alex limping toward them and Dena beside him and, waving wildly at him, Layla, her thoub flying and the wind lifting up dust at her feet.

Mustafa let go of his hand and flung himself at Alex and Dena. William sprang into a trot. Immediately he had to stop—his legs were rusty, painful. He was light-headed with hunger and thirst. He walked, keeping his eyes on Layla, who was slower than the others, hindered by her thoub. He was suddenly aware of what a mess he was, in clothes he hadn't changed in weeks. But the sight of her drove him on. She was breathless with laughter; as he drew closer, he saw that she was crying as well as laughing, sunlight glinting against her wet cheeks.

Finally, he was face-to-face with her. He checked the urge to reach for her—impossible out in the open, with the soldiers. And he feared that he was quite disgusting. They had to settle for a show of formal greetings—How are you? It's good to see you—until Alex winded William with a hug, and Dena reached for him.

In happy chaos, talking over one another, asking a thousand questions, they made their way to the parked truck. William learned that peace negotiations were in motion; a cease-fire had been in place since late June; something called a Machakos Protocol had been signed in Kenya; a prisoner exchange had been agreed; the office in Khartoum had lobbied for his release. In prison he had existed in timelessness, no news filtering in from the outside world, and it seemed a miracle now that so much had happened while he was inside.

When they got to the truck, he was amazed to see Layla take the driver's seat. Yes, she had driven all the way from the compound, she said, and she would drive them all the way back. Alex and Dena and Mustafa bundled into the backseat. He took the passenger seat and was terribly happy and proud, looking at her in wonder as she started the car.

On the way back, he saw that the landscape was changed—there had been more rain during his time in prison. The air was rich with moisture and fresh grass had sprouted. The soil had taken on a dark tinge. In the villages he saw women and men hoeing and digging, yoked oxen plowing furrows. Acacias were covered in blue-green leaves. It felt as though the land were celebrating his release, had put on ornaments of grass and foliage, adorned itself with sun-speckled pools of water.

That evening, he and Layla decided that he would go to her family and officially seek permission for her hand. Peace or no peace, they needed to be married as soon as possible. But they had to convince her father first.

ſ

HE'D WAITED only long enough for his bruises to heal to visit Layla's father. Though he'd often driven her home in the truck after work, when they'd steal half an hour or an hour so she could practice driving, she'd always insisted that he drop her off outside the village, so she could walk the final stretch.

Upon arrival he was met by a collection of unsmiling male relatives—a stern-faced father in a tattered sirwal, a potbellied uncle, and Layla's two brothers. Layla's mother and the uncle's wife, along with Layla, remained on the other side of the homestead tents. Two dogs lolled under the shade of a thorn bush, one of them with her teats suckled dry, though there were no pups in sight.

He had been self-conscious, aware that his appearance signaled the gulf between him and the men who sat across from him in their threadbare jellabiyas and sirwals and their bandaged-together flip-flops, drinking water out of tin cans instead of cups. For Layla's family was poor, poorer even than he'd imagined. The homestead was made up of a handful of tattered tents. There was a metal bed and some old chairs: he sat on one, the father, uncle, and brothers sat opposite him. There was one room made out of brush and leaves. The camp was enclosed with a fence of branches.

When he made the proposal, the men exchanged meaningful looks with one another.

After a pause the father asked, "You say you work for these white people, as a translator?"

"Yes."

The uncle appraised William. The brothers hadn't said a word since greeting him.

"You'll be able to take care of Layla?"

"I wouldn't be asking to marry her if not. I care about Layla. I'm coming to you because as you know there's been a lot of trouble in the district these past months. It's quiet now with the cease-fire. I don't want to lose the chance. I'd like us to be married so I can look after her."

The father asked him more questions then. How long William had worked for the organization, how much he earned. His gaze lingered on William's watch, the leather shoes. William made it clear that he was well-off. He even exaggerated a little, knowing that the family's poverty gave him an advantage. They might look down on him because he was a Nilot, but they could use him all the same. And indeed, there was a change in the men's attitude over the course of the conversation. When he mentioned how much he earned, the uncle looked at the father. Some calculation, some message passed between them. They invited him to share a meal with them.

Over the meal they exchanged news about the cease-fire. Layla's father told him about losing their cattle the year before. William listened attentively, expressed sympathy.

It was after the meal, over another tea, that they returned to the marriage. It was almost evening. Layla came to clear away a tray and smiled at him fleetingly. It gave him courage. It occurred to him that during his visit she had barely said a word—negotiations over her fate were reserved to men.

"I'm willing to consider your offer," her father began, "though you're not one of us. But it's also true that our people and your people aren't strangers. The most important thing is that you're a man who has your affairs in order. She wants you," he said. "So I'm ready to give you my blessing."

Her father wanted one hundred head of cattle for a bride

wealth—a fortune. The usual amount was around fifty, at most, if the groom was rich. But this was the calculation that the father and the uncle had made: that William could afford it.

"Fine," he agreed.

A round of hand-shaking and back patting and then Layla herself was there, congratulated by her mother, her father, the uncle, her brothers.

He was marveling over how smoothly everything was going when, in the midst of the congratulations, her father said, "There's one more thing. Before the marriage can take place, you must visit the mosque."

"The mosque?"

"To become a Muslim."

William stared, started to speak, and then stopped. He should have known. Nomad women were sometimes allowed to marry strangers, but never outside their faith.

Layla sensed his unease. The next day, when they met alone, she was full of remorse, saying that they should call it off, that she didn't want him to go to the mosque, that he was already giving up so much—a fortune of a bride wealth—it was too much to give more. But Layla's father was adamant that if William didn't become a Muslim the engagement was off.

And so now he was here, at the mosque, wondering what his schoolteachers, the Catholic priests, would think of him becoming a Muslim. Most of all, he dreaded his mother. He hadn't yet told her that he was converting. He wondered about himself— was he going too far? He told himself it was a formality, but there was a lingering doubt, a feeling that he might be betraying himself. Though sometimes he thought that his only true religion was his father's—the Nilot religion his parents practiced before the war took his father's life, and which he grasped only vaguely. The war had erased everything. He wasn't certain what he believed, if he believed in anything. He was only sure he wanted Layla.

Fewer and fewer people came out of the mosque. A herds-man passing by chastised a wayward cow. Merchants across the street closed up their shops for the day. He heard laughter, and again became conscious of the happy, hopeful mood envelop-ing the town, in spite of the still heavy presence of soldiers and militiamen.

Finally, he turned to the gate. He passed a group of men standing in the archway and crossed a small courtyard to the main prayer hall. He took off his shoes and stepped into the large, sparse room. Windows lined the walls. The floor was covered in a worn green carpet, bulbs dangled from long cords extend-ing down from the high-domed ceiling. Along the far side of the room a row of taps overhung a concrete basin. A handful of wor-shippers sat on prayer rugs with heads bent, palms upward on their knees,

William spotted the imam rolling away his prayer rug near the windows. He was a small, kind-eyed, gray-haired man. He knew William, as he knew everyone in the town, and when he saw him, he greeted him warmly. He was a Sufi, and friendly with Nilotes, which made the authorities suspicious of him.

As with every conversation in Saraaya these days, their talk turned to the good news of the agreement. William announced that he'd come to convert. In the midst of picking up his prayer rug, the imam stopped, looked at him. William explained that he was getting married.

"A nomad woman?"

"Yes."

The wish to convert, the imam said, had to be sincere. Was he doing it for the bride's family, or from his heart? William told the truth—he simply wanted to get married; the bride's family was insisting.

"And you love this woman? Truly and sincerely?"

"Yes. With all my heart."

He was afraid the imam might turn him away, but after a moment of thought he said, "How can I refuse young lovers? My own grandmother was a Nilot, my grandfather a nomad. They married over everyone's objections. Come this way."

He led William to the middle of the hall and motioned for him to sit opposite. Soon William was repeating words—no god but God, Muhammad his prophet—speaking the script three times, the phrases strange in his mouth.

It was done—he felt no different. It was all for Layla. Just a few words uttered. A loss but also a new beginning. They would be married; they'd begin a new life.

The imam led him to the taps and demonstrated the ablutions. William reached his hands under the faucet, washing between the fingers, up to and around the wrists. He splashed warm water against his face. He rolled up his shirtsleeves, soaked his arms, ducked his head and ran his palms over his hair and neck, drops dripping from his ears and chin.

They came to the prayer. He stood behind the imam and followed his motions, touching his head to the ground as the imam recited verses. When he felt the imam rise to a sitting position, he rose too, his limbs unfurling as he knelt and sat and bent his head, a last flush of light coming in through the window and falling on the embroidered filament of the prayer rug.

His muscles loosened. He relaxed on his folded legs, sensed the ceiling soaring above. Through the tall windows, muted light warmed his hands and neck. He was not giving himself up. He was opening himself to more. He was a Nilot, and a Catholic. Now also a Muslim. There was room in him for many things. For everything. He was flooded by a sense of his own largeness, his own possibility. He breathed faintly, feeling the soft weight of his palms on his knees, everything but the warm glow of light and the imam's voice fading away.

ſ

"MUSTAFA, COME HERE," Dena called.

She watched as he climbed down from a ladder by the gate, decorations draped over his shoulder. He and William were busy with wedding preparations. The yard had become a construction site, workmen coming and going through the door, planks of wood and fabric strewn everywhere. Two hundred chairs were stacked against the kitchen wall. A giant tent supported by metal poles covered the clearing. A dais for the bride and groom had been built under the gazebo, on which sat two wooden chairs decorated with plastic flowers.

Layla was staying with her family, in seclusion for another week until the wedding day. A few days ago, William's mother and sisters had arrived from Juba. The mother was a tiny, sharp-tongued woman with a mane of white hair. She was unhappy about her son's choice of a nomad bride. When she found out, on top of it, that he'd become a Muslim to appease the bride's family, there were scenes of devastation. She wept and prayed and followed William brandishing a cross, while William's three sisters tried to hold her back. She alternated between weeping inconsolably and parading through the compound giving imperious orders to the workmen, often contradicting William's own. William had finally persuaded her to move to a neighboring compound, where she was now being looked after by his sisters. This left William and Mustafa to arrange things. Mustafa was up early every morning painting a chair or sorting lights or hammering a tent peg. He scolded sloppy workmen. He was terribly excited about the wedding, but he wasn't the only one—the whole town was looking forward to it. People were in the mood to celebrate the agreement, to enjoy the cease-fire, and the wedding was the occasion. A mixed marriage between a Nilot and a nomad, as though fate had decreed that the cease-fire was to be capped by a union across a divide that had seemed impossible to bridge only weeks before.

Dena, too, was venturing out more. It had taken courage to go to the garrison to welcome William out of prison three weeks ago. But that day, when she saw him step out holding Mustafa's hand, she forgot her fears and went running with Layla and Alex. She'd missed them so much that she hugged William right there in front of the soldiers and took Mustafa—whom none of them were expecting to see—in her arms.

On the way back to the compound, Mustafa jabbered on about prison. William made light of it, but she could see by his swollen face and his limp that he'd been roughed up badly. He was gaunt, his clothes hanging off him, his cheekbones sunken. Still, his eyes shone. In the passenger seat beside Layla he grinned from ear to ear, occasionally reaching to touch Layla's hand. Layla laughed as she drove. She and Alex asked questions, William and Mustafa answered in a jumble of Arabic and English. It had felt good to be together again.

She took courage from William. In spite of prison, he wasn't afraid of soldiers, or militiamen, or security men. They were still out on the streets. But when she walked with him through town, she reminded herself that there was a cease-fire. An agreement had been signed. Even if militias wanted to disrupt the peace—it was common knowledge that they resented the agreement—no one else was in a mood to fight. Now that people had gotten a taste of tranquility, they wanted more of it.

One afternoon, Dena, Layla, and Alex sat listening to William talk about prison. His eyes clouded and his voice dipped as he spoke. He told them about the stench in the cell, how he was always on the brink of retching. He told them about the chained men who made animal sounds. The beatings, the hunger, the filth and the dirt, and the despair. Worst of all, the uncertainty. He'd been so happy to be free again that it had taken time for the horror of it all to sink in.

When he went quiet, Dena found herself speaking about the day of the raid. Alex knew the story, but she'd never told William and Layla. As she spoke she looked down at the tablecloth, tracing her hand along a pattern of sunflowers. Soldiers saw her filming and dragged her into her room, she said. There were two of them. She tried to fight them. They took her camera. They took her clothes off. They touched her. They filmed her.

Impossible to convey what it had felt like. She wondered how the women in the villages survived it, those with children, without money or shelter—much worse happened to them. She was weaker than she imagined herself to be. Really she was lucky. Unlike most people she could leave Saraaya, she could leave the country anytime she wanted.

When she looked up, she saw by their faces that they understood. Something in Layla's eyes made tears well up in hers. It was a relief to share it with them, and in the days following she felt lighter, less afraid. She began going out more often, though without the camera, and always with William.

In town, people often stopped them to congratulate William on the engagement. Tea ladies, herdsmen, merchants—all recalled a kind word, a favor of his. Children remembered his jokes and little gifts. The villagers who had sheltered at the compound had a special place in their heart for him.

Invited or not, everyone planned to attend the wedding, and they had fantastic expectations. Rumors that there would be as many as four hundred wedding guests spread like wildfire. The menu was discussed and embellished—roasted sheep, cakes as high as hills, stuffed pastries, nuts and dates stewed in honey. People gasped at the bride wealth given for Layla—a whole one hundred head of cattle. A wedding worthy of a big city. Unlike anything anyone had seen in these parts for years.

She'd promised William she'd film the wedding, but she'd been thinking what to do with the camera after the night. She was done shooting Alex. And she wanted to give the device away.

Now, having climbed down from his ladder, Mustafa went up to her.

"Here." She held out the camera. "I want you to have this."

He stared at it, then at her. "You're giving it away?"

"Yes. To you."

"How come?"

"I'm done with it. I promised William and Layla I'd film the wedding, so I'll have to borrow it for that night. Otherwise, it's yours. You can sell it even, if you want."

"You won't make films anymore?"

"I will make films, just not with this camera. This one . . . well, I don't want it."

He reached for it tentatively, as if expecting her to change her mind. It weighed him down, and he struggled to turn it one way, and then another.

"I won't sell it," he said. His face lighted. "Can I film you?"

Before she could object, he pulled her toward the gazebo and positioned her in front of the ridge pole. He struggled to haul the camera onto his shoulder, pitching it over like a sack of coal. It was so large on his small body that he looked like a giant-headed insect.

He told her to sit down on a chair and came closer, the camera teetering and wobbling.

"Hold it steady."

"It's heavy."

"Then stand in place and zoom in. The buttons on the top."

He planted his feet apart to steady himself, found the zoom, and disappeared again behind the lens. He giggled. "Your teeth are big."

"That's it," she said. "Now try following me."

She got up and walked toward the kitchen. He was slow in catching up, the giant eye trundling upward so late that he lost her.

He jogged after her, but the camera seesawed on his shoulder and he stopped, frustrated. She walked a little slower, and he followed her as she passed by the gazebo and the storage room. Amused workmen put down their tools to watch.

At the office, she knocked. Alex called them in. He'd been cooped up for days finishing his report. Papers were piled in front of him. Maps were pinned to the window shutters and taped to the walls, many of them torn, blotted, or covered in children's scribbles. He still hadn't told Dena how he planned to finish the report, given that much of his documentation had been damaged or destroyed.

He turned in his chair to face them.

Mustafa rushed into the room, almost crashing the device again, and Alex reached to stop it from tumbling.

"Dena gave it to me!"

Alex looked at her. "Really?"

She nodded. "He's filming me. For practice. Why've you stopped?"

Mustafa leapt to work. He made her stand beside Alex, in front of the filing cabinet. He came closer, then moved back, then adjusted the zoom; he went out and got the tripod and set it up. He made them pose—Dena behind Alex, both standing together, Dena seated and Alex standing. Alex draped maps over his head and made silly faces, and Dena laughed, and Mustafa pretended to be annoyed.

She could see that in an hour his grip on the camera had improved, as had his balance. He would be very good at this, she could tell.

∫

SINCE PRISON, everyone was being nice to Mustafa. In the days after his release, Layla had hugged him often and fed him until he was stuffed to bursting. She felt bad about their meeting under the tree, when she'd pushed him away, and made up for it by spoiling him. Alex invited him into the office to show him maps. And now Dena had given him her camera. The two of them were back under the gazebo; they'd left Alex to work. William was visiting Layla's family at the homestead.

He and William were back to their old friendship, but still Mustafa was eager to prove himself. With only a week until the wedding, he threw himself into the preparations, going with William or on his own to chase down cooks and musicians, to distribute wedding invitations, to find tablecloths, or to put up decorations.

The only dark spot was his mother and siblings. The week before, he and William drove to his village. They found his mother's house occupied by a strange family. Mustafa shooed off children playing in the yard while William spoke to their parents. They came from a village a day's walk away. Militias had destroyed their home there. Passing through this village they had found this house intact but empty. They took shelter, planning to stay only a little while, but when no one came they decided to remain. William convinced Mustafa to let them stay until his mother returned—this way the place would be looked after.

The only person who'd seen Mustafa's mother was a neighbor two houses down. She told them that his mother had fled in May, when the fighting was heaviest. One morning she saw her and the children heading in the direction of Saraaya, along with other families. She couldn't say what had happened to them after that; she herself had fled the village the next day and returned only with the cease-fire.

On the drive back to Saraaya, Mustafa stared glumly through the windshield. William told him that his mother would turn up.

And in the meantime he'd arrange for Mustafa to come with him and Layla to Khartoum—they were planning to go there after the wedding. This lifted Mustafa's mood, but then he wondered if it was right to leave his mother and brother and sister behind. What if he never saw them again? He frowned at the road to stop himself from crying.

He distracted himself by diving into the wedding preparations. He grew frustrated with William, who—considering that this was his own wedding—was careless with important details—whether the tablecloths should be blue or white, whether the plastic roses decorating the bride and groom's dais should be gold or red, whether the cooks should set up their coal stoves by the kitchen or behind the storage room.

"Any which way is fine," William said, and Mustafa clutched his head. He took it upon himself to look after the details, leaving bigger problems to William—arranging the meeting between his mother and sisters and Layla's family, or notifying the security police about the wedding, just to be sure that the celebration proceeded smoothly.

And so he worried over plastic roses and gold paint and tablecloths. He looked forward to Khartoum. He'd see the huge markets William told him about and the Nile and the Presidential Palace and the buildings that were ten and twenty stories high. William promised to put him in school there. There was no reason to feel bad about leaving. Once he finished school, he'd come back for his mother and brother and sister and bring them to the big city.

And now he had this camera. He thought about all the things he could do with it. He might film his journey to Khartoum, he might film the market, he might film his new school. Maybe he'd grow up to be a filmmaker, like Dena.

What he loved about the camera was that you could put in or leave out what you wanted. You could make Dena small by zooming out and moving back—which he did now—and then Dena was just a speck amidst the tents and the poles and the wedding decorations. Then what was around her became more important. He liked seeing all the things around her, the chaos of the compound, a happy chaos, the chaos of the forthcoming celebration.

Dena smiled, her eyes crinkling in the frame.

"You're a pro," she said in English.

He looked at her quizzically.

"Professional." And then in Arabic, "Means you know what you're doing."

"Pro-fes-sion-al." He snapped closed the camera display with a flourish.

ſ

SEVEN P.M. and Alex still sat in the office, working. It was growing dark. Bugs flitted in and out of the window, drawn to the lamplight on his desk. Outside, cooks were setting up their stoves. Above the din of the generator, he heard Mustafa scolding someone and William pleading with his mother in Nilotic.

The wedding was tomorrow. A pickup truck had arrived earlier to deliver more tables and chairs. William was very busy, and it was especially hard now he was separated from Layla, who was staying with her family until the wedding day.

Alex helped where he could, accompanying William when he wasn't working on the map report. Since news of the Machakos Protocol, the market was up again, people thronged the streets, and even some who had left town were returning.

William, Layla, and Mustafa were going to Khartoum after the wedding, though William hoped they, too, would eventually go elsewhere. Alex was heading back to the United States. Dena was also going home. She had friends in Boston, she told him. She'd settle there and see where things led—she was thinking about going to film school. And so they were all leaving. The wedding would mark their farewell to Saraaya, and he resolved to finish his map report in time to celebrate.

Now it was done. His back was sore from sitting. The laptop screen gleamed a faint blue as he scrolled to the top, looking over the document one last time.

THREAT AND RISK SURVEYING PROJECT—
SARAAYA, SOUTH KORDOFAN PROVINCE, SUDAN.

FINAL REPORT.
AUGUST 18, 2002

Introduction

The Threat and Risk Surveying Project commenced in the state of South Kordofan, district of Saraaya, in November 2001. The project lasted approximately ten months, including an extension of two months beyond the initial planned project period, due to civil war–related disruptions. It had two main objectives:

a) to update maps of the district, given that outdated maps have been in use by the local authorities, and b) to provide accurate information to better support aid and development projects by supplying a more precise picture of environmental, conflict, and other threat and risk hazards. Key components of the mapping project include: villages, cattle migration routes, water wells, and grazing pastures.

Currently, many maps in use by authorities and other non-governmental entities and humanitarian relief organizations are derived from surveying maps created under the Anglo-Egyptian Condominium Administration (1898–1956), when the 1 million square mile territory was effectively under British control. These maps consolidated colonial boundaries and reflected new administrative states and districts. These external borders, as well as internal state and district lines, have largely survived into the present day, though they are under heated contestation in the civil-war conflict that has been ongoing between North and South Sudan—with only short breaks—since the country's independence in 1956. Recent developments regarding the signing of the Machakos Protocol on July 20 of this year and a possible comprehensive peace agreement are promising.

The topography of the country ranges between desert in the north and tropical climate in the south, and between alternating dry and rainy conditions in regions in between. Dry- and wet-season topography predominates in Saraaya, which falls between the Sahara Desert and the White Nile drainage basin. However, accelerating climate change over the past decades has had dire consequences. Most especially, grazing and agricultural lands have shrunk, and rains have become more irregular, thus leading to livelihood uncertainty for those in the district relying on pastoral activities, those relying entirely on agriculture, and those relying on some combination of both. These changes have rendered existing cartographic representations largely unreliable in capturing the fluidity of the current changing situation. And while new mapping and surveying technology is evolving—most notably, the recent widespread introduction of Global Positioning System (GPS) mapping and other surveying satellite-based tools have been immensely helpful—this technology is still basic and limited in its uses, and reliance on field-site visits and informant interviews was necessary for the collection of accurate information. It is for this reason that the project was overseen and directed by a Field Survey Officer (myself), tasked with conducting site visits and interviews, as well as gathering data and environmental information to assemble a more comprehensive picture of the current state of affairs.

The district of Saraaya was chosen as the basis of the project because of its strategic location between North and South Sudan, its place as a flash point in the civil war between the Southern rebel movement and the Northern government based in Khartoum. It is a resource-rich region, with the primary commodity—oil—of interest both to the government and the rebel movement. In addition, the district—because of its location on the peripheries of the Sudd swamp region—contains rich agricultural soil and grazing pastures, the latter accessed by Northern nomads who move with seasonal rains. During the dry season (December–May), they settle in the district for six months to graze their cattle on local pastures. The district's more sedentary population—Southern Nilotes—undertake both agriculture and pastoralism as livelihood activities. Agricultural activities consist of the farming of staple grains such as maize, millet, and sorghum. Because of shrinking grazing pastures and the loss of herds, nomads are increasingly settling in the district and engaging in agricultural activities as a means to sustain a secure livelihood. This has led to increasing conflict over land distribution and resources.

The situation has deteriorated radically over the past decade and a half, as the civil war has escalated. In response to the threat from the rebel movement based in the South, and because government troops have been spread thin fighting rebel forces, the government resorted to arming and deploying informal militias whose ranks are drawn from nomadic clans that move into the district seasonally. Nomad men have been recruited into militias to attack both Southern rebel forces and Nilot communities suspected of aiding them. This counterinsurgency *strategy serves the interests of the Northern government eager to contain the rebel threat, as well as the interests of nomads suffering from loss of herds and land by allowing them to accumulate war loot of cattle and property.*

As of the writing of this report, an initial agreement—the Machakos Protocol—has been signed, which paves the way for further peace negotiations between the government and the rebel movement. The cease-fire declared in the district of Saraaya on June 19 has held for two months. As stated, these developments are promising. However, things remain in flux, and it is yet to be seen whether peace will hold.

Data and Maps

In accordance with project objectives, maps below provide an overview of current conditions. Clashes related to the civil war disrupted the work and affected some of the information gathered over the course of six months of surveying. This is reflected in the maps presented.

Definitive information is difficult to establish. Firstly, while the project commenced with the assumption that some consensus existed between groups about general boundaries and access to resources, such consensus has been dissipating in recent years, especially under conditions of civil war. Maps vary according to the informant. Furthermore, environmental degradation has led to increasing unpredictability in seasonal patterns. The climate is becoming severely unstable and is in a rapid state of decline. Such change is only likely to accelerate with time. These instabilities are reflected in the following maps, updated by informants (ages 2–12) who sheltered at the NGO compound during a recent wave of attacks. Cartographic revisions provide an overview of current conditions.

Urqud
Abu Deleiq
Burush
El Hilla
Bir
Umm Bel
J. ESH SHAMI
2366
ABU HUMEIRA
2367
Umm Shanga
Damm Gamad
J. KURO
J. EL KABSH
Wad Banda
J. BA'SHO
Daqqaq
Wad Ashqar
Suqa el Gamal
Raj...
Umm Sileia
...nama
Buta
En Nahud
O...ARE HILLS
Wad Gellad
Tom Bishara
J. ABU
Umm Gurraba
Taweisha
Beringil
Rahad et Ta...
Ghabeish
El Odaiya
Muhageria
Ab Sufyan
Dalil
Sharaf
Tabila
Ez Zarga
Wad Nassib
Nugara
Sunta el Zumaqi
Bukhit
Abd ed Daim
Umm Dubban
Sherif Uqeil
Abu Gabra
Muglad
...awa Koo
Abu Matariq
Rahad Kuweis
Bang
Curasa
Kubba el Managu
Umm Didarr
Mereiwin
Ed Daer
Sinun
Gabras
El Burma
Seitaib
Haiyaf
Halluf
Dawas
Safaha
Umbogom...

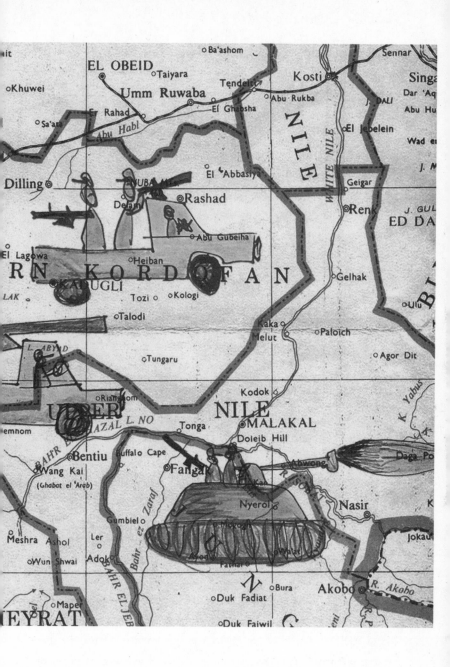

More shrill shouts came from outside. He hesitated over the report again but decided he was satisfied. He saved the file and closed the laptop screen.

He stepped outside. Lights illuminated corners of the yard. Workmen were drawing tents taut. Two women swept carpets. Mustafa was up on the dais painting the bride's and groom's chairs. William led cooks hauling carcasses of sheep toward the kitchen. Dena, along with William's sisters, was setting chairs around tables. William's mother sat by the kitchen giving orders. The compound gate was open; children, neighbors, market women, and the occasional stray cat or goat sauntered in. Visitors lent a hand, or simply looked on at the commotion. The excitement was contagious, and he plunged into the tumult.

∫

IT WAS A COOL EVENING. Wedding tents billowed in the breeze. Lights twinkled along the compound walls, drawing guests to the entrance also sparkling with lights. The shouts of children, the chatter of women, the deep laughter of men mingled with the thrum of the generator keeping the electricity going for the night. In the space cleared by Dena's room, musicians coaxed sounds out of their instruments. The aroma of coal-sizzled meat wafted from the kitchen, where cooks had been preparing the wedding feast since the day before.

Mustafa wove his way among the tables. All morning he'd helped with last-minute arrangements. Now the courtyard was transformed into a magical scene. Under the gazebo, two golden chairs with backrests fanning out like peacocks' tails—where Layla and William would sit to receive the good wishes of the guests—were beautiful. He had spent the previous evening painting the chairs himself—his fingers were still stained with golden paint.

There was a canopy of fairy lights over the music area,

for dancing. He had spent all morning up on a ladder, helping a workman drape the lights. He'd unfurled the red carpet that lay beneath the band's feet. He'd helped mount the whirling red and green and white fabric of the tents, an opulent backdrop to the finery of guests: nomad men in white jellabiyas and turbans, women in colorful thoubs, Nilot men in shirts that they wore for special occasions, Nilot women with elaborately braided hair, jewelry in their ears and on their arms.

He felt a sense of proprietorship over the tents, the band, the carpet, even the guests. The yard was already so full of people that new arrivals were pressing up against the walls. He went from table to table distributing Pepsi bottles. He tried to keep the crate of drinks from brushing against his suit. A frustrating smudge of dirt had appeared on his white shirt. He'd been waiting to wear this suit for days. Had wanted to strut around the market with it, to show off, but was coaxed and then threatened by William. He could wear it as much as he wanted after the wedding, William said, but it was to be put away until then. And so it had remained wrapped up in its plastic bag until tonight, when the moment he'd been waiting for arrived. He had put on his suit.

The decorations were under threat by the boys and girls tumbling among the guests, climbing up tentpoles, chasing one another, and shrieking. He saw a group dressing themselves with strings of fairy lights they had detached from the wall. He put down the crate of soft drinks and went to scold them.

The children—lights in their hair and around their necks and belted around their waists—flashed white and yellow at him. Seeing that he was only a little bigger than themselves, they paused only for a moment.

"And who are you to tell us to put them back?" a girl carrying a toddler said.

He'd labored over those lights, as he'd labored over everything that was beautiful there tonight. He marched over and pulled lights from the girl's hands. The children shuffled him. But the oldest of them was no more than six or seven, and he managed to make them scatter. He got a chair and rehung the string along the wall—upset to see that there was now a patch of darkness in the middle.

⸎

LAYLA WAS SO HAPPY to see Dena through the open tent flap that she ran to her and hugged her.

"Dena, thank God. Help me."

Dena smiled. "Who did this to you?"

"My aunts. Don't laugh!"

She was distraught. She'd trusted her aunts to do her wedding makeup, but, after looking at herself in the mirror, she'd wanted to cry. She looked as though she'd buried her face in a bowl of flour. Orange lipstick overran her lips. Two pink smears bruised her cheekbones. A horrible purple-gold eye shadow reached all the way up to her eyebrows, making her look permanently surprised.

She had banished her aunts, along with her mother, from the tent, telling them that she would take care of herself. Just as she was despairing over what to do—she'd never worn makeup in her life and didn't know how to put it on—Dena arrived.

"We'll do it over," said Dena.

"Do you know how?"

Dena gestured at her bare, boyish face. "I'm no expert. But we'll manage."

Layla led her into her tent. On the ground a suitcase lay open. Dresses were spread out on two chairs, shoes tossed on the mat, jewelry on a table. She'd never had so many things. William's bride wealth not only came with livestock for the family but also gifts for her—clothes and perfumes and small, delicate handbags and jewelry.

Dena held up a necklace. "Lovely."

"Yes. All William. He's so good."

She didn't know how he'd managed to arrange everything in time—such a big celebration, and so many odds and ends to see to. And his going to the mosque for her—that was what had really touched her. Two days after meeting her family he returned to tell her father that he had converted. That the religious contract would take place in the mosque. That he would provide the bride wealth as agreed, on the condition that the wedding take place within a fortnight. She had been stunned, and overjoyed, and grateful.

And then to have these lavish gifts. Her family was dazzled by the treasures that emerged out of the suitcases escorted by William's sullen mother and sisters.

He made light of it, but she knew that he'd been shouldering a lot. They could spend time with each other only fleetingly, as when he came to visit, he was mostly with her father.

She sat down in front of a mirror and tilted her head up, and gushed forth her complaints. Her mother and aunts were crowding her all the time; she had no say in what to do or where to go. She was ashamed of her family's behavior toward William's mother and sisters, who had come to deliver the bridal gifts three days ago. Her family had been rude and superior, and Layla had sat through the visit, trying to make up for them.

She was deluged by an endless stream of well-wishers. Dozens of relatives had arrived from far-flung encampments and pitched their tents and sleeping mats in the homestead. It was as if the family, knowing that they were giving her up for good, were rising one last time to assert their dominion over her.

Dena dipped a cloth into a bowl of soapy water and wiped Layla's eyelids and forehead. She rummaged in a plastic bag full of makeup.

"No powder," said Layla. "Just kohl and lipstick. The red, not the orange."

"OK, close your eyes."

She felt the nib of the kohl pressing along her eyelashes, then looked up as Dena ran it along the rim of her lower eye.

She asked, "What will you wear to your wedding?"

Dena looked at her. "I told you, I'm not getting married."

"I mean if you marry—" She stopped. "If you marry a girl. Like you were telling us."

Dena picked up the lipstick. "A suit," she said. "And a flower in my hair."

She closed the lipstick tube and tossed it onto the bed, then looked at Layla. "I think we need a little blush."

"Just a little," Layla said. She tilted her face so that Dena could brush along her cheekbones.

Layla asked, "And would your parents be there?"

"No, they'd never come."

"I'd come."

Dena smiled. "Good. But let's get you married first."

She appraised Layla's face. "Perfect."

Layla leaned into the mirror. Yes, she looked like herself, but better. Her eyes larger, her skin glowing, her lips saturated with color. She turned her head this way and that, enchanted by her own reflection.

"Thank you."

She jumped up and kissed Dena on the cheek, leaving a trace of lipstick there.

∫

WILLIAM MOVED to the neighbor's, where his mother was staying, to dress for the wedding. He stood in front of a mirror, listening to the party starting up next door—a thrum of laughter, shouts, traffic of cars parking to unload guests. For days now he'd hardly slept and was exhausted. But tonight, he felt the exhilaration in his fingers as he buttoned up his wedding shirt, as he brushed his hair—the barber had given him a haircut free of charge, as a wedding present. Not just the barber but the whole town was coming to celebrate.

He wondered at the strangeness of these past weeks. From prison to fussing over wedding lights and music. Looking forward to a new life with Layla. When he went to visit her father, as was the custom for a soon-to-be son-in-law, Layla sometimes emerged from one of the tents and they sat together making plans. They'd go to Khartoum first. Mustafa would come with them. His mother had vanished, and William had no luck in tracking her down.

A knock at the door. Mustafa burst in, cheeks gleaming with Vaseline. He was in the suit he'd been waiting to wear for days, a miniature man in black trousers and a small double-breasted jacket and a white shirt and a clip-on red tie, identical to William's.

He took in William's shoeless feet, his beltless trousers, his half-unbuttoned shirt.

"What's taking you so long?" he scolded. "The yard's full of guests!"

He complained about the disorganized cooks and the wobbly tables and the stained tablecloths, which weren't as white and bright as they should have been, and about the musicians, who still hadn't finished setting up, and the children, who were destroying the decorations.

William listened. This was more Mustafa's occasion than his. And what would he have done without him? Over the past hectic weeks, Mustafa seemed to have developed the ability to be in three places at once. Always ready to go to the butcher's, to carry an envelope of cash to the cooks, who needed an advance payment to buy their cooking supplies, to hire equipment for the band.

William crouched. "The musicians might be a little late but it's OK."

"But—"

"And no one will mind if the tables are wobbly and the table-cloths aren't perfect."

"So leave the tablecloths?" he asked anxiously.

"Leave the tablecloths."

"What about the children?"

"Chase them away."

Mustafa nodded.

They heard more guests in the street, and Mustafa rushed out the door.

He reached for his shoes, the scent of polish rising to his nose, and slipped his feet in. He smoothed his trousers and put on his jacket and patted his neck with cologne. In the mirror, he looked himself over, taking in the dark face, the body that had caused him so much consternation in his early days with Layla. Remembering those days, months ago now, he thought of the corpse. His fear at the cemetery, thinking that perhaps he was burying Layla, and his euphoria when she'd returned to the compound.

The corpse was a memory. It was his wedding night. Full of anticipation, he walked out toward the lights.

∫

ALEX REPLUGGED THE power cord and signaled. A musician tried the microphone. A high-pitched electric shriek engulfed the yard, and guests covered their ears. He shifted the speaker away from the microphone—this time the musician's voice came through crisply. He gave a thumbs-up to the band.

He walked around, savoring the festive atmosphere. He'd never seen the townspeople so dressed up before. The compound, too, was transformed. He himself had shaved, bought a shirt and trousers especially for the occasion. He waved at people he knew from town. The gaping stares he'd encountered in his first days in Saraaya were gone. People had gotten used to him just as he'd gotten used to them.

"Need some help?" he asked Mustafa, who was handing out soft drinks.

"Yes," said Mustafa. He pointed to tables by the kitchen. "Over there." His English had improved over the last few months.

Alex took bottles and made his way to the guests. They asked him questions. He was lost at first, but finally understood that they were asking about his departure. He told them he was leaving in five days' time, on Saturday.

He saw Dena, dressed up in a blue shirt and a pair of dark pants, the camera on her shoulder. He went over. She took the Pepsi he held out to her.

"Nice, isn't it?" he said as they both stared out over the tables.

"Yes," she said. "Strange that we're leaving so soon."

People moved toward the gate and she grabbed his arm. "William's here," she said, and lifted the camera.

ſ

MEN CLAPPED HIS SHOULDERS, old women embraced him, children tugged at his tie and stepped on his toes. He was crushed in from all sides. Market vendors, Nilot friends, nomad herdsmen, tea ladies, neighbors, bus drivers—some had come from as far away as Hasaniya and Malakal to celebrate with him. The band struck up a tune as he stepped into the yard. Lights twinkled along the thatched roof of the gazebo, the walls, the kitchen doorway. He saw Mustafa elbowing his way toward him and reached to hug him.

Alex beamed at him. "Congrats," he said, embracing William.

He was spruced up in a blue shirt and trousers.

"Thanks," said William. "You look good."

Alex grinned. "So do you." He pointed to the dais. "Your throne awaits you."

By the time he arrived at the groom's golden pedestal his throat was dry. His palms were damp. His lips ached from smiling. The speakers blasted music into his ears. Layla's father and her uncle came up to congratulate him. They were warm, even deferential, impressed by the opulence of the wedding.

He glanced over the guests. Layla would be arriving any minute now, and he longed to see her. Women began ululating by the door. Mustafa climbed up on the footrest of William's seat.

"Layla's here!" he announced.

The ululations grew louder. The instruments under the gazebo went into crescendo—the keyboard gave a flourish. As he approached the gate the crowd thickened, but now guests picked up Mustafa's call to clear the way.

*

SHE WAS WEIGHED DOWN by jewelry on her head and arms, around her ankles and neck, by the high heels that made her wobble, by the heavily beaded thoub that was three kilos at least. She was uncomfortable, hot, unsteady. The press of women around her was oppressive, fingers adjusting her dress, her necklaces, her hair. Her mother kept pulling her thoub over her head. Her aunt fiddled with the nose ring, which had come out of place. Her thoub snagged on the rings on her fingers, and she had to keep untangling it.

While she was dealing with all this, the women kept giving her contradictory commands. To step into the yard. Not to step into the yard—wait until the groom arrived to greet her. To cover her face. Not to cover her face. To watch out for the hem of her dress, which was dragging in the dirt. To watch out for the strap of her dress, which had fallen off her shoulder. They dabbed at her forehead with handkerchiefs to clear away beads of sweat collecting there. They checked her teeth to make sure they weren't

smeared with lipstick, they fiddled with the bracelet that was biting into her upper arm, so that, before she had even stepped into
the yard, she was already longing for the moment when she could
have quiet again, just herself and William.

Deciding that it was impossible to execute a hundred con-
trary orders all at once, she made a definitive move toward the
entrance, tottering in her shoes, and having to reach out an arm to
steady herself. When the gate opened, she was dazzled by the sea
of faces. There were hundreds of people there. Decked out with
tents and lights, the courtyard was illuminated as though in a
dream. She was accosted from every side by people she knew and
didn't know. It took her a minute to spot William moving toward
her through the throng. He had stopped, as if afraid to approach.
In the suit he was all beautiful lines. The red tie and white shirt
set off his jawline, the gorgeous smile, the warm, generous eyes.
What she felt at that moment was not only pride but relief. They
had done it—they were married at last.

*

HE SAW HER in a shimmer of gold and red. Her feet and hands
were covered in a pattern of henna that echoed the embroidery of
her dress, delicate flowers and vines wrapping around her ankles
and wrists. Her arms, neck, and head were covered in the jewelry
that he'd given as part of the bride wealth. Over the bridal wig
woven out of black thread she wore a helmet of gold coins. Kohl
around her eyes made them seem larger, and the bright-red lipstick made her smile more radiant.

The effect on William was that he suddenly grew terribly
shy—she seemed a miracle under the twinkling lights. Little girls
stared up at her, dumbstruck. Men commented on her beauty. She
was so engrossed in handshakes and hugs that she didn't see him
until someone called, "The groom's here."

People prodded him forward. As he drew closer she seemed to grow more brilliant. He leaned in. He could smell her sandalwood perfume. He whispered in her ear that she was beautiful. He held her hand and Mustafa cleared a path for them toward their chairs.

At the dais, he helped her up. The band turned toward them and played music. She said something to him that he couldn't hear over the noise. They laughed instead. A line of well-wishers formed near their chairs, and Mustafa stood at the edge of the dais, ushering people up and down, directing the flow. They spent the first hour shaking hands, being kissed and embraced by old women and men. Children jumped into their laps.

Guests gathered to dance under the gazebo. William turned to her and asked if she might dance with him.

"My shoes," she said.

"I'll help you."

Women ululated as they approached and Dena followed them with the camera. Alex and Mustafa made way for them. William led Layla into the throng of dancers. He hadn't danced in a long time, but as a young man, he had loved it. His hands inched up and his shoulders rose and fell; his limbs recalled those moves he'd watched in Bollywood films, and the crowd clapped for him as he circled around Layla, who laughed trying to keep up.

*

ALEX DANCED WITH Mustafa and William and Layla. He convinced Dena to put down the camera and danced with her. Occasionally, William led Layla away to sit and rest her feet. But Layla didn't like missing out. An hour into dancing, she unclasped her high heels, and flung them away. The crowd roared. Other women took off their shoes, and, freed from their foot gear, took over the circle, awing the men who stood mesmerized.

Alex gobbled the plate of food someone handed to him—he'd never tasted such delicious meat. Whenever he felt himself flagging, he gulped down a cup of coffee. Some guests sprawled out on chairs to rest, others rushed around with plates of food, still others splashed water on their faces to refresh themselves. Women gossiped, men told jokes, the bride's and groom's chairs were invaded by children who squeezed on top of each other, pretending the dais was a flying boat. He was accosted by young women who made him speak Arabic and Nilotic so that they could flirt with him.

He danced with William's mother and with children, making a spectacle of himself. The young Nilot herdsmen made him join them, and so did the nomads. Everyone laughed at his clumsy steps, and he laughed with them.

Mustafa was high on Pepsi. Eyes glazed, grin plastered on his face, he bounced around the circle of dancers like a firecracker, his red tie askew, his white shirt untucked, his double-breasted jacket flapping. He could tell by Dena's flushed face, sparkling eyes hungry to capture the feast of color and light—that she was happy. She plunged in and out of the crowd with the camera, like a pearl diver at sea. Even she couldn't help moving to the music—it had been a long time since any of them had been to a party.

At one point, needing a break in spite of the caffeine, he sat down on the edge of the dais and reached for a paper plate to fan himself. Two minutes later William appeared, a sheen of sweat on his forehead, his eyes as bright as the overhead lights. He collapsed beside Alex, sighing with happy exhaustion.

Mustafa found them. He was so disheveled by dancing that he looked like he'd stepped out of a brawl.

"People are asking for you!" he called.

"In a minute," said William. "Come here."

Reluctantly, Mustafa came. William pulled him onto his lap. "You need a break. Sit for a minute."

Mustafa fidgeted and squirmed in William's lap, impatient to get going again, until William finally let him go. He bounded up and away into the circle, and they laughed as they watched him.

∫

SOMEONE HAD SNUCK IN bottles of sorghum beer, which were now making the rounds amongst the guests. People were getting tipsy. Music pulsated. Lights flashed. Beef bone littered tables. Empty soda bottles had toppled over as though exhausted from dancing. Demure grandmothers rose from their seats, shedding half a century of age to dance their old, forgotten bridal dances. Children flitted about the yard like whirlwinds. Babies lay swaddled on tables, sleeping as peacefully amidst the noise as though in the silence of their mothers' wombs. Young men fell in love with young women. Young women settled on husbands. The cooks, finally done with cooking, had been ushered into the circle of dancers and applauded for the feast they had prepared. Sweat stains bloomed on the musicians' orange shirts. They were exhausted, but the euphoria of the crowd kept them going.

Dena moved through it all, filming embroidery on women's dresses, cooks' faces lighted by the glow of coal embers, girls in lace dresses and frilly socks, toothless women with tattooed lips. Turbans sat on men's heads as opulent as palace domes; long-limbed Nilot men moved like princes amongst the crowd. The yard was a tableau of color, the air a sea of scents. Powdery dust and aphrodisiac perfumes and bone marrow and coffee and the whiff of alcohol and the dense heat of exertion. Musicians played diplomats, switching between Nilot and nomad songs. When the Nilot songs came up the young, tall men and the delicate Nilot girls faced one another and danced. When the nomad songs came up, turbaned men raised their canes and saluted the nomad women whose eyes were as expressive as their gracefully twisting arms.

Even William's mother forgot her sourness. The frown knitting her brow unraveled into laughter. She danced with Layla, showing her Nilot steps. Amidst the gaggle of his beautiful sisters William was a god amongst goddesses. Layla was an angel forged from fire and gold.

Neighbors who'd hidden away during the troubles reunited, catching up on news, sharing stories of their war plights. Distant relatives embraced one another. Displaced villagers forgot that they had lost their homes, surprised to catch themselves laughing rather than crying for a change. Between the music and the beer and the pleasure of celebration, nomads rediscovered the Nilotic tongue they had learned as children. A bountiful night, full of food and music and laughter and goodwill, when the war seemed but a dream from which the townspeople had awoken. The elders spoke of the ancient amity between Nilotes and nomads, recalling the time when you could march with cattle for weeks and not reach the end of a pasture, when rains arrived as regularly as the beat of a heart.

*

HAVING DANCED for two hours, and before that having run around chasing disobedient children, and before that having helped set up the compound, Mustafa was in a state of emergency. In between distributing soft drinks, he'd been drinking bottle after bottle himself. And so now he desperately needed to pee.

The dancing hadn't let up, and he was afraid that he might lose his spot at the front, from where he could see William and Layla and William's sisters, and from where he had a good view of the boldest dancers—those who broke out from the crowd and moved into the center, impressing everyone around. He himself had jumped in twice or thrice, adrenaline pulsing through his veins as he flipped and bent and semi-somersaulted, the crowd's noisy encouragement pushing him to ever greater feats of dexterity.

But he could no longer concentrate on dancing—his bladder was about to burst. He pulled on Alex's arm. Alex looked down, flushed, happy, sweaty.

"Keep my place," he said. "I come back."

"You OK?"

"Toilet."

"OK, see you in a minute."

Carefully, he uncrossed his legs—no way to walk with them tangled up—and pushed his way through, shielding his stomach with one arm against wayward jabs. He squeezed in between hips and arms and torsos. The music receded behind him. The same children he'd told off earlier over the lights were now wreaking havoc on the potted plants. He ignored them and rushed to the latrine.

A few minutes later he emerged, light and free as a feather. The children were gone. A few very old people—those too ancient to dance—remained seated. Three mothers fed their children. Otherwise, the space was strewn with plates piled on top of one another and overflowing ashtrays, tablecloths pulled askew, chairs hastily pushed back. A row of prayer rugs faced east. The decorations were the worse for wear—the streamers at the door had disappeared, but most of the lights still twinkled.

A breeze lifted. He looked up as the tent filled with air, patterns on the fabric rippling and sagging. The gate opened and a group of men stepped into the yard. Nomads in jellabiyas and old, mangled turbans, who paused just inside the gate, taking in the lights, the tents, the guests.

One of the men leaned over an old lady seated close to the door. She seemed confused by something he asked. Another man picked up a plate of half-eaten food and dipped into it with his fingers, then gestured to his friends, who searched the table, but finding no food, went to the kitchen. They came out again with plates from which they ate hungrily, their cheeks bulging, their fingers smeared with fat. One of them lifted a soda bottle to his mouth, his Adam's apple bobbing like a sharp stone in his throat.

Mustafa watched. Something about the men's faces—a wildness that he recognized. One was older, slim, with a beard and pinched features. Two others looked alike, both smooth-cheeked. Another one was dark-skinned, tall, wearing sunglasses even at night. Suddenly he saw that two of the men carried guns half-hidden under their vests.

He turned toward the dancers and elbowed and pushed. The deeper he went, the more closely people were packed together. He was smothered, his head squeezed in between bodies and his arms snared and immovable legs trapping him. Blurs of velvet and polyester blinded him, sequins scratched his skin, sweat and perfume enveloped him. Brain-rattling smacks landed on him as he stepped on toes and scratched and pushed forward, infuriating people.

The music grew louder, thumping, exacerbating the panic in his chest. He threw himself forward and lights brightened. In the split second in the air, he reached out, landing on his hands and knees in the middle of the dance floor, right at Layla's hennaed feet. She looked down, alarmed, and helped him up, and for a moment he was awash in the glitter of her thoub, her scent of sandalwood. She dusted off his suit, her braids brushing against his face. He tried to tell her that militias had arrived, but she couldn't hear him. William whipped him round. His tie was loose and there was a high sheen on his face and a wild gleam in his eyes. He was tipsy and swung Mustafa's arms, wanting him to dance. Mustafa jerked free and tugged at his jacket.

"What?" William bent down.

Mustafa reached for his neck and shouted in his ear that militiamen had just come in.

The laughter faded from William's face. He straightened and looked toward the gate. Layla touched his shoulder, and he said something to her. She frowned, then held his arm. Hemmed in, Mustafa stuck close to William, uselessly standing on tiptoe trying to see. Across the circle, Alex and Dena were oblivious—Alex drunkenly twirled one of William's sisters and Dena danced with two children.

A crash reverberated through the speakers and unintelligible words echoed. The guitar twanged and went silent; the same electronic note repeated over and over on the keyboard. People stopped dancing, heads turning toward the corner of the gazebo where the musicians stood. An instrument tumbled to the ground, the sound amplifying across the yard. Someone unplugged the microphone. In the sudden silence, only the generator thrummed.

William moved away from Layla. Mustafa followed him through the press of bodies. Ahead of them, the militiamen. One held the guitar upward by the neck. A musician was on the floor, wincing, holding his arm. Another musician had ducked behind the drums, only his eyes peering over the rims.

Guests shrank back. Others pressed forward, wanting to get a view of the brawl. William's gaze lingered on the injured musician, then swept up to the militiamen. A vexed expression came over his face.

"What's going on here?"

The militiamen turned. They looked William up and down, taking in the fancy suit, the handsome face. The one wearing sunglasses raised them briefly to get a better look.

"And who are you?" asked the older man. The hem of his jellabiya was frayed, one breast pocket unstitched, his boots worn. His hand sat casually on the gun dangling from his shoulder.

Across from him Mustafa saw Alex and Dena step to the front of the crowd.

"I'm the groom," said William. "You're welcome to the wedding. But we don't want any trouble. We have permission from the authorities."

Immersed in drink and pleasure, the guests watched as though this were the next installment in the night's entertainment; many didn't see the guns, and those who had a view of them remained glued to their places, thinking there was a cease-fire. Surely the men with guns would join the dancing.

There was a flurry of movement. Layla, left behind when William had moved toward the noise, pushed her way out of the throng, appearing in her dazzle of red and gold. She went to stand beside William.

The older militiaman stared wonderingly at her, then at William. "She's your bride?" He looked at her again, then turned to his friends and shook his head in astonishment. "It's a mixed marriage. Nomads and Nilotes."

The men turned back and stared at Layla.

The bearded one leveled his gaze at William. "Who gave permission for this wedding?"

"The security office," said William. "You can check if you like."

"Well," the man said. "We weren't informed." At eye level with his arm Mustafa saw the gun rise. "Let this be a lesson to any Nilot who thinks he can mix with ours."

He pointed at William. A shot rang out, and as William fell other people dropped; Mustafa made out the ripple of Layla's thoub just before he, too, was pushed to the ground—near him a man crawled under a table, then someone fell on him and for a moment he couldn't breathe; there was carpet in his mouth and his eyes burned; the smell of burst lightbulbs in his nose, and the yard was full of screams. The weight lifted off him and he breathed and looked up to see men tumbling down from the compound walls, their hands bleeding from glass shards jutting from the top. Alex and Dena huddled behind one of the oil drums used as planters. By the kitchen, William's sisters clutched their children. William's mother stumbled about dazed, even as one of her daughters tried to pull her to the ground.

A breaking noise behind him and he looked and saw the bride's chair crash backward from the dais. Tents teetered and collapsed, so that whole parts of the yard were covered in fabric under which people flailed. Plates of food flew and then lights dimmed. He raised his head to see the militiamen moving toward the street, scattering people, stepping over terrified men and women, some of whom stampeded ahead of them into the night.

The space near him cleared. Across the carpet he saw William lying on his back, head tilted, lips parted, eyes open. Dead.

EPILOGUE

SHE HAD THOUGHT THAT IF SHE SAW WILLIAM BURIED, she might understand that he was really dead. The day after the wedding, still in her bride's clothes, she went with Dena and Alex and Mustafa to the graveyard. There she found market merchants, tea ladies, herdsmen, children, villagers, refugees—just as everyone had come to his wedding, so they gathered for his funeral. There was a fight over whether to bury him in the nomad cemetery or the Nilot one. The nomads claimed him; he'd become a Muslim. His mother said over her dead body. Layla stepped forward then. He was murdered by nomad men; she wouldn't let him be buried with them.

She watched Alex dig the grave along with others, while Mustafa cried against her dress. On the other side of her Dena wept. Only she remained tearless. She forced herself to look at the shrouded corpse, but the effect was to make her doubt herself. How could she be sure it was really him?

The following days were a haze. She lay in Dena's room, her family coming and going. Her father agitated, her mother pleading with her, her brothers scolding her. William's sisters wailing. William's mother pounding her chest. From the yard the sounds of mourning. Women weeping beneath the tattered decorations, music replaced by lamentations, laughter by somber whispers.

She had to muster up her courage to face her family, who wanted her back. But she couldn't imagine going back. Not after William, not after all she'd lived through. How could she? She and William had had a plan: to go to Khartoum and take Mustafa with them, and so now she decided to make her own way there and take Mustafa along.

Ten days after the burial, the two of them boarded the bus to Khartoum. Mustafa carried Dena's camera on his back, while she pulled a suitcase and purse containing their most valuable belongings—an envelope of money, the piece of paper that Dena had given her with an address in Khartoum, William's gifts—clothes, jewelry, perfumes—the belongings of a bride, though she was now a widow.

The two of them waved goodbye to Alex and Dena through the window. Wheels trundled. Saraaya drew away—earth-colored houses and thatched roofs, faint strips of dirt road through green plains growing fainter. The sun leaked light. Bodies swayed in motion with the bus. Mustafa leaned against her shoulder, blinking in the brightness. For the first three hours they drove along the highway to the northeast. Wind whipped hair into her eyes and beneath her the bus moved, lurching over stones. Hills rose from the plains; they were approaching a mountain range. Her gaze drifted over the scenery, slopes ahead like the limbs of a giant sprawled out in sleep.

Five hours into the journey, a village—more a camp than a proper settlement—came into view, and the bus stopped. People descended, stretched their limbs, drank water, children chased one another around the bus.

A woman offered them drinks.

"Your boy?" she asked Layla, nodding at Mustafa.

They had left Saraaya still with no news of his mother. What had forced her not to lose herself in those days of the funeral was the knowledge that if she didn't decide wisely, he might end up on his own.

She was too young, but she answered, "Yes."

A little later, Mustafa touched her arm.

"Do you think Dena and Alex will call us?" he asked. "From America?"

"Sure they will," she said. "They promised to."

He stared at his shoes, the new ones he'd worn for the wedding, and she knew he was thinking of William.

They climbed back into the bus and soon were passing into desert. Through the window, the horizon kept receding. The land lay shadowless; wadis yawned dry throats up at the sky; a lone tree made a stand against the elements. Every so often, something knotted in her chest—a sudden expectation. That William might surprise her at a crossing or appear at a bend in the road. Even on the wedding night, as she looked on at his corpse laid out under the gazebo—his white shirt stained crimson, his breath still— she'd expected him to get up, to come to her, to reassure her that it was a bad dream—they'd be leaving for Khartoum tomorrow.

The sun arced across the sky, tucked itself into the land. At night, in the darkness of the bus, her mind kept going back to that moment of the shots—she'd dropped to the ground at the sound, burying her face in William's shoulder. She remembered the scent of his lemon cologne and a warmth against her skin. When she opened her eyes, her gold bracelets were oily with blood. She glanced up at him, but his face was turned from her. She raised herself and saw Mustafa across from them. That's when she knew—she saw it on Mustafa's face.

Had he died while she'd held him? Or the moment the bullets entered him? Had he wanted to say something to her? Had she missed the last seconds of his waking, her head buried in his shoulder? It had happened so quickly, she was still reeling.

Early the next morning, they arrived in Khartoum. Mustafa's white shirt was rumpled from the ride, one of his socks had
fallen from his knee, his cheek was creased from where he'd lain
it against her shoulder. They gathered their things and stepped
down onto the log-jammed clearing.

Hawkers called out their wares and impatient drivers honked
and buses pulled in and out of the station. Families embraced in
greeting or waved goodbye. Mothers laden with groceries walked
past, leading children licking lollipops. Beggars spurted through
the tangle of cars, knocking on windows and promising God's
mercy in exchange for a coin.

Weighed down by bags, she bumped into a man who glared
at her. She walked forward to cross the street, Mustafa following
her, and a car screeched to a halt inches from where they stood.
She stepped back as Mustafa clung to her, his eyes staring, his
lips closed.

"You all right?"

He nodded. But the fear she sensed in his tight grip echoed
her own. How to make their way in this strange place where
things moved so fast. In spite of herself, she searched for William. She imagined him amongst a group of passengers, turning
just in the nick of time to see them. She saw him making his way
through the throng toward them. She pictured him reaching for
their hands and saying—I'm here. Come.

ACKNOWLEDGMENTS

Deepest thanks to Peter Carey, Colum McCann, Claire Messud, and the Hunter College CUNY MFA Program in Creative Writing, which changed my life.

Huge thanks to the fabulous team at the Wylie Agency, most especially Sarah Chalfant and Jackie Ko, for their invaluable guidance and support. Deep thanks to Jill Bialosky, Drew Weitman, and the whole team at W. W. Norton, with whom it has been an absolute pleasure to work.

Thank you to John Freeman for publishing an excerpt from the novel in *Freeman's: The Best New Writing on Arrival*, which opened all kinds of doors. Thank you to Rana Dasgupta for publishing another excerpt in *Granta: The Magazine of New Writing*, issue 151.

Thank you to Hans-Uli Feldman for invaluable conversations and insights about the history and practice of cartography.

Thank you to the cultural institutions and residency programs that provided me with space, time, and money to write. Special thanks to Sally de Kunst and the Arc Artist Residency in Romainmôtier, Switzerland; the Miles Morland Foundation in the UK; the Cité internationale des arts in Paris; the Iceland Writers Retreat; Villa Sarkia Residency in Sysmä, Finland; the Jan Michalski Foundation for Writing and Literature in Montricher, Switzerland; the

Maison Baldwin in St-Paul-de-Vence, France; the Austrian Federal Chancellery/KulturKontakt Artist-in-Residence Program in Vienna; the Akademie Schloss Solitude in Stuttgart, Germany; Mophradat in Brussels and Athens; the Schloss Wiepersdorf Cultural Foundation in Brandenburg, Germany; and last but not least Art Omi in Ghent, New York. Thank you to Michel and Catherine Soublin for providing me with a DIY residency in the form of a place to write one summer.

Deepest gratitude to my friends, whose support and company kept me going through the years: Marie Constantinesco, Divya Awal, Lana Dinić, Neşe Doğusan Alexander, Sanjay Pinto, Maya Pinto, Uraline Septembre Hager, Elizabeth Park, Xiao Kun Kora Park, Charles Lang, Ritva Koistinen, Katariina Záborszky, Shams Yazdani, Ghazal Ramzani, Niusha Ramzani, Samira Mohammed Ali, Paul Joachim Schulze, Olga Gerstenberger, Nursemin Sönmez, Silke Nagel, Inken Sarah Mischke, Manjiri Palicha, Matthias Haase, Simran Sodhi, Sonita Bindra, Adam Bresnahan, Sabrina Mandanicci, Claire Debucquois, Josuah Merkl, Agata Lisiak, Hélène de Givry, Duygu Kaban, Todd Sekuler, and Camille Fontaine.

Deepest thanks to Sara, Fadwa, Bayan, Layla, and Thorne. I can never say thank you enough to my mother, who made everything possible. And to my father, who also made everything possible, beginning with our long-ago walks, hand in hand, to the bookstores.

ſ

Map on page 277 designed by Duygu Kaban.

Map on pages 278–279: A. Nicohosoff, cartographer. The Anglo-Egyptian Sudan. [Alexandria, Egypt: Engr. A. Nicohosoff, 1949]. Retrieved from the Library of Congress, www.loc.gov/item/20 19589297/.

Thank you to the Geography and Map Division, Library of Congress, for access.

Map on pages 280–281: Maṣlaḥat Al-Misāḥah. Sudan. [Khartoum, 1976]. Retrieved from the Library of Congress, www.loc .gov/item/76693428/.

Thank you to the Geography and Map Division, Library of Congress, for access.

Graphic design on all maps by Niusha Ramzani.